Five Things

Lynne Marino

Publisher's Note:

This is a work of fiction. All names, characters, places, and
events are the work of the author's imagination.

Any resemblance to real persons, places, or events is
coincidental.

Solstice Publishing - www.solsticepublishing.com

Five Things

Lynne Marino

To Lizzy and Tony and Dan. Because of you I only have two things every day before I make my five.

Chapter One

Gina Ferrari didn't want to go, but she knew she couldn't stay. Quiet as a fifteen-year-old with a set of keys to the family car, she tiptoed toward the exit. Her clothes were strewn from the bed to the door like bread crumbs in an enchanted forest, and she picked up each piece as she went. If this was a fairy tale, it wasn't going to end with "they all lived happily ever after". She'd blown that one in the opening paragraph.

Her short, black leather skirt slipped on without a hitch, but the boots were a different matter. The zipper came to a stop when it reached her slightly thicker-than-average calves, and she had to push the leather together with one hand while pulling the zipper up with the other. When she stood, the balls of her feet reminded her why she stuck to comfort shoes in real life. The walk back to her hotel would be torture, and maybe that was what she deserved for masquerading as someone she wasn't for the past three days.

No one back home would ever know about this, although she might tell Rachael. Rachael would probably tell her she was nuts. Either that or she would ask why it had taken so long in the first place.

She took a step and winced. How did the women of Rome walk in these heels all day, gliding effortlessly from rutted streets to uneven sidewalks? Every time she put her feet down on the pavement, she felt them protest, but she loved these boots because they made her short legs look long and lean. Well, almost lean. To her, the boots said Gina Ferrari walks on the wild side. The minute she got back to St. Louis she would change right out of them, and the skirt too.

"Arrivederci, Marc." she whispered her goodbye to the still sleeping man, then opened the door slowly, making sure the lock clicked into place softly as she shut the door behind her.

Out in the hallway, she walked toward the elevator that would take her down to the main lobby while her eyes scanned the freshly painted molding and new carpeting. It was a nice hotel, with a sitting room, bar, and a computer room downstairs. Much nicer than the one she was staying in.

A middle-aged man and woman, six feet ahead of her in the hallway, weren't getting along. She couldn't make out every word, but she could hear their British accents as she followed them into the elevator. They all stood three inches apart as the lift, which is what her temporary companions would call it, slowly made its descent to the lobby.

"Are you quite sure breakfast starts at seven?" The British woman asked the British man.

"The brochure stated seven a.m. sharp in English, Italian, German, and Japanese," the British man replied. "If you'd bothered to read it, you would know. Surely you can, at a bare minimum, read in one of those languages."

Ouch, Gina thought. The man uttered the words *bare minimum* with a pinch of condescension that only the British could insinuate into two little words. They must be married. They had to be. No woman would ever ask a question with a tone that implied the man was an idiot unless he was her husband. On the other side of the equation, no man would ever reply to a woman like that unless she was his wife, or he had a death wish. Maybe they were travel weary, and a few more hours of sleep would render them as sweet as Cadbury chocolates. Or maybe this was what marriage ultimately did to everyone. It certainly had to Andrew and her.

She kept her eyes on the toes of her boots and hoped the ride would be over before the Brits really got into it. When the elevator reached the ground floor, the husband insisted, in poorly pronounced Italian, that she exit first. He must have thought she was a native like Marc had when they'd met. Given that the two Brits started arguing again, she was happy to comply.

"*Grazie,*" she murmured and exited as quickly as her high-heeled boots would allow.

The two men behind the reception desk grinned with an appreciative gaze as she passed them. It was so seldom she got looks like that anymore. Maybe it was the skirt. She would have to email Daniel when she got home and thank him for helping her locate the Prada outlet, but not tell him precisely why she was so thankful. There were certain things mothers and sons didn't discuss. Men who eyed you from behind hotel desks were one of them. Having the best three days of your life with a man you'd just met was another. She shook her head and turned down the Via Nazionale past the ruins of Trajan's Market, then headed left toward the Piazza della Rotonda.

Why had she done it? Certainly, there'd been men before Marc she'd been attracted to, although she couldn't think of any off the top of her head. Why him, and why did she feel compelled to give herself the third degree about it? Did there have to be a reason for everything she did, and did she always have to analyze her decisions ad nauseam? Couldn't she have three measly days of fun without making a federal case out it?

After rounding the corner into the piazza, she sucked in her breath and stared in wonder. The Pantheon affected her that way. How could this amazing structure still be intact after two thousand years when so many things had returned to dust? Its name in Latin meant "every god," and like countless people before her, it was to every god, goddess, and saint she would plead her case to. She hurried toward the entrance and tried hard not to glance at the fountain in front because it was there she'd met Marc three days ago. This visit had nothing to do with him.

"*Buongiorno*," the guard said, as she passed through the colossal bronze doors.

"*Buongiorno*." She smiled back and swept past him. There were only a few precious minutes to spend here. Then she had to get back to her hotel, grab her suitcase, and hightail it to the airport.

"Please," she whispered as her eyes turned to the round opening in the middle of the high, domed ceiling. Had they designed the oculus to mimic God's eyeball, staring down at desperate souls? She straightened her skirt and patted down her hair. "Please help me."

Her eyes stung with the beginning of tears. She wiped them away and cast her gaze toward the Porphyry floor, then turned to look back up.

"It's not really about me," she said to the hole in the middle of the ceiling. "I'm fine. Even with the divorce, I'm fine. I'm always fine. Seriously. What I need is help for my son."

It wasn't working. She could feel it wasn't. She hated asking for help, and if anyone at the university saw what she was doing right now, she'd be laughed out of the next faculty meeting. Make that the next ten faculty meetings, and it was quite possible her colleagues would vote to impose a lifetime ban.

This time she wet her fingers with spit, as her mother had when she was little and patted her hair down again. Closing her eyes, she put her whole heart into it.

"Please. Help my son find the right path." There. That was truer to the overall concerns of existence and therefore more inviting to whoever was up there, if anyone or anything was up there at all. She had her doubts, but she was willing to try.

And then she heard it. The word flashed in her mind like the winning answer in a game of Scrabble. Three small letters that came together to make the word:

Joy

Gina coughed on the thought. "Jesus, Mary, and Jupiter...or Wonder Woman. Whoever is in charge up there today, and believe me—I am not picky. I just need a little guidance. I mean, my son does, and he's plenty joyful already. Can you help him? Please?"

Although it was beautiful to behold, the ceiling remained silent. Gina waited, then turned and walked out the bronze doors, getting as far as the outer steps before teetering on her heels and falling on the stone floor. She picked herself up and marched back inside.

"After all those years in Catholic school you finally answer me, and this is what you have to say? What am I supposed to do with joy? He needs to finish his PhD. That has absolutely nothing to do with joy—trust me on that one." She got nothing more from the hole in the ceiling, but she did receive a curious glance from the security guard.

This is what desperate people do, she thought as she turned to leave again. They plead to amorphous entities about things outside of their control and then convince themselves that they've received a message. Human beings had been doing it forever, long before they put two and two together and figured out that ducking into a cave during a rainstorm was a brilliant idea. She'd always considered herself smarter than that, but the truth was, she'd never been this desperate. Until now.

These past three days had been an exercise in labile insanity, and this last trip to the Pantheon had been yet one more run at it. What had she been thinking? She shook her head and kept walking. Maybe she would tell Rachael about meeting Marc, but she was not going to tell her, or anyone else, about this.

***

He barely made the flight. In fact, Marc Edwards was the last person on the plane. For this act of near negligence, he received a dirty look from the two flight attendants who were waiting to latch the door and get the plane off the ground. He slid into his business class seat seconds before the captain gave his "*Buongiorno*. Welcome to Alitalia" spiel over the loudspeaker.

The woman in the window seat turned to him as he settled in. "Oh," she said, "I thought maybe I'd have this row all to myself."

"Sorry." He smiled his routine, automatic, polite smile, the one he gave to the checkers in the grocery store and the secretary at work. She was, he figured, around his mother's age, if his mother had still been alive.

"Well, you did pay for it." She shoved her purse under the seat in front of her. "Unfortunately, I'll be crawling over you to use the restroom. Incontinence. It happens when you get old."

"Would you like me to take the window?"

She smiled as she scanned his lower half. "No. Your legs are much longer than mine. But thank you."

Marc closed his eyes and thought about Gina. When they'd stumbled into the hotel together last night, he hadn't bothered to ask the desk for a wake-up call (why ruin the night with petty details about the morning), and he'd hadn't set his own alarm either. She'd left so quietly that she hadn't woken him, nor had she bothered to say goodbye. What had he expected? Breakfast in bed? Well, yes actually, but given the rowdy cab ride through Rome to the airport, it was better he hadn't had anything to eat, with or without her. Unfortunately, they'd never exchanged addresses, or phone numbers, or anything else for that matter. And he'd wanted to. He traveled to Rome often, and if he knew how to contact her, his trips would become even more frequent and enjoyable.

"They'll want you to put your seatbelt on," the woman next to him leaned toward him and whispered.

"Thanks." He opened his eyes and buckled up, then stole another glance her way. She seemed normal, although her incontinence was a little more than he wanted to know. Nevertheless, she wasn't wearing any overt religious symbols, no buttons on her lapel pronouncing her politics or the solution to life's ills in one to three words. And given the fact that her sweater appeared to be a blend of natural and man-made fibers, he would more than likely not be receiving a sermon about saving the planet one strand of hemp at a time. Fantastic.

She handed him the menu from the seat pocket and gave him a mother's smile. "Tell me what you want, and I'll order for you if you're asleep. You look exhausted."

He happily complied, then fell into his dreams.

True to her word, she didn't nudge him until the food and beverage carts arrived. He was halfway through his meal when a woman with ample curves walked into the business class section from coach. She tapped the flight attendant on the arm. Her backside resembled Gina's, as did her clothes. But many women wore black leather skirts and had hair that was thick, long, and tucked neatly behind their ears. He would probably be seeing Gina Ferrari in anyone who resembled her for months to come. Damn, he should have gotten her number.

Marc heard the woman in the aisle speak in perfect American English, and he stuck his head out for a better scan of her backside. He'd always liked full figures.

"Excuse me. The other flight attendants sent me to get you," she said. "We've had an accident in coach. A couple of kids threw up on their parents, and a few other people got splattered, too. It's a real mess."

Marc tucked his head in as she turned to walk back to coach with the attendant on her heels. How could it be her? His Gina hadn't known English, and she wasn't an American, much less one on a flight heading for, of all places on the planet, St. Louis's Lambert International Airport. He put his drink down and smacked his head. "God, I'm an idiot."

"You all right?" The woman next to him asked.

"Yeah, I'm fine." Then he added, "If you like being a chump."

"I don't know about the chump part, but you do look like you saw a ghost. Or maybe an ex-wife."

"Neither."

"Old girlfriend?"

"Sort of, but not really. Excuse me for a minute." He straddled his food tray, somehow managing to get into the aisle without spilling anything, and walked to the entrance of the coach section. Once there, he snuck a peek, using the curtain that divided the two sections as a shield. No mistake about it, it was her. He watched as she helped wipe off the two kids who were crying and covered in a layer of crud he didn't want to know the origins of, although the odor was making its way toward him already.

The flight attendant from business class who had been recruited to help, flashed him another dirty look. He took it as a cue that he should return to his seat, and within ten seconds of his behind making contact with the cushion, the woman sitting next to the window started in.

She cocked her head and spoke in an imploring tone. "So do you mind me asking what's going on? I'm curious, because the look on your face when that woman in the black leather skirt went by, reminded me of the look on my four-year-old son's face when his older sister told him that Santa Claus and the Easter Bunny weren't real. I could have throttled her for that one. Four years old, and no one will let you believe in Santa Claus."

Marc nodded in agreement but said nothing. Instead, he downed his wine and wished for more. The whole situation reminded him of one of those goofy Doris Day movies his mother and aunt used to love. The ones where Doris meets that Rock guy or some other hunk type in an unbelievable coincidence. They fall in love after loathing each other through at least half the movie, because they really were in love with each other from the start but didn't want to admit it. This couldn't be happening to him because that's not how real life worked. Ever. And yet, here he was.

"Here, drink this." She handed him what was left in her mini bottle of scotch. "Just down it."

He obeyed. "Right now, I feel like I'm in one of those goofy romantic comedy movies. You know the ones I mean?"

"I do. I love them. Everything turns out happy in the end, but they haven't met their in-laws yet. So which one are you? The hero or the comic relief?"

"Comic relief?"

"You know, the Tony Randall guy."

The woman signaled the flight attendant who had returned from coach slightly rumpled, and requested four more bottles of scotch and two glasses of ice. "My treat." She smiled.

"Thanks. Who's Tony Randall?"

"Ah," she said, looking at the plane's ceiling. "The younger generation and the things they don't know. Tony Randall is the one who loves the heroine but is too much of a schmuck to ever get her, so he loses her to the handsome cad who, by the end of the movie, has been transformed by true love into a decent sort of fellow. I think Gig Young played the schmuck in a few of those movies, too."

"Actually, I was referring to the unbelievable coincidental aspect of those movies. You know, the kind of situations that never happen in real life, but you're ready to swallow it whole in a movie."

"Oh, the fates," she said with delight.

"Yes, the fates."

"Well, that actually happens sometimes. At least it did to me."

"Really?"

"Yes," she said with certainty. "Sometimes life hands you a gift, if you're smart enough to take it. My husband and I literally ran into each other. On bikes. He was staring at another girl with nice legs in a pair of short shorts. They called them hot pants in the late seventies. Or was it the eighties? I forget. Anyway, she was on a bike going the other way, and he smashed into mine because he was looking at her. Then he had to take me to the university health center, and I made him take me home after that. The rest is history."

"And the other girl?"

"Who knows? I hope she and her shapely legs had a happy life."

Marc swallowed. "But this woman— "

"And it happened to my grandmother in Germany. She almost missed a train because she didn't want her friends to think she was riding on a third-class ticket, which she was. After her friends left the station, she made a mad dash for the train car, and all the seats were taken, so she went and stood by my grandpa. According to Grandma, he was the only one who didn't look like a bum. He gave her his seat, she gave him half her sandwich, and the rest is history. So you could say that my whole family and I are the direct results of fate, chance, and luck, and so are my kids." She sucked the scotch off her ice cubes and smiled. "Thank god for life's toss of the dice, huh?"

"But this woman— " Marc began again.

"Oh, and my husband and I quickly realized we were in two lecture classes together that semester, and we hadn't noticed each other before he crashed into me. So, sometimes I think fate decided we needed a kick in the ass." She grinned at him.

This woman might have been his mother's age, but she was not like his mother. "That's good," he said reassuringly. "But this woman—"

"The one in black who came through here about the puking kids?"

"Yes. That one."

"She's certainly voluptuous."

"Yes, she is, but she lied to me. She pretended to be Italian. And now she's on this plane headed for St. Louis and speaking perfect English."

"She speaks Italian?"

"Yes, she does."

"That's nice. I always wanted to speak another language."

"And now," Marc continued, "obviously she speaks English, which she never told me. She just let me limp along in Italian for three solid days."

"You speak Italian, too?"

"Um-hmm. And she told me she lived in Rome."

"God, those Italians ooze sex, don't they? Did you go to bed with her?"

Definitely, not his mother. "Just once." Well, he didn't want her to think Gina was a slut. But wait a minute. What did he care? She'd lied like a rug to him for three solid days.

"Hmm. You know, it's the whole female dichotomy that makes us do these things."

"Excuse me?"

"The virgin-whore thing. You have to be so good in real life that sometimes you need to let the not-so-good-girl out. And Rome is about as far away from St. Louis, Missouri, as you can get. Besides, I bet you can be really charming." She smiled like the Cheshire Cat.

The woman rendered him speechless. "Um, thanks."

"Either that," she continued, "or she's married, in which case you'd better watch out. People carry weapons in the US. You wouldn't want to get stabbed or get your ass shot off."

"Good point."

"Are you married?"

"No. No, I am not."

"Kids?"

"None of those either."

"Family?"

"A sister."

"I'm glad to hear that. Everybody needs somebody. Don't you think?"

The flight attendant arrived with the extra scotch and ice. Marc was grateful for a break in the conversation, because he didn't want to be interviewed about his lack of a family, or a love life, nor was he sure he wanted to follow his impulse and go demand the truth from Gina Ferrari, if that was her real name. Really, whose last name was a car? She'd probably made that up and was laughing about it at this very moment.

He watched the woman unscrew the cap off her scotch and pour the contents directly onto the ice, then followed her lead. She raised her glass to him and said, "Here's to coincidence. Think of it as life giving you a wake-up smack."

Marc lifted his own glass half-heartedly.

"Then there are omens, the portent of the future." The woman put her glass down hard on her collapsible table tray. "Remember when I told you my husband was staring at the girl in those short shorts?"

"Yes."

"Well, they weren't the last pair of legs he was attracted to. The bastard."

"Sorry?"

"He wasn't a perfect man, but then again, I wasn't a perfect woman."

He glanced her way but said nothing.

"I didn't cheat on him like he did on me. I just made his life miserable when he did. Maybe we deserved each other, but it was mostly love, and that's why fate threw us together." She shrugged, then sighed. "For everyone there is someone."

Marc didn't believe in omens or fate, and he hated the adage that things happen for a reason. Things happened, and then people found a rationale for them. Logic ruled life, not some predetermined plan. And maybe he didn't have anyone anymore, but being alone was far better than being with someone for the sake of not being alone. That, he could testify to. At least his life was full of possibilities of his own making, not the grand plan of some god playing chess with his life. And the woman sitting in coach who was supposed to be from Rome? He wasn't quite sure how to process that one, but it most certainly wasn't fate. Sometimes life hands you a gift, if you're smart enough to take it. Hmm.

***

"Gina." Rachael called to her as she wove through the crowd of people dragging their luggage out of customs, and she looked up to see her ex-sister-in-law waving like a maniac. "Welcome back, kiddo."

After the long, tiresome flight with those poor, sick kids, she could barely keep her eyes open, but her aching calves and ankles were the alarm clock of pain that woke her with every step she took. She couldn't wait to put her Birkenstocks back on.

"You look different." Rachael scrutinized her as she walked out of the security perimeter. "Is that really you?"

"It's me."

"Here, let me get that." Rachael took the handle of her suitcase, which she released without a second thought. "What happened to you? You look like you've been through an Italian version of a fashion-makeover show. Is this your postdivorce look?" She eyeballed Gina's clothes with an incredulous grin.

"I thought about changing before I boarded, but I ran out of time and checked my suitcase in at the airport." She shifted her purse to her right shoulder. "I can't tell you how much I want a shower." She could still smell the vomit on the tips of her fingers after she'd washed them three times. Those poor parents. "And maybe a toothbrush. But I don't know if I have the energy to use it."

"Uh-huh."

Rachael started up the carpeted walkway toward a sign that read, Parking Garage, still stealing glances at her. Her long legs were hard for Gina to keep up with, especially given her current state of exhaustion.

"So where'd you pick up the modern-day fertility-goddess outfit?" Rachael asked.

"At the Prada outlet, outside of Florence. Kimmy told me about it before I left for Italy. She gave me a wish list, and Daniel helped me locate it. I went there to get some things for her and ended up getting a few things for myself." It was more than a few things, and it was completely impulsive. But somehow, the shopping spree had helped her cope with Daniel's decision. After years of hunting and pecking through second hand stores and scanning clothing catalogs at midnight with her fingers crossed that what she ordered would fit, who knew she was capable of being a shopaholic? Then again, who knew she'd do what she did in Rome? Maybe she didn't know herself as well as she thought.

"Your daughter is the biggest fashionista this side of the Mississippi," Rachael stated with her usual certainty. "She probably has a map of the world with pushpins marking every high-end store on the planet. And the ones that show the designer outlets blink on and off."

Gina laughed. "Don't give her any ideas." She pressed the elevator button for down. It was already lit, but she did it anyway in the useless hope that the door would open quicker. "I'm never wearing these boots again. I'm only going to look at them."

Rachael rolled her eyes. "How's Daniel?"

"Angry." She felt her eyes starting to water and swallowed hard. "Mostly at Andrew, but at me, too. I think it's more than the divorce. We really messed up somewhere."

Rachael nodded as though she understood completely, and Gina felt both relieved and ashamed.

"I called a friend of mine from college who works in administration at Madison U. She said Daniel has a year to change his mind," Rachael said. "Just so you know."

Gina sighed and wished for a nice, warm stretcher so she could curl up in a fetal position and be wheeled to the car. The cold, wet winter weather bleeding through the elevator shaft seeped into her skin and made her feel worse. "I still can't believe he did it," she said, turning to Rachael. "Even if he was mad at us, it doesn't make sense. He left without saying a word. Do you realize that he's gone to the same city my father scrimped and saved to get out of?"

"Did you check the pizza school out?"

She swallowed. "No. I didn't want to go to Naples and see Uncle Giorgio. I'm still hurt that he and Gino set this whole thing up and didn't tell me. I met Danny in Verona, then we went to Florence. He's my son, not theirs."

"G, he's twenty-two."

She stared at Rachael, hurt and angry.

"He can think for himself," Rachael continued, ignoring Gina's look. "God only knows the kid can operate better than the rest of us using only half of his brain."

"Then why ditch your PhD to go make pizzas? And I'm fully aware that he's an adult. Legally speaking."

They stepped into the elevator that had conveniently appeared in time to cut off Rachael's reply, which Gina was certain involved some comment about the fact that she and Andrew had pushed Daniel too hard.

Gina leaned against the cold, metal side bar for support and eyed Rachael, whose dark hair stuck out around her face and shoulders as if she'd put her finger into an electric socket. Rachael had given up trying to tame it into anything other than what it was, thick, coarse, and bushy. For the first time, Gina noticed streaks of gray in the strands that surrounded Rachael's face, and it left her feeling unsettled.

"Did you know that the male brain doesn't reach maturation until the age of twenty-six?" she asked Rachael.

"That explains a lot of dates I had in college."

She swept past the joke. "My point is that he's only twenty-two. He's still maturing."

"I read an article while you were in Italy about this thing that goes on there between mothers and their sons, and I thought of you. They have a word in Italian for it. *Momismo*. Isn't that funny?"

"Hilarious."

"Apparently, sons stick around till their mid-thirties, while their mothers cook and clean for them."

"And your point is?"

"Maybe you need to let go."

"If you had—" She stopped herself. If she hadn't been so tired from the flight, she never would have said it in the first place, and she regretted it immediately.

"I know," Rachael said quietly. "If I had a kid, I'd be worrying about him, too. Or her. I didn't say I wouldn't, okay? You know the whole Jewish mother thing is almost as big as the Italian mother thing, except we share our recipes."

But Rachael hadn't had children, and she'd ended up divorced because she couldn't.

"Rach, I said you could have the recipe for fig cookies anytime you wanted it."

"I have it. They don't taste the same as when you make them. I think you're holding out on me."

Gina switched the subject again. "I met someone."

"That's nice."

"And I slept with him."

The elevator door slid open almost as wide as Rachael's mouth. Cold air from the parking garage hit them like a sharp slap on the cheek. Gina grabbed her suitcase and rolled it behind her as she followed Rachael toward the car.

After they settled themselves into Rachael's aging, tan-colored Volvo wagon, Gina turned to her. "That doesn't make you uncomfortable, does it? You are my sister-in-law." She buckled up her seatbelt.

"Technically, I haven't been your sister-in-law for the last two months, and I would like to remind you that I'm the one who supported you divorcing my idiot brother in the first place. Uncomfortable, no. Surprised, you betcha, and also very interested." The heater roared to life as Rachael turned the engine on.

"You're surprised?"

"You're not exactly known for bed-hopping, my friend."

That was an understatement. Her ex-husband had been her one and only lover.

"In fact," Rachael went on as she tended to do, "I'd give you the lifetime achievement award for being a very good girl. Almost nun-like. It's probably fallout from your divorce."

"I didn't fall right into bed with him, okay? We were together for three days."

"Wow. Three days. Seventy-two whole hours. Now I get it."

"Rach, the guy flirted with me in Italian, in front of the Pantheon, on the steps of the fountain. And he was interesting. Do you know how long it's been since anyone flirted with me in English, let alone Italian?"

Rachael sighed as though remembering a nice dream. "Decades?"

"Pretty much. I'm telling you there's something in the water in that city. And get this —he's a professor, too. Not that it matters, but it was a turn-on at the time." She hesitated, then finished what she wanted to say. If she couldn't tell Rachael, she couldn't tell anyone. "Last night was amazing."

"Too much sharing." Rachael held her hand up. "Are you going to see him again?"

"He doesn't know who I really am."

"What do you mean?"

"He thinks I'm Italian."

"You are Italian."

"No, he thinks I live in Rome. That kind of Italian."

"You mean for three days you posed as an Italian and never told him the truth?"

"I know, it's crazy, but it's not like I was trying to pass as Korean. He came up to me and started speaking in Italian, and I didn't correct him, even though I could tell he was an American because of his accent. His verb endings and prepositions were incorrect, but not so bad I couldn't understand what he was trying to say. And I didn't think I was going to spend three days with him, but one thing led to another, and I just couldn't say, oh, hey, you know yesterday when you thought I was from Rome and I let you? Well, I'm not."

"Okay, whatever, Gina."

She stared blankly into space, remembering the past three days. She could have had a different life, a much different life than the one she had today. Sometimes, life gave you a gift, and those three days had been hers.

"Hello," Rachael called out. "You really are jet-lagged, aren't you?"

"Yes." Gina rubbed her eyes, drier than normal from hours spent on the plane. Her black hair exaggerated the circles under them. On the way home, after the kids puked, she piled her hair on top of her head, held up by a feeding frenzy of bobby pins and clips she'd pulled out of her purse.

"So were you wearing that outfit when you were with him?" Rachael's eyes darted to Gina's clothes again.

"Part of the time."

"Oh, well that's why you passed for the real thing. You said he was a professor?"

"Um-hmm."

"Not to press the point, but he's a professor. How do you know you'll never see him again?" Rachael put the car in reverse and began pulling out of the airport garage.

"He said he goes to Columbia. The university. And he teaches business and finance, not child development. That's not a related field unless you're a policy wonk or a grant writer or you want to start a daycare."

"Are you sure he didn't mean your Columbia?"

"He said Columbia, as in Columbia University. That's in New York. Whenever someone says Columbia, they mean New York."

"I know where it is." Rachael always got a bit testy if it seemed like someone was questioning her knowledge base. "And did he say that in Italian?"

"Yes."

"And you said his Italian wasn't that great. Right?"

"It wasn't that bad, either. I could understand most things he was trying to say."

"But…"

"Rachael."

"Okay." Rachael cocked her head in Gina's direction. "You're the bilingual one in the family. But the word *Columbia* stands for a lot of different places. Let's see. There's Columbia the university, which we've already established, the town in Missouri where you live, Columbia, South Carolina, Columbia in Chicago. There's the Columbia River, and there's a Columbia Cosmetology School, also in Columbia, Missour—"

"He meant New York," Gina interrupted. But there was that small moment on the bus where she had tried to clarify what he'd said. "You mean," she'd inquired in Italian, "that you work at Columbia, the university?" He'd smiled and nodded yes, then added that he was going to Columbia soon. She hadn't pushed the point because by then they'd gotten off the bus that went to the Aqueduct Park and had started talking about more important things, like food, espresso, gelato, ancient Rome, and the Italian countryside.

"Whatever you say," Rachael said, with a heavy dose of doubt icing her words. "If he meant Columbia, he meant Columbia."

They drove in silence as they made their way out of the area surrounding the airport, then Rachael asked, "What was his name?"

"Marc."

"Does signore Marco have a last name?"

Gina was afraid that was coming. "Yes."

"And what is his last name?"

"Edwards."

"You know, you could Google him. See what turns up."

Gina kept quiet.

"Maybe he was lying like you were."

"I wasn't lying. I *am* Italian. I just don't live in Italy."

"Whatever. Maybe he's a spy with faulty Italian language skills."

"Rachael."

"Okay, okay. We'll drop it, Venus." She turned right onto the highway. "So I'm assuming you don't want to swing by the bakery and see your brother?"

Her lips formed a straight line. "I need some sleep and a clear head before I read Gino the riot act." She pointed the toes of her boots down, and then up in a useless attempt to stretch her aching calves. "Do you know how Kimmy is? I haven't heard from her in a couple of days."

Rachael kept her eyes on the road. "She's fine, healthwise."

"What do you mean, healthwise?"

"I said it wrong," she said, shaking her head. "Don't start worrying about her, too. She's fine. As far as I know."

Chapter Two

The two-hour drive from St. Louis to Columbia gave Marc plenty of time to think. He managed to trail little Ms. Gina-whoever-she-really-was through customs and out to the parking garage. It was no small feat, trailing her at a safe distance. The successful execution of his first surveillance mission had been surprisingly exciting. Ha! If Gina could lie, he could spy.

How fortunate that there had been a curtain between first class and coach, and for the fact that the flight attendants had agreed to let him stay in his seat until everyone was off the plane. Gina had turned around once when they were in customs, but he had been three rows over, ten people back, and wearing sunglasses for extra measure. If her eyes had scrolled his way, she didn't recognize him. He wasn't supposed to be there in the first place. Well, neither was she. Obviously, she wasn't Gina Ferrari from the Eternal City, but was she Gina Ferrari at all? Probably not.

He'd heard her friend yell the name *Gina* when they'd met at the airport, but that didn't mean her last name was Ferrari. Maybe she used the name as a private gag. The whole thing had probably been an enormous joke that she and that friend of hers were probably laughing about at this very minute. Maybe she had a husband, and maybe the guy couldn't be bothered to pick her up, so her friend had come to get her. He wished he didn't care, but if she was his wife he'd have been there to pick her up.

It was a silly coincidence that they'd ended up on the same plane. He wasn't Rock Hudson, nor the other actor the woman on the plane mentioned. Tony something or other. He was Marc Edwards, professor of business and finance, on sabbatical, and currently unattached.

When he watched them get into that dented Volvo and drive away, he'd written down the license plate number. What he would do with it he had no idea, but the internet could produce marvelous bits of information if you knew how to massage it or were willing to pay money to someone. Maybe he could learn to do that sort of thing on his own. Being slightly older didn't mean your brain was addled. Yet.

The bleakness of the winter landscape made him shiver as he drove the interstate, even though his car was toasty inside. Midwestern winters were going to take getting used to again. New Mexico winters were no picnic, depending on the altitude you were at, but in Missouri, the wet mixed with the cold was enough to make the bones of a five-year-old feel arthritic.

He reminded himself of the good things. He was now only two hours away from his sister instead of a two-day drive. It was a straight shot from Columbia to St. Louis, and he intended to make the journey at least twice a month. He wanted to see more of Betty and get to know the person he'd made a point of avoiding most of his life. She needed someone, and so did he.

Before he knew it, he'd pulled into the driveway of his friend's house, who, luckily, was also on sabbatical and had offered him his house for the semester. Coincidence? Fate? Of course not. He knew people in academia, and he and Jim Kirby had been friends since grad school. He'd gotten an appointment in New Mexico, while Jim had gone on to Mid-Missouri University. Sometimes things simply worked out. Since he was officially house-sitting, Jim and his wife, Lisa, had insisted he only pay the utilities. Now, if that was fate, he could use a little more of it and a lot less of what had happened over the course of the last year.

Jim's Tudor-style cottage was within walking distance of the university. It was one of the few houses left where the one-acre lot had never been divided. The backyard, courtesy of Lisa, was a gardener's paradise, complete with an English boxwood maze. Come spring, he looked forward to sitting on the lounge chair in the middle of it.

He noted that the front door of the cottage across the street opened as the trunk of his car popped up. The figure of a teenage girl made her way out of the picket fence surrounding the house and across the street to where he stood.

"Evening," he said, as pleasantly as his tired mind and cold body would allow him to.

"Uh, hi," the girl replied, tentatively.

Judging by her hunched shoulders coupled with her uneasy greeting, he thought she had a bad case of teenage shyness. She was slightly overweight, and even from where he was standing in the dark, he could tell she had a bad case of acne. He remembered suffering from reoccurring bouts of it himself. Not fun. But any assumption on his part regarding this girl's lack of confidence disintegrated the minute she started talking.

"I have been waiting for you to get here all day. Didn't your plane get in around two?"

"Yes, it did, but I stopped off to visit my sister. Excuse me." Marc squinted at her. "Who are you?"

"Sydney Sheppard, professional house sitter, dog walker, and errand runner. Also, your new neighbor." She stuck out her hand. "Oh, and I don't clean houses."

Marc grabbed his carry-on and checked bag out of the trunk, then shook Sydney's hand. "Nice to meet you. How did you know my plane got in around two?"

"The Kirbys told me, and I checked online. Oh," she said, reaching into the back pocket of her jeans, "here is my letter of introduction and recommendation from them."

He took the folded paper from her and slipped it into the outer pocket of his carry-on.

"They've known me since I was ten."

"And how old are you now?"

"Almost eighteen."

"So that would make you seventeen?"

"Technically, yes."

"Well, thank you for the letter." He was so tired. All he wanted was to get inside and collapse on the bed. But she wouldn't go away. Why wouldn't she go away?

"Here, let me help you with your carry-on. Free of charge, of course." She took it from his hands, then stopped halfway up the sidewalk, and reached into her other back pocket. "Oh, and my rates are reasonable. Here's a list of them."

"Thanks, uh— "

"Sydney. Sheppard. You know, like the sheepherders. I live across the street. White picket fence." She put his carry-on down in front of the door and backed away. "We'll talk, okay?" She called from the sidewalk.

"Okay." Thank god, she left. He pulled the key to the front door and after a few seconds of jiggling,opened the door and found the switch in the entry hall. Light flooded the living room as well as the art deco stained-glass windows on either side of the thick oak door. Yes, this would be wonderful while he figured out where he was going from here. With any luck, it would not be back to New Mexico.

Within seconds, he heard their steps, a quick clicking on the floor. She appeared first, with a smile on her face that went from one oversized ear to the other.

He reached down to stroke Victoria's small red head and heard Albert coming toward him at breakneck speed. Amazing how fast corgis could run on those three-inch stubby little legs. "Hey, kids. Miss me?"

Each dog jumped up and demanded its quota of affection, then tried to herd him toward the laundry room where he found their treats and chow sitting on top of the washing machine. A note next to the treats bag from Lisa explained that they'd left yesterday morning, earlier than expected, and had put Sydney Sheppard in charge of feeding the dogs for one day.

He reached into the treats and pulled out two biscuits, giving Victoria hers first, because if he didn't, she'd immediately go after Albert's. They devoured them like they hadn't eaten in a week, which, by the shape of them, couldn't be farther from the truth. "Hustlers," Marc whispered.

Sometimes he thought the dogs understood him, and when he thought that, he knew he hadn't been around people enough. As he rolled his suitcase into the bedroom, they followed an inch from his heels, herding him down the hallway.

He pulled the bedroom shades down and collapsed on the thick comforter. After weeks of sleeping alone, except for one night in Rome, he still had trouble getting used to it. Although he missed few things about Elaine, he did miss her feet, which were like small space heaters under the covers. His, always cold, went to them like missiles on a search-and-destroy mission, seeking out their warmth. It had been one of the few things Elaine had begrudgingly tolerated in their years together without having, as she was fond of saying, a negotiating session. Negotiating, to Elaine, usually entailed her telling him how it was going to be. He should have known something was up when she'd bought him a pair of thermal socks.

He scrunched one foot under each dog. Unlike Elaine, they never seemed to mind. They positioned themselves so that one faced the window, while the other kept watch on the door. The duo always worked in tandem. They were pals for life. He'd wanted a pal for life, but he'd chosen the wrong person for that wish. Even though she considered herself open and forward-thinking, Elaine did not like change, and he'd had the audacity to do just that. He sighed, thinking that his life would have been so much simpler and infinitely more enjoyable if he'd opted to be a dog. On that note, he rolled over, shut his eyes, and scanned his mind for five things.

It wasn't hard today. The Kirbys, which he would count as one, warm beds, the woman he thought was from Rome, maybe coincidences (something he would give serious thought to), and the fact that he could see his sister more. Like he ever thought he'd be grateful for that one. But he was. It was a constant source of amazement to him that so many of the things that he'd thought in his youth that he'd never end up doing or believing, he'd ended up doing and believing. Age was humbling. It wiped the arrogance right out of you. So maybe tonight he had six things to be grateful for instead of five. Or, perhaps he should save humbleness for tomorrow, just in case.

***

Gina hated St. Louis. Though she'd grown up there and had many pleasant memories in and around the city, her fondness for the past did not encompass a love for the place. Why her father had decided to settle in a city of gray skies, red brick, and stuffy attitudes was beyond her. Well, no, it wasn't. He'd been sponsored by a cousin in Kansas City, who somehow thought that bringing him to America also meant choosing a bride for him. After that fact had become apparent, her father had boarded a Greyhound bus for St. Louis. It was as far as he could get from Kansas City on the money he'd had, without leaving the state and breaking the terms of his sponsorship. Daniele Gino Ferrari was a baker who'd started his own business, Ferrari's Bakery, in Old Florissant, a small town that had collided with the northern part of greater St. Louis about a century before.

At forty-three, Daniele had made it back to Naples and picked out his own bride from several introductions his mother had arranged. A month later, Maria Francesca Ferrari had boarded a plane with Daniele for her new life in the glorious US of A. Despite their age difference, it had been a love match. Not surprisingly, the lack of sunshine coupled with St. Louis's bone-chilling winters had about done Francesca in. But it had been Gina's brother, Gino, who'd dealt the fatal blow, or so Gina fervently believed.

The hands on the kitchen clock registered seven before she and Rachael stopped talking about Kimmy, and it was seven-thirty a.m. before they made it out of the house . At five minutes to eight, Gina parked her lapis blue Ford Focus on the curb around the corner from Ferrari's Bakery, having left it in Rachael's keeping when she'd been in Italy chasing Daniel down.

There was a parking spot directly in front of the store, but she took a pass on it. She wanted the advantage of surprise. Now, she sat in the car staring at the face of her wristwatch, waiting for the bakery to open, and wishing she'd had a third cup of coffee.

Hearing from Rachael that Kimmy had moved in with her father had wounded Gina more than Daniel's wingnut flight to Naples. Kimmy blamed her for the divorce, and while Rachael had done her best to try and make Gina feel that she should be proud to have such independent children, she felt anything but pride. Their decisions left her feeling scared for them and hurt. A few months ago, they had been crammed together, complaining about the fact that there weren't enough bathrooms. Starting today, Gina could take her pick. In fact, she could leave the door wide open, and no one would care.

The minute hand on her wristwatch moved to the middle of the number twelve, while the small hand rested on the number eight. Gina got out of her car and marched to the entrance with as much of a determined gait as she could muster in her plodding Birkenstocks. The familiar tinkle of the brass bell announced her arrival seconds after she turned the handle to Ferrari's Bakery. When she was a child, she had loved the sound, but when she was a teenager, she'd come to dread that tinkle because it meant she had to put down her book and wait on a customer. Gino, with his bluntness that bordered on rude, couldn't be trusted with the job. This morning the sound of the bell meant her brother had been forewarned as much as he deserved, which was not at all.

A dark woman with rounded hips that were not as large as her chest, came through the small, open doorway behind the counter. Her smile evaporated the second she saw Gina, then reappeared with a note of caution reflected in her eyes.

"Is he back there?" Gina asked.

Shauntel nodded slowly. She walked out from behind the counter and turned the sign on the door to closed as two customers walked up. "How long's this gonna take, Gina?" she asked.

"I haven't a clue."

"We'll open in ten minutes," Shauntel yelled through the door to a customer with a put-out expression on her face. "Sorry for the inconvenience. Free loaf of bread when you come back." Smart woman. No wonder bakery sales had gone up in the five years since Gino exercised his first bit of common sense and married Shauntel Johnson.

"Oh, and by the way," Gina said before she stormed into the back room. "Good to see you, as always."

Years ago, her mother had sewn flowered curtains to cover the opening between the shop and the workroom. They were long gone. The bakery looked like a man ran it, though Shauntel's soft touches were beginning to make an inroad. Nothing fancy came out of this bakery unless it was special ordered. The standard fare was good bread, rolls (especially at Christmas and Easter), biscotti, and small layered cakes with sliced burnt almonds around their sides. Ferrari's was also famous for wedding cakes, on order. A few months ago, Shauntel told Gina that folks were coming all the way from South and West County now to order them.

"I've been meaning to make some curtains for that opening," Shauntel said, as though she'd read Gina's mind. "You know, spruce the place up. I was thinking thick red and white stripes to match the awning over the door. What do you think?"

Gina turned to her sister-in-law and smiled. "I think that's a great idea. My mother had—"

"I know. Your mother had flowers. Gino's told me that about ten times now. I like stripes. You know, Gina, your brother meant well."

"He ruined my son's life."

Shauntel put her hands on her hips in defiance but said gently, "He thought he was helping. I'll be upstairs waiting for you two to finish whatever it is you two are going to say. Come on up before you leave and tell me about your trip, okay? Gino keeps saying he'll take me to Italy, but he never does. At least if you tell me about your trip, I can pretend like it's mine for a little bit."

The short passageway between the storefront and the back of the bakery opened into the workroom. She spied on her brother at the far end as he leaned over one of the high wooden tables, rolling out dough for something. His tattoos moved along with his lean, tight biceps, and for a split second, Gina thought it was like watching a cartoon. When he picked up a generous handful of pine nuts and sprinkled them over the dough, she knew he was making biscotti.

Under thin, white cotton cloth, on a side table near her, small ping-pong ball–sized dough lay in perfect rows on trays, waiting until they were ready for the large oven. Gina pulled back the cloth, grabbed three of them, and started throwing. Each one hit the intended target. First her brother's left ear, then his right. She hoped the one that hit his earring smacked the post against his neck. The third dough ball hit the top of his head, although she was aiming for his aquiline nose. When she had been with Marc in the Capitoline Museum and saw a bust of Julius Caesar, it was like seeing a well-groomed likeness of her brother, minus the ponytail. Too bad Gino acted more like the impulsive Marc Anthony.

"Ah, hell, Gina, *che cazzo*. Stop."

She grabbed another ball and threw again, this time hitting his arm.

"Stop it already. You're destroying my profits."

"*Che stronzzo*, you horse's ass." Like she could care about his stupid profits.

"Ah yes, the professor with the mouth of a fishwife."

"I'll never forgive you. What you did, going behind my back like that, you broke my heart."

"Settle down, sis. This isn't a Godfather movie."

How dare her impulsive, self-destructive, volcanic brother instruct her in self-control? When she went off, it was for a good reason. When he went off, it was to wreak chaos. "How could you do that to me?"

"I didn't do it *to* you. I did it *for* Daniel. He was miserable. And stop with the rolls, okay? That was an order for the Knights of Columbus, and I'm doing it on a discount already because of Papa." He threw up his hands in disgust.

"If my son was miserable, you should have told me or Andrew. We're his parents." She watched Gino grimace when she said her ex-husband's name.

"Danny begged me not to. He made me promise. You and Andrew put so much pressure on that kid to be the

Boy Wonder he couldn't tell either of you, especially during the divorce."

"I never pressured him. I followed his interests." She knew she was lying the second she said it, but how could she admit that to Gino? She was the one who always did things right. She had a goddamn PhD in child development. At least he didn't know about Kimmy. Or did he?

"Oh, come on, Gina. You would have had him on *Jeopardy* when he was still in diapers if you could have. It scares him, how invested you are in his intellectual success, and he resents it. That's why he couldn't tell you how miserable he was. He wanted out, and I helped him because he's family."

"So, you helped him leave everything to go make pizzas. Wow, Gino, thanks a lot."

Gino put the lid back on the tin of pine nuts and started to pick up the dough balls. "It's more than making pizzas."

"Like what?"

"Like I can't tell you."

"So now you and my son, *my son*," she said her voice rising, " keep secrets ?"

Gino let his breath out and shook his head back and forth slowly. "All I can say is that it was his idea, not mine." He collected the thrown dough balls and pitched them into the trash can.

"You should be glad he didn't get into drugs or start drinking. Or worse." Gino turned to face his sister. "The kid's twenty-four now. Let him go."

"He's twenty-two. It's hard to keep track when you're in prison. Or rehab, for the second time." She crossed her arms over her chest.

"Okay, now you've hurt me. Are we even?"

"No, we are not. My son isn't your business. He's mine. You should have stayed out of it."

Gino let out a sigh. "I would have loved to, but he felt he couldn't go to you, partly because of the divorce."

"What do you mean, the divorce?"

Gino let out a breath and shook his head slowly. "He thought everyone had enough on their plates already. He didn't want to upset you. Gina, trust me. I helped your son."

What was the point in arguing with her pig-headed brother any more than she already had? Gino did what he wanted regardless of who it hurt. He always had, and she'd said enough mean things already. Still, she wanted to lunge at him with her fists, wailing as she had when they were little and another mother in their neighborhood wouldn't let her daughter play with Gina because of her brother.

She let the last ball of dough she had been holding, roll to the floor. It stopped at the tip of her brother's black, lace-up work boot, and somehow Gino managed to flick the dough ball onto the top of his boot, kick it upward, and catch it with his right hand. Damn him. He was always the coordinated one, involved in soccer since he'd been five, while she had sat on the bleachers, reading next to her mother. Her brother had blundered through life like a bull with a blindfold on, and she had tried to make up for his actions by getting awards instead of detentions. Yet she loved him. He was her brother.

He moved forward and gave her a tentative hug. Gina didn't reciprocate. "You raise a bird with an open cage—when they fly away, there's a chance they'll come back. You raise a bird in a locked cage—the minute you open it they're gone for good. That's what Mamma used to say."

Gina produced a weak smile and considered for a minute asking her brother if he thought Daniel's cage had been open or shut. But why invite input from a man who'd never raised a child and could barely take care of himself? "How long did he feel this way?"

Gino threw up his hands and turned his palms out, but not as dramatically as the people in Rome had. His gesture was muted, as though he was speaking perfect Italian with an American accent. "Before the divorce. A year, maybe. He'd come here on the weekends and make cookies with Shauntel and me." He sighed. "He'd start talking, and we listened."

She'd known without knowing. The last semester, his coursework had been filled with more Bs than his usual straight As, and he'd been dragging his heels when it came to his research.

Gino scanned her up and down with pursed lips. "I thought you picked up some clothes when you were there. Daniel told me you went up north near Milan."

Just when she was feeling warm and fuzzy. There was nothing wrong with Birkenstocks and sweatpants and extra-large sweatshirts. "What are you trying to say, Gino?"

"You'll never get anyone if you go around looking like a reject from the gym."

"You have to ruin it every time with your big mouth, don't you?"

He shrugged.

"What makes you think I want anyone? Maybe I'll sleep around for the rest of my life."

"If that's your goal, you still need to ditch those shoes."

She grabbed a warm roll out of a baker's dozen and took a sizable bite out of it, then put it back in the box. "I've had enough of you today."

"Ah Jesus, quit eating the profits."

"You eat it, Gino." She swallowed. The roll was quite good, but there was no way she was going back for the other half. "And I don't mean the rest of your stupid rolls." After one last dirty look at him, Gina put her fingers under her chin and brushed them forward. He knew what it meant, and he returned the gesture with an extra dose of drama.

"I am your big brother."

"You're my twin."

"I came out first."

"Big deal."

"Only sluts sleep around."

"I can't believe you said that. That is so disgusting. Hey, *testa di cazzo*." Ha. She'd gotten him with that one.

Her feet hit the back stairs that went to the flat above the bakery, where the first eighteen years of her life had been spent. They led into the second-floor pantry and through the kitchen. Two large windows next to the old enamel table always left the eating area warm and sunny in summer and winter. That kitchen was something she missed.

Shauntel smiled as she got up from the table. "What can I get you?"

"A new life."

"Never works."

"Well, then how about a cup of coffee?"

"I can do that." Shauntel put the kettle on the stove. She and Gino didn't have a microwave because they believed microwaving foods often rendered them soggy and rubbery. They were both food snobs, which was the only thing the two of them were snobs about. Despite her many complaints about her brother, she did appreciate his good points. She just wished it took two hands to count them instead of less than one.

"That fight was over in under ten minutes. You two are getting better. Must be age. Can I turn the sign to open now? I got a business to run here."

Gina smiled. "Go ahead. I'll take my coffee downstairs to the shop, and we can talk about Italy there. Then I have to head for home."

Chapter Three

Marc Edwards had a productive and busy morning, studying Gina Ferrari. The real one, not the imposter. After he'd woken up and drunk three espressos, he'd gotten on the computer and Googled her name. That produced a landslide of Gina Ferraris, most of whom lived in Italy. He hit pay dirt when he'd refined his search to Gina Ferrari, Missouri. Much to his shock, there she was, living in Columbia, and a professor to boot. Coincidence? Luck? Divine providence? Or had he gotten knocked in the head and was now in some Twilight Zone coma state, trapped in an eternal rom-com?

He wanted to pick up the phone and call the woman who sat next to him on the plane, but he had no idea who she was. There was no one to share this with. He couldn't call his friends in Albuquerque, because they were Elaine's friends, too. They were still processing their breakup and what it meant for future interactions with either of them. Whose friends would they be?

Dr. Gina Ferrari had published a mountain of articles on various aspects of intellectual development in young children, with particular regard to the effects of family influences. He continued to peruse the books she'd published, the conferences she'd spoken at, as well as the academic journals her articles had been published in.

With the priority-level password the chancellor's office had already given him, he'd done some extra snooping. Yes, it was unethical, but he figured when someone made a chump out of you the way Gina Ferrari had him, one must fight fire with fire.

Changes in her administrative records and tax-withholding information indicated she was recently divorced (thank god), had two kids on her health plan, and lived three blocks up the hill and around the corner from where he was right now. This was getting creepy.

If she had fessed up to who she really was, they could be eating dinner together right now, and maybe even have had that breakfast they'd missed. While he admired her moxie, he wished he hadn't been the recipient of a scam because it made him feel naïve, stupid, and used. Then again, on a few levels, he was quite thankful to have been on the receiving end. It had been the most enjoyable three days he'd had, well, since forever. He stretched his arms and laughed, thinking about it.

Anytime Marc sat for more than thirty minutes, he had to get up and do something. When he was a boy, the cleaning lady used to say he had ants in his pants, so walking the dogs again in spite of the cold, sunless day sounded like an inviting activity. He grabbed his coat, harnessed up the dogs, and headed out. The minute he made it to the sidewalk, the door in the house across the street opened, and Sydney Sheppard bounded out. He suspected she'd been waiting for him.

"Hi." She studied her feet while gathering up steam, then let it rip. "I was wondering if you'd made a decision about hiring me."

Before he could answer no, Albert and Victoria surrounded her, then jumped on her legs.

"Oh, that's sweet," she said as she bent down to pet them both at once. "They missed me." She glanced up. "Albert and Victoria are a much better choice of names than Diana and Charles, huh?" She stood up, grinning. "Are you going to breed these two?"

"No. He's neutered, and she's spayed."

"Oh." She blushed. "I guess I should have looked at Albert for the answer to that one. You know, the real Victoria and Albert had a passel of offspring, which is one of the reasons there are so many royals in Britain today."

Marc jerked his head back. Who was this kid? "Puppies were more than I thought I could handle. Have you ever walked two dogs at once?"

"No. But I'm sure willing to try."

"Okay. But first, tell your mother."

"Which one? I have two. You know, as in *Heather Has Two Mommies*.

Marc frowned in confusion. "Um, either will do."

"You don't know about the book, do you?"

"What book?"

"You don't have children, do you?"

"Regretfully, no."

"Nice answer. A lot of men don't want to admit they have any, much less pay for the ones they have, like my dad when he found out my mother was gay. Like I had anything to do with that one. And yet that's his excuse for not paying child support." She turned and headed for her house, then turned back quickly, and added, "Sometimes, you can't make this stuff up."

The dogs pulled him across the street in hot pursuit of Sydney.

When they all reached her front door, she turned to him and said, "Wait right here. I may like dogs, but one of my moms is strictly a cat person."

Sydney opened the door and yelled. "I'm going on a walk with the corgi guy across the street. He wanted you to know so you don't think he's a pervert and have him arrested or something." She turned to him and grinned.

"It's okay," a chorus of two female voices answered through the door. "We know all about him from Lisa," one of the female voices added.

Marc had to laugh. He stuck his head in the door and yelled, "Hello, and thanks."

"You're welcome," they answered in unison.

He handed over the dogs' leashes. "Here. Let's see what you can do on a test drive."

"Cool." Sydney started off down the hill, the opposite way from where Marc had determined Gina Ferrari lived.

"Wait," Marc said, thinking this would be perfect. "Let's go up the hill, not down."

"Whatever you want, Professor Edwards." With the expertise of a professional at the Westminster Dog Show, Sydney turned the corgis around without tangling either leash.

"Impressive," Marc said, smiling. "And you can call me Marc."

"I gave you a sheet detailing my rates, right?"

"It's on the kitchen counter."

"And you can call me, Syd."

They two of them walked in silence while Marc scrolled through his brain to find something appropriate to say to a teenager. "What year of high school are you in?"

"I'm graduating this spring."

"That would make you a senior."

"Yeah, and don't ask me what I want to do for the rest of my life because I don't know, and I'm tired of people asking."

"Okay. I won't ask."

"I'm thinking about being a vet."

"Very interesting."

"I guess. Or maybe I'll study history."

"Why not do both?"

She glanced at him and snorted. "Whatever. Like I said, I don't want to talk about it."

"Okay."

"I guess I could do both, huh?"

"Yes, you could." Marc took note of the way she directed the dogs along the sidewalk.

"So, what's finance like?"

"How'd you know I was in finance?" he asked. Then it dawned on him. "Lisa talked to your mothers about me, didn't she?"

"Yeah, you were the number one dinner discussion last week. The guy who's going to gut Mid-MO's budget. My mothers work in the art department."

"Oh. So you do know all about me."

"Yep, but nobody else does. Yet. My moms don't talk to too many people, and I don't have any friends."

"How come?" He shouldn't have asked that. He knew it the minute he said it.

"I'm blunt, I don't like to party, and I'd rather read than go on Facebook."

"Oh. I'm sorry. Not about the reading part, but about the friend part."

"Don't be. It's not like I'm going to off myself or anything." She gave him a rueful grin after she said it.

"That's reassuring." Marc grinned back.

"Besides, like I said, my dad won't help me financially, and my bio mom's a nude model in the art department. If I want to go to college, it's either loans or a scholarship, and I'd like to not be in debt for the rest of my life, unlike the rest of my generation, so I'm shooting for the best scholarship I can get."

"Sounds like a plan. A very good one, too."

They walked on for a half block more in silence.

"And I want to get away from here as far as I can get," she said, breaking the silence.

"That's how I felt my last year of high school."

"Where'd you go to high school?"

"Webster Groves. In St. Louis."

"Oh wow, you got far away. Two whole hours west on Highway Seventy."

"Hey, look, smarty pants, I've been all over this planet. I'm back here to be closer to my sister, and why I feel the need to explain myself to an almost eighteen-year-old—" He stopped mid-sentence, watching a horrified expression spread on Sydney's face, then broke out in laughter.

"Sorry," she said.

"Don't worry about it."

"My mouth gets me into trouble. A lot."

"Really, don't worry about it, okay?"

"So you think you want to hire me?"

He nodded as they trudged up the hill. "Can you walk them after you get home from school? That would help."

"I'll do it every day. I'll text you if something comes up, but it never does." She grinned at him again. "Like I said, not much of a social life. And what about the errand running?"

The kid was relentless, and Marc admired her for it. "Let's keep walking, and we'll talk."

* * * *

One of these days, Gina told herself, she would own a house with an attached garage. Either that or she would live someplace where subzero temperatures were forbidden by law. She gritted her teeth against the cold and yanked her suitcase out of the trunk. It landed on her toe, and she winced while making a promise to herself that she would ditch her Birkenstocks as soon as they wore out, which in truth might be never. Someday, future archeologists would dig up those strangely shaped soles and speculate about whether they had been some sort of spoon rest.

Holding onto the porch rail, she pulled her suitcase up the back steps. Lord, how she loved this wreck of a house. When they'd moved to Columbia, she and Andrew had bought the two-story Craftsman style home because it was in-between Winston College, a small, private liberal arts school where Andrew taught, and the university—a perfect compromise and a state seldom attained during their marriage. The brown brick house had a large pebble-stone porch that covered the entire front. Every other winter, at least one pipe sprang a leak, and on the years that didn't happen, a river of rust-colored water came running out of the upstairs toilet as it overflowed. Old houses were money pits, yet somehow when she ran her hands along the thick, solid walnut banister, it felt worth it.

She turned on her computer the minute she got inside, and scanned her email for any messages from Daniel or Kim. The first to appear was from her son, and she thought for a minute what it must have been like for her grandmothers in Naples to wait weeks for a letter from her mother or father. How immediate life had become.

From: Daniel<dferrari@gmail.com>
To: Mom <gferrari@hotmail.com
Subject: You

Mom,
Wanted to make sure you got home safely. This is my choice and I want you to respect it, although I do not think you do. I am enjoying myself. For once. I love you, Mom.
Daniel

God that hurt. She respected him. Of course, she respected him, but that didn't mean she thought he'd made a wise decision. And as a mother, wasn't it was her duty to tell him so?

She noticed he used her last name instead of Andrew's in his email address. Was he going by Ferrari now, instead of Ellison? That could cause some trouble. She hoped Andrew wouldn't find out. Divorce or not, she still wanted everyone to get along. It was possible. She'd read several research articles about positive postdivorce communication.

Kimmy's email, dated two days ago, announced she was moving in with her father because he needed her. It sounded like a page out of Andrew's playbook, and it meant at least one of three things. Either he was still angry and wanted to get at her through their daughter, his cleaning lady quit, or his recent girlfriend ditched him and he needed someone to listen to him talk about himself. All three together were also a distinct possibility.

She closed her email and pulled her suitcase upstairs, pausing to peek in Kimmy's bedroom as she flipped on the light. The closet was open and stripped of all her clothes, and the hangers jammed together at odd angles as though someone had pulled off shirts and sweaters in clumps, instead of one at a time. More telling was that her laptop, iPad, and cell phone chargers were missing from the now empty desk, their outlines visible by the dust left behind.

The phone rang as she opened her suitcase to empty it, and she picked it up without checking the caller ID. Even a telemarketer was better than the onerous task ahead.

"Mom?"

"Kimmy? Honey, I—"

"Mom," Kimmy's voice quivered. "I need your help."

"What's wrong?"

"Dad won't let me keep my dog."

"What dog?" She was in Italy for two measly weeks, and her daughter now had a dog?

"My dog. He was Jennifer's, and her parents made her get rid of it, so I took him, and now Dad won't let me keep Hairy either, so you have to. Please."

"Harry? Like the wizard guy?"

"H-a-i-r-y."

"Oh, Hairy, as in dog hair." Wonderful. "How big is he?"

"Not very."

What was she saying? Why didn't she tell her, sorry I can't do this? But if the dog was here, Kimmy might move back in, or at the very least come after school every day to walk him. They could have dinner together and talk like they used to.

"Okay, bring him over, and we'll check this Hairy dog out. And I'm not saying yes, but I'm certainly not saying no. Do you need me to pick you up?"

"No. Dad's letting me borrow his car to drive Hairy to your house."

I'll bet he is. "Okay. Fine. Bring him over." She hung up the phone, but not before she heard the joyful screams of two girls on the other end.

***

Hairy turned out to be the ugliest dog Gina had ever seen. His tail was too long for his medium-sized legs, and his floppy ears went on for three more inches than they should have. If she were to guess, the dog was a cross between a sheltie and a beagle, although at least one more canine breed was in there someplace, passing on to him patchy fur the texture of twenty-year-old, stained shag carpeting. He was the kind of dog you winced at upon seeing until he wagged his tail and looked at you like you were the best thing he'd ever set his dark-chocolate eyes on. Gina melted at once.

She smiled to herself as she and Kimmy walked down the sidewalk together with Hairy, thinking that it was wonderful to be doing something other than trading barbs with her daughter about doing her homework or cleaning up her room, or the fact that there wasn't much of a future in being a professional cheerleader. Let Andrew deal with it for once.

She turned to Kimmy and said, "Okay, I'm convinced Hairy is not the dog from Hades and won't chew up the house or pee on the carpets. So why didn't Jennifer's parents want to keep him?"

"They're getting divorced. Like everyone else, I guess."

This did not surprise her one bit. Jennifer's parents had been unhappy in their marriage since the girls had been in middle school. She ignored her daughter's dig and asked, "How is Jenn doing?"

"Okay, I guess." Kimmy was silent for a second, then said, "Her dad's girlfriend hates dogs, and her mother is moving into an apartment that won't take animals."

"If I take Hairy—"

"Mom, I'll watch him. I promise. He'll be my dog. Really. You won't have to do a thing."

"If Hairy stays at my house, and I'm not saying yes yet, I expect you to come over and walk him. A lot." She watched the cogs turning in Kimmy's head. "Agreed?"

Kimberly sniffed. "I was going to anyway. He's my dog. I love him."

"How long have you had him?"

"Since yesterday."

They walked half a block in silence, then Gina said, "The scarf I brought you back from Milan looks wonderful, by the way." While Kimmy hadn't told her she loved it, she had put it on along with the new leather gloves as they were leaving to walk Hairy.

"How come you didn't get the paisley pumps I showed you on the internet?"

"Those shoes were eight hundred euros. At the outlet."

"But this is nice, too." Kimmy patted the scarf. "Thanks."

"Would you like to stay for dinner?"

"That'd be great. Then I don't have to cook. Do you want to ask Dad? I'm sure he'd love to see you, Mom. You know, find out about your trip."

Gina forced her face to stay neutral. "I don't think that's such a good idea." She paused for a moment, then said as casually as possible, "So your dad has you cooking?"

"Yeah. He says it's good practice for college. You know, for when I live on my own."

"Uh-huh." She watched Hairy's behind as he led the way, his hips wagging from side to side as he walked. The tufty hair on his butt stood straight up around his tail and gave the impression that he had double Mohawks on his backside.

"So are we going to talk about you moving in with your father?"

Kimmy put her head down and handed the leash to Gina. She stuck her gloved hands into the pockets of her black wool coat. Her hair, dark and thick like Rachael's, acted like a complete shield for her face.

"When you were in Italy and I was staying with Dad, he seemed so..."

"So, what?"

"Lonely. I think he misses you. And then Jane broke up with him."

"Is Jane the woman he was dating?"

She jerked her head toward Gina. "You're not supposed to know anyone broke up with him, okay?"

"Okay. Let's get back to why you moved in with your father."

Kimmy started again. "I've been living with you since you made Dad move out—"

"Kimberly, it was a mutually agreed upon decision."

"Whatever. But he's the one who's sad. So I thought, and Dad agreed, that I should live with him until I graduate. So we could spend some quality time together."

"I see. Okay, if that's what you want before you go away to college, that's fine with me."

"Well, Dad and I have been talking about that, too."

"Not the Cardinals cheerleader thing again. Please tell me you are not going to pursue that. You're smarter than a cheerleader." Gina wished she could grab her words back the minute she said them. They'd been getting along so well.

Kimmy stiffened. "The Cardinals moved to Arizona."

"No, they didn't."

Kimmy's chin jutted out. "You're thinking of the baseball Cardinals, but the football Cardinals are now in Phoenix. As in Arizona."

"Really? Do they have Cardinals in Arizona? You know, the birds?"

"I have no idea. And I am going to try out for professional cheerleading someday, but Dad thought it would be better if I got a few years of college under my belt first."

At least she and Andrew could agree on a few things. "That's wise. Your grades and test scores are excellent." *So why do you want to be a cheerleader?* "I think you have a good shot at the colleges you applied to. Especially Ann Arbor."

"Well, Dad thinks staying here and living with him for my first two years before I tryout for professional cheerleading is a good plan, too. So maybe I won't go away. Maybe I'll go here."

A three-alarm fire went off in Gina's head. "I thought we were all settled on you going away to college."

"But Dad needs me."

"Kimmy, *kids* are supposed to need their parents, then they spend some time hating their parents because they still need them, even though they don't want to, then they go away." She put extra emphasis on the words *go away*. "Then they come back from time to time, and their parents miss them. And the kids don't understand that until they have their own children. It's a process called *growing up and establishing your own life*. You are way too smart to be a cheerleader." Gina chose her next words with care. "Maybe you should consider an alternative career path."

"Phys ed?"

"That sounds…interesting."

Kimmy turned away from Gina, and stared at the floor. The curtain of hair covered her face once again.

"If you go away to college, your father will be fine without you."

"I applied here."

Gina blinked. "Here? At Mid-Missouri?"

"Yeah, here. And I'm going to audition for the Golden Girls this summer."

"When did you get into acting? Aren't you a little young to play a retiree?"

Kimmy sighed, then looked directly at Gina. Although her voice was coated with defiance, there was a look of hurt in her eyes that made Gina realize she'd crossed a line with her daughter she didn't know was there. "Mom, not the television show. The Golden Girls is the name of the cheer squad for Mid-Missouri U. The school colors are red and gold. You work there. You should know these things."

"Oh, of course. I knew that. Isn't it past the deadline for applying?" She brightened at the possibility, and hoped it didn't show.

"I had to pay a fine for a late application, but it was only fifty dollars, and Dad put it on his credit card. He says I'm a shoo-in, late or not."

Where had she messed up in her parenting? She'd read more about adolescence than anyone she knew. Raising her children had been a carefully laid plan, as though she'd been cooking a great, wonderfully complex recipe in which every ingredient had to be weighed, measured, and mixed at the precise moment. Somehow, it had all flopped in the oven. One son, one brilliant, handsome, cherished son in a goddamn Pizza University, and another equally smart and beautiful daughter conned into being her father's housekeeper through the most critical years of young adulthood. This couldn't be fallout from the divorce alone.

They rounded the corner and started down the hill toward home when Kimmy reached out and jerked hard on Hairy's leash. "Hold up, Mom." She motioned her head toward a man next to a girl with two dogs who had extremely short legs. They were at the bottom of the hill about a hundred feet in front of them.

"Isn't that Sydney Sheppard?" Gina asked, squinting. "I can't tell exactly."

"Yes, and please don't say hi. Let's go." Kimmy took Hairy's leash and started walking back up the street.

Gina followed on her daughter's heels. "What's wrong?"

"I don't want to talk to Sydney Sheppard."

"You two used to be such good friends."

"Things change, and no, I don't want to talk about it, okay?"

They turned into the driveway and started toward the front door.

"Still staying for dinner?"

"Depends. Can I try on those boots you brought back?"

"Sure."

"I can't believe you bought them."

Me either.

"So, they were cheaper than the pumps I wanted?"

"Much."

"Can I wear them?"

"You can try them on."

"Can I borrow them sometime?"

"No. Getting back to dinner, is it a yes or a no?"

"Will you leave me alone about college?"

"Yes."

"What are you making?"

Gina laughed. "Whatever you want."

"How about fettuccini with clam sauce."

"Red or white?"

"Red has fewer calories. And can we make enough for Dad? I'm sure he misses your cooking."

She opened her mouth to speak, then shut it. Instead of saying what she wanted, she said as evenly as possible, "If there are leftovers, you may take them home."

"You're the best, Mom. I really appreciate it."

Gina beamed. Modeling maturity had its rewards.

"Could you help me do some of Dad's wash, too? It's in the trunk of the car."

***

Marc and Sydney made it back as the phone rang, and it sent the corgis into a barking frenzy. Any unauthorized noise did unless they were eating. "Hush," he hissed at them as he picked up his cell phone from the kitchen counter.

"Marc," a woman's voice said, "can't you get those dogs of yours to be quiet for one phone call?"

One phone call? He knew she meant it to be funny, but it still irritated him.

"Elaine, how are you?"

Sydney made a motion with her hands about feeding the dogs, and Marc nodded in agreement.

"Excellent," Elaine said. "Did you have a good holiday?"

She knew he celebrated Christmas. They both did. Why couldn't she say Christmas? It wasn't like they were at a faculty party. This was a private conversation between the two of them. And yes, he had to acknowledge the pettiness on his part for allowing himself to be annoyed by her word choice, but that's what happens when people break up. All the things you ignored to make the relationship work come rushing to the surface when you split. "Christmas was pretty good," he said. "I went to Rome for part of it, and that was particularly wonderful."

"Of course, you did. You'd live there if you could."

"And you?" He asked, hoping to reroute the conversation before Elaine went on her rant about Rome's terrible traffic, its horrific drivers, and the graffiti. Personally, he found the graffiti fascinating. Romans had been writing on walls for thousands of years, so why stop now?

"Spent it with my sister and her family in Charlotte." She laughed derisively. "They're such bourgeois yuppies. Their sons both play lacrosse. Next thing you know they'll be applying for Duke."

He had to admit, Elaine's sister-in-law was vacuous in a genteel Southern sort of way, but vacuous or not, he was glad Elaine had family to visit. Maybe he wasn't in a relationship with her anymore, and her proclivity for elitism might bug the hell out of him, but that didn't mean he didn't care. Not by a long shot.

Silence ruled on both ends. Two people who'd lived together for twenty years now had nothing to say. It was sad, he thought, very sad.

"The reason I called is that I decided not to buy you out of the house. I think I'd rather sell it," Elaine said.

"Fine." They'd fought about this a month ago. He'd made the mistake of mentioning to her that she should give serious consideration to not taking on the house by herself. Elaine wasn't great with home repairs or cleaning or maintenance of anything, including relationships. She read books, went to plays and movies, sat on faculty committees, and attended political functions. A walkup flat or a condo in a high rise was what she needed. Still, she had taken it as a chauvinistic insinuation that she was incapable of doing those types of things, and had gone ballistic.

"Thanks for giving me some time to think it through."

"No problem. Can I leave my stuff there until the house sells?"

"Of course. And you're still good on not wanting any of the furniture?"

"It's all yours." Minus his camping equipment, he wanted a clean break. Besides, she'd picked out all the furniture anyway, and he'd never taken a shine to her taste. Too much chintz.

"You're being awfully nice about all of this, but then you always were. Nice."

Too late Elaine. "Call me when you locate a real estate agent. I'd like to be included in the negotiations."

"Of course. It's half yours."

He put the phone back down on the counter, then remembered Sydney was standing at the far end of the kitchen. She stared at him, her arms crossed.

"Getting divorced?"

He crossed his arms back at her. "Technically, yes."

"Is that why you left New Mexico?"

"You know, you ask an awful lot of questions for someone your age."

"She didn't like the dogs, did she?"

"No, she did not."

"You should have known, then."

Marc cocked his head. "Known what?"

"Never trust someone who doesn't like dogs."

"I'll keep that in mind next time." Marc walked Sydney toward the front door and opened it for her.

"When do I start?"

"How about Wednesday? I have to make a copy of the key and tell the Kirbys you'll be coming in and out of the house."

"Don't bother. I have a key already. They were my designated run-to house for emergencies. Plus, I was feeding the dogs and walking them before you got here."

"Oh yeah, I forgot."

"Did the woman in New Mexico like cats?"

"Not that it's any of your business, but no, she didn't like cats, either."

"Duh. There was clue number two."

"Goodbye, Sydney." He shut the door and tried to stifle his laughter because that kid needed no encouragement whatsoever.

With the dogs on his heels, he made his way back to the bedroom, thinking about his chance encounter with Dr. Gina Ferrari. She hadn't even recognized him. But in the very near future, he would be running into her again, and this time it wouldn't be by chance or coincidence. Nor would it be a fate smack. Next time he'd be the one holding all the cards, and the joke would be on her.

Tonight, he was not exhausted to the point that when he climbed into bed he couldn't take the time to survey his surroundings. Lisa Kirby had decorated the bedroom in warm colors. The beige bedspread and muted rusty-red throw pillows contrasted well with the brightly colored prints that lined the wall opposite the bed. It all worked to bring the eye quickly to the four, framed prints, each of the same maple tree rendered in a different season. He liked the fall one best, although the starkness of the winter print was surprisingly interesting.

His sister Betty would like the prints if she ever saw them, but every time he brought up leaving the group home, she refused. After a lifetime of never being given a choice about anything, he suspected she rather enjoyed saying no to everything she could. Good for her.

With that thought in mind, he arranged the top of the comforter around his shoulders and thought of five things. Tonight, they didn't come as fast as they had the night before, but he forced them to the forefront from sheer habit, something that performing any ritual for a solid year will get you. He was grateful for the corgis, which tonight would be counted as two separate entities instead of one. Yes, it was cheating, but he allowed himself a pass, and that made him think of a very real number three, that he could forgive himself for being less than perfect and all too human. Number four was, of course, his sister Betty's burgeoning independence. This brought him to tonight's big one, drum roll, please. Number five was not only the fact that he'd landed a post that took him out of New Mexico for the next year, but also that somehow in some inexplicable intersection of the cosmos, he had landed right smack dab next to Gina Ferrari.

Chapter Four

Gina loved the front doors of Prichard Hall, home to the Department of Child and Family Development. The large, thick-beveled-glass door was framed in even thicker oak and surrounded by stone scrollwork instead of the aluminum and steel used in the newer structures around campus.

The first time she'd walked through those doors it had been for her faculty interview, the new Cornell graduate proud to be called Dr. Ferrari. She also remembered the sadness that engulfed her because her mother had passed away and wasn't alive to see her get a faculty appointment. Most days, she slipped in through the side door, as she did today, an hour before most of her colleagues were up, anticipating their first cup of coffee. Unfortunately, most of her colleagues did not include Dr. Roberta Cooper, the department's chairperson.

"Stop right there, Dr. Ferrari." Roberta stuck her head out the door and grinned. "We need to talk."

Gina was caught midstride. She remembered telling Andrew when she had first been hired that Roberta Cooper had eyes in the back of her head and the nose of a bloodhound. Nothing and no one ever got past Roberta Cooper.

"Get your coffee and beat it back to my office, pronto." Roberta grinned and scrutinized her watch. Her perfectly spaced teeth appeared particularly white against her dark-chocolate skin and pitch-black blouse. "We've got a good hour before the rest of our esteemed colleagues burst through the doors, and we need to talk."

Oh, that did not sound good.

Gina took another sip from her cup as she sat and listened to Roberta wind down. Hopefully, the action of swallowing would buy her some time to process the words, but instead, she choked from the heat of the French roast as it bulldozed its way down her throat and into her stomach.

"Why me?" she asked, coughing. "Couldn't you come up with someone else who knows more about budgets than I do?"

"You were requested."

"By whom?"

Roberta sighed. "By the chancellor and the shill who's going to be making his way to every department. The guy is using this as his sabbatical research, and he'll be writing a paper about the process. We're his guinea pigs. It's insulting."

"Do you know the shill's name?"

"Don't remember. We'll be meeting him on Monday. You should be getting an email about it." She squinted at her computer. "I have no idea why he decided to start with Child and Family Development. I guess he wanted to test out his method with the little fish before he moved on to the sharks. And, as far as why the chancellor requested you to be the liaison for Child and Family Development, do you know anyone who might have put your name up?"

"No."

"Well, I'm sure it was a coincidence, then. He probably went down the list, and your name stuck out. You know, Ferrari. Like the car, or Gina, like Gina Lollobrigida. He probably likes Italians. And I'll never admit to saying this, but I'm glad he picked you. You have social skills and nice manners. In fact, sometimes I think you're the only one in the department with either. Except for me, but I didn't say that, either."

She watched Roberta chuckle. Besides having superior hearing and eyes in the back of her head, the woman could be insightfully sarcastic and finish off any opponent with a mean verbal bite. Simply put, Roberta Cooper was the department chair because she could and would employ any arm-twisting method without a drop of regret. Gina sighed. There were times she wished she could do the same.

"When do I have to do this?"

"The first budget meeting is Monday morning, and it's mandatory. After that, you'll make your own schedule with the faculty, and with the Shill-boy—and I didn't say that either. Shouldn't take more than two or three meetings, but truthfully, I have no idea how long this process will take with our esteemed faculty."

"Can we talk about the other committee you put me on?"

"Of course."

"Since I got picked for this budget fiasco, can I get off this one?"

"No. I put your name in before I got this email from the chancellor. I can't take it back now." Roberta rolled her desk chair to the door again, checking the hallway to make sure it was still empty.

"I'm going to get you a motor for that thing," Gina said as Roberta rolled back to her desk.

"Go ahead. This chair makes up for the go-cart I never got as a kid." She grinned like the devil she was. "My brother had one, but my daddy wouldn't make me a go-cart because I was a girl. Some things you never get over." She cleared her throat and said, "Go ahead and talk. The coast is clear."

Gina unbuttoned her navy peacoat, crossed her legs, and readjusted her worn, denim skirt. "I understand you had nothing to do with the budget committee request, but what have I done to be put on the committee for handwashing policy with Marty Schmidt?"

"Like I said earlier, you have social skills."

Wonderful. Another fantastic reward for being good. Maybe Rachael was right: she was a nun. "And that woman from public health—Barbara Goodshanks? Roberta, she and Marty Schmidt are impossible apart, but together? I was at a party with Barbara Goodshanks once, and as I picked up one of the canapés, she asked me if I'd washed my hands."

Roberta waved her hand in the air as though she was swatting a fly. "She was joking."

"If drop-dead serious is the new way of joking, then okay, she was joking."

"But you didn't say anything, did you?"

"Of course not," Gina bristled. "I didn't even give her a dirty look, but boy, I wanted to. And as for Marty Schmidt, are you aware that every Valentine's Day she sends out a mass email about chocolate, with an attachment that breaks down the calorie count and fat content of every brand known to man?"

Roberta nodded sympathetically while tapping her foot impatiently.

"And," Gina spoke quickly to avoid being interrupted, "she has this thing about coffee. She claims it's a dangerous brew and should be regulated by the FDC. You should have heard her."

"But you didn't say anything back, did you?"

"No, but I shou—"

"That's my point." Roberta stuck her finger out and pointed it at Gina. "You wanted to, but you didn't. And that's why I need you for this job. Dealing with miserable people with big egos is your specialty. You know your way around them. You never lose your temper or get snippy and sarcastic like I do. But then again, I get away with it because I'm the boss." Roberta smirked again, then made a motion like she was playing golf and had taken a shot off the tee.

"But they make *me* miserable."

"They make everyone miserable. They're bullies with high IQs. Worst possible combination. And if we don't get someone on that committee who knows what they're doing, the guidelines for handwashing in infant-toddler and preschool programs are going to be the germ-free equivalent of the McCarthy trials. These people do not understand the nature of childhood. In fact, I wonder if they ever were children. Maybe they popped up in an organic, sugar-and-dirt-free cabbage patch. Oh, that's all off the record, too."

Gina's eyebrows shot up. She felt oddly grateful that Roberta wasn't the one assigned to the handwashing committee.

Roberta picked up a stack of stapled-together manuscripts from her desk and handed them to Gina. "Here are the guidelines as they stand. The top one is the most recent. Take a gander at them when you have a minute, and you'll understand what I mean. Pour a stiff drink before you do it. The first meeting is in about a week, at six-o'clock in the morning, in Marty's office."

"Six?"

"Hey. I talked her out of five thirty. Schmidt's an early riser." Without missing a beat, Roberta asked, "How was Italy?"

"Memorable."

"And Daniel?"

Gina shut her eyes for a moment, as though she could wish it all away. "I don't get it. All he has to do is finish his dissertation. Just two hundred little pages, give or take a few. It should be a no-brainer."

"I know, Gina. I know."

"So why does he bag it and run off to Naples?" Gina couldn't help herself. She'd wanted to keep it a secret almost as much as she wanted a kernel of insight from someone who might know.

"Because he's young. You know the risks when people pursue advanced degrees at his age. It isn't for everyone."

"That's why he was at George University instead of back east, so he could be close to family. I thought we had all our bases covered."

"Humans are not an exact science." There was a gentleness to Roberta's voice. "If we do start messing around with DNA someday, we'll be shocked in yet one more way that our children didn't turn out the way we expected them to. But you know, Daniel is a good kid, whatever he ends up doing." She paused for a moment, then asked, "And your daughter? How is she?"

Gina stared into her coffee. "She moved in with her father."

"Sheesh."

"She's talking about being a professional cheerleader."

Roberta chuckled outright. "Where do they come up with these things?"

"She's thinking about living with Andrew until the end of her sophomore year. Who do you think gave her that idea?"

"Not you."

"Andrew should have called and told me, but he hasn't even called to ask about Daniel." She stood and picked up her coffee cup.

"What are you off to do?" Roberta asked.

"Go through my mail, my email, my voicemail, my class lists, and check out what my grad students have been up to. Basically, everything I can cram in before my office hours begin next week and my students start lining up to tell me that their entire future depends on taking this class this particular semester. Then I'm going to call Andrew to see if we can meet for lunch sometime this week." She turned at the doorway and said, "See you at the meeting on Monday."

Gina got halfway down the hallway before Roberta stuck her head out again.

"Hey," Roberta called. "You didn't say anything about my new shoes." Half a leg came peeking out from the bottom of Roberta's door to reveal a cherry-red leather high-heeled pump.

Gina grinned, in spite of her mood. "They're awfully sexy for the Child Development Department. Someone's bound to make a comment."

Roberta glanced up and down the hallway before she returned the grin. "And I'll tell them, how do you think those kids we study got here?"

***

Marc sat at the dining room table with his cell phone by his fingertips, waiting patiently. One of the volunteers at the group home was working with his sister on phone skills. She'd called ten minutes ago to let him know that Betty would be phoning if he was available to chat. Like clockwork, his phone had rung. Also, like clockwork, both corgis had come barreling in from the living room the second they'd heard the ringtone, which this week was Johnny Cash singing, "I Walk the Line."

"Marc, Chancellor Webber here. You made it in okay?"

Not who he was expecting, and it threw him off guard.

Before he had a chance to respond, the chancellor continued talking. "I got your email last night."

"Good."

"Any reason you wanted to start with the College of Home Economics?"

"You mean Human and Environmental Sciences."

"Right. It used to be called Home Economics, then they changed it. Didn't up their enrollment any, though. Is there a reason you wanted to start with them?"

"Is there a reason I shouldn't?" He reached down and scratched Albert's ears.

"No, but they're the least of the university's worries. It's only three small departments. There's Child and Family Development, Nutrition and Dietetics, and Interior Design. And I'm warning you that Roberta Cooper, I mean Dr. Cooper, the chair of Child and Family Development, is a force to be reckoned with. The chair of Nutrition and Dietetics is difficult too, but Cooper is a real ball buster. That last comment was strictly between you and me."

No fooling. "I'm sure Dr. Cooper and I will get along amicably."

"It was smart, requesting one of her faculty to be the liaison between the budget committee and you. Put a peer in charge, then you don't have to work with the entire department. Wouldn't want to be her, though." He added quickly, "Or him. What's that saying? Kill the messenger. But it'll work. In fact, it's downright genius." Marc could hear him laugh through the phone. "Whoever it is will be the most hated person in the department. At least it won't be me."

"Cutting five percent out of every department's budget isn't going to be easy," Marc told him. "You could take more from the hard sciences. They can make their budgets up with grants a lot easier than liberal arts or social sciences."

"Five percent across the board. A shared sacrifice. Everybody takes a hit. As chancellor, that's what I stand for. Equality. We've all got to share the pain. No pain, no gain."

Marc rolled his eyes and made a face of total disgust. He was glad they weren't on Skype. He'd already seen the numbers. Five percent from departments like Gina's was going to hurt more than five percent from a lot of others. But then again, he'd never known of a program without some fat that couldn't be cut here or there.

"The email announcing the process went out to all the colleges five days ago. You got a copy of it, right?" Stuart Webber asked.

"Yes, I did." He smiled and kept scratching behind Albert's ears. Watching him get all the attention, Victoria made her move and jumped up on his other leg. It felt good to be fought over. "I'll email Dr. Cooper myself later today," Marc told him.

"Sounds like a plan."

"Would you mind putting me through to your office assistant?"

"Is there a problem?"

"Nothing for you to bother with. She keeps spelling my name M-a-r-k, and it's M-a-r-c, and I don't want any confusion out there. You know, forget I said anything. I'll email her later today."

"No. I'll put you through. That way she can schedule a time for us to get together at the end of next week. I'm curious to know how it goes with the College of Ho—, Human and Environmental Sciences."

Marc ended the call then got up for one more cup of coffee. This was his fourth. He wasn't quite over his jet lag yet, but he was working on it. He pitched two treats to the dogs, then sat down, and wondered what Gina was doing right now. Probably having fun. Judging by how much she'd smiled when they'd met, she probably had fun all the time.

His Johnny Cash ringtone went off again, as did the dogs. This time he checked the caller ID, which said, Friends Forever. It was the name of Betty's group home. He shushed the dogs and picked up the call.

"Hello," he said slowly and clearly like the volunteer had instructed him to. "This is Marc Edwards."

A conversation took place in the background on the other end of the call, then his sister yelled into the phone. "Hello. Marc Edwards. This is Elizabeth. Edwards."

"Hello, Betty. How are you?"

He could hear another conversation in the background as the volunteer told her what to say next and to lower her voice. "I am fine, Marc Edwards. Are you fine, Marc Edwards?"

"Yes, I am well."

"But are you fine?"

"I am also fine."

There was silence, then Betty said, "You are my brother."

"Yes, I am."

"You come to visit me where I live."

"Yes."

"Soon?"

"This weekend." He made it more specific. "On Sunday."

"When you come, you will be fine?"

"Yes. I will be fine and well."

"Goodbye. My brother. Marc Edwards."

He heard a click and put his phone down. Well, that went better. The last time they'd worked on phone skills, there had been long pauses between their conversations. Betty had hung up on him, then called him back to say goodbye, and then hung up again before he could say goodbye to her.

The group home supervisor told him that Betty needed to take small steps toward her skill acquisition. Everything needed to be broken down. He was immensely proud of her. After decades of living in his mother's house with little stimulation, and no independence, she now lived with others and was a contributing member of her group home. Still, it made him sad. Betty could have had a fuller life. He should have fought for his sister more and dared to challenge his mother's dictums. Instead, he'd fled the second he'd turned eighteen, eager to start his own life and avoid the turmoil at home.

He could have had a different life, too, but it had little to do with his mother and much more to do with his own choices. How could he be this old and still have so much to learn? When he was a kid, he thought that when you were done growing physically you were all grown up, and then you strode through life with all the answers. Boy, had he been wrong.

His phone rang again, and he picked it up without seeing who the caller was. Luckily, it was Betty.

"Marc Edwards?"

"Yes, it's me, Betty."

"I forgot."

But she didn't say anything. After a long pause he asked, "What did you forget?"

"I love you."

***

If Gina had known that her ex-husband was going to agree to meet her for lunch on the same day she called, she would have put on something better than her worn denim skirt, imitation Uggs, and her five-year-old, recently mended, button-down red cardigan. Usually, Andrew made a production of checking his schedule and getting back to her, but not today. It wasn't that she wanted to appear attractive for him anymore. What she wanted was to avoid his snide remarks about the way she dressed. Through the course of their marriage, his disparaging comments had only served to make her dig the heels of her comfort shoes in deeper.

What had he expected? They'd had Daniel when she had been finishing her sophomore year, and Kimmy when she'd been working on her masters degree. Between school, the kids, and teaching, it hadn't been like she had a lot of time to think about herself, and it hadn't been like Andrew was willing to roll up his sleeves and help.

When they had first been married, she had tried to let Andrew's criticisms slide, but thinking back on it, she realized they had acted like water torture. The accumulated, incessant drip of his criticisms had finally broken the back of their marriage, and in the end, all she'd wanted was to leave.

Andrew was already seated in the far corner of the last train car turned restaurant by the time she got there, ten minutes late. Lizzy's Station, a restaurant in Columbia's abandoned train depot, was one of the town's better eateries. It consisted of a maze-like constellation of old dining cars nestled in the rear of the old depot, which now served as the bar.

Andrew claimed that he liked Lizzy's Station because it was private. Gina suspected it was because, even though he declared himself a vegetarian at least once a month, Lizzy's had the best hamburgers in town. Andrew ordered his with shiitake mushrooms and made a big deal of the fact that she ordered hers with cheese. Like cheese was the deal breaker in the clogged artery department when you were eating a hamburger in the first place. How had she married such a fussy man?

She slipped into the booth without any acknowledgment on Andrew's part. "Hello," she said to the newspaper in front of his face. His repertoire of subtle put-downs had been labeled and cataloged years ago. Besides, she was ten minutes late, an egregious act in Andrew's book, so what better treatment could she expect than his paper-in-the-face routine?

She put her purse down and started to unbutton her coat. Andrew folded his paper and picked up the menu.

"They've added some new items," he said, without glancing up.

"That's nice."

"Stir-fried vegetables with shrimp, chicken, or tofu, in a ginger-sesame sauce, and a salad with arugula and sweet baby greens. There's also a grilled vegetarian sandwich with gorgonzola cheese. It's about time they brought out more meatless selections."

He put the menu down and surveyed her. His eyes narrowed infinitesimally. "What's going on? You were rather cryptic on the phone."

As if he didn't know. "I thought we should talk about Kimmy. And Daniel."

"She made the decision."

"And I'm glad you're spending time with her." She was quite proud that she had not inserted the word *finally*. "She knows she's free to move back home anytime."

"Home? That house isn't a home to anyone anymore."

When they had been younger, and Andrew had played word war with her, she'd found it challenging. The amazing Andrew Ellison paid attention to Gina Ferrari, the baker's daughter. Well, not anymore.

"And thank you for letting her use your car so she can come over and walk Hairy. I'm sorry she couldn't keep him at your place. He's really a very sweet dog, and she loves spending time with him." The award for killing someone with kindness goes to—Gina Ferrari, PhD.

Andrew said nothing. Instead, he studied the menu until the server came to take their order. "Hamburger deluxe with mushrooms on your whole wheat, multigrain bun, and make sure it's toasted dry. I don't want trans fats coating the surface. And make my hamburger rare, not very rare or medium-rare. Rare. Pink. Not running red or grayish brown. Exactly the median between the two." He turned to scrutinize the server.

Gina watched the girl's eyes shoot up, then recover quickly. There was a tip to be had at the end of this ordeal, or so the server falsely believed.

"I'd like your cheeseburger deluxe with a large order of onion rings. And could you bring a bottle of catsup, please?" Gina watched the server flee and wished she could go with her.

"My, Gina, that's healthy."

She wouldn't waste her time trying to point out to him that he'd ordered a hamburger, too. It was pointless, as were most of the years they'd been married. "You know I saw Daniel when I was in Italy."

He picked up his newspaper and turned the page over, holding it up again to cover his face. Once upon a time, Gina had been in awe of that face, its high cheekbones and piercing blue eyes, thick with dark lashes. Once upon a time thick, brown hair had framed his face to perfection, shoulder length and often held back loosely in a ponytail, like his sister Rachael's. Now, it had thinned, and he cut it to where it could be tucked neatly behind his ears so that it whispered, I was once a hippie.

"That's nice." He flipped the newspaper down to give her a withering look.

"He's fine," she answered, as though he'd asked. "I'm not sure why he's doing what he's doing, but he's fine."

He stared at her and said nothing.

"I thought you'd want to know."

"You thought I'd want to know about a son that has embarrassed both him and me by leaving his PhD program? He's not getting my attention this way."

"I don't think it's about you, or me, or our divorce."

"And thank you for telling me he was going," he said stiffly.

"I didn't know until he got there. That's when I contacted you."

Andrew nodded curtly and avoided any eye contact.

"I'll send you his email address." She suddenly remembered he was using *dferrari* instead of *dellison*. "Uh, I meant his international cell phone number. I'll send it to you *in* an email. Then you can call him if you want. Or text. I think he gets texts, too."

"He bought the damn cell phone with my money. He can call me. And you can tell him I'm not paying for someone to get a job at Pizza Hut."

Gina spoke, knowing full well that she would never tell Daniel what his father had said and, more importantly, how his father had said it. "All right, Andrew. Would you like me to tell you when I hear from him?"

"If you want. It makes no difference to me one way or the other."

Why did this man have to pout like a little boy? To this day Gina never understood what had come between Daniel and him, not that their relationship had ever been good.

"And how do you like Kimmy living with you?"

"We're getting along fine. You know, you can't have them both, Gina. You've got Daniel on your side. It's only right I should have Kimmy."

She gathered herself together. "That's not what I meant, and Daniel is not on my side. Our children are not possessions to be divided up because we divorced. I do not have Daniel, and you do not *have* Kimmy. They're *our* children, and we need to focus on supporting their growing maturity and independence."

He made a face. Gina had to admit, her last sentence did sound a bit pedantic, but the words had kept her from reaching out, grabbing the newspaper, and smacking him with it. "I love them both. And you do too. I know you do."

The deflated expression on his face used to leave her flustered and in search of something to make it better. It was a sad fact of life that she no longer cared about the man in front of her, and she had once thought she loved him.

"Please don't lecture me, Gina. I'm not one of your students."

"Why are you encouraging Kimmy to stay here for college?"

"Because there are two perfectly acceptable institutions for her to attend right here. My college and your university. Besides, she wants to be a cheerleader."

"That's a silly pipe dream."

"I think she really wants to do it."

"Andrew, we filled out five applications to good schools out of state and sent them off this fall. You knew that. She worked on them at your condo, too. With her SAT scores, she's competitive for all of them."

He smirked at her.

Gina's hands went up to her forehead. "I leave for Italy to see why our son has gone off the deep end, and our daughter moves in with you. Then she tells me she's not going away to college but staying here and continuing to live with you so she can be a cheerleader. Why would you encourage her to be a cheerleader? Do you think that's in her best interests?"

"You always were insistent that they choose their own paths. Isn't that what you used to say? Let them make their own choices whenever possible so they know how to initiate the decision-making process as adults. And she's decided. She's going to stay here."

"It's not in her best interests." She considered warning him about her suspicions that Kimmy harbored a desire to reunite the two of them, but she didn't. As far as she was concerned, it was never going to happen, so why bring it up?

"You can't stand the fact that your daughter is doing something different than what you think she should do."

"And you can't stand the fact that your son refused to be micromanaged." God, she was better than this.

She could see his fingers starting to grip the edge of the newspaper. As luck would have it, the server came with their order, and he relaxed as they both unfolded their red cloth napkins instead. Now they would eat, go back to speaking polite dribble, and say goodbye. Nothing had been accomplished.

Andrew looked at their server. "I sincerely hope this hamburger is rare like I ordered. Otherwise, I'm sending it right back."

"Yes, sir," the server said, as she put the catsup bottle down next to the onion rings.

Without asking, Andrew grabbed an onion ring with his fork, opened his whole wheat, multigrain bun, and laid it on top of the mushrooms. It was what Gina had expected. She should have stopped him. She wanted to stick him with her fork as he reached over and confiscated her onion ring, but why escalate things further?

He scrunched the top of the bun down on his hamburger, then said, "Kimmy needs to stay at your house this weekend. I'm busy."

Chapter Five

Although it was a quarter to eight in the morning, the sun remained hidden behind thick, gray clouds. Gina trudged up Wilson Avenue and crossed University Drive, headed for the department's first budget-cut meeting. What a way to start the semester.

She had enjoyed her daughter and Hairy this past weekend, until the very end when she'd reminded Kimmy that her homework wasn't done. Unfortunately, that bit of direction had followed closely on the heels of telling Kimmy that she was not to bring her father's wash over and expect it to be done by her. She'd suggested that, together, they could find a YouTube video for her father to watch, and he could learn to do his laundry on his own.

Kimmy's reaction had been to slam her bedroom door, the front door, and the car door before telling Gina that maybe if she had been a bit more helpful when she was married, they'd all still be together as a family. No one could inflict a wound better than Kimberly, and although Gina ached to defend herself, all it would have done was prolong the argument.

Thankfully, thoughts of coffee, the sacred brew of the overworked and underappreciated, crowded out her thoughts as she made a beeline into the small faculty kitchen. Much to her surprise, she saw that the coffee had already been made and that two-thirds of it was missing from both pots. With her coat still on, she walked down the hallway to the conference room where the budget meeting was to commence in a matter of minutes. There, she saw the entire faculty, with Roberta herself sitting at the front of the table.

"The meeting started at seven forty-five," Roberta said, looking straight at her.

Gina opened her mouth, then shut it. She didn't want to argue in front of everyone that her email from the administration had distinctly said ten minutes after eight. She scanned the room for a chair and observed that the expressions on the faces of the faculty appeared as though someone had told them their tenure was revoked, their article had been rejected (again), and by the way, there was a deadly virus sweeping across the country that was going to hit Columbia, Missouri, no later than Tuesday.

And then she saw him.

"Dr. Ferrari?" he asked. "You're Dr. Gina Ferrari?" he asked again, this time saying the word *doctor* with an ever-so-slightly mocking tone in his voice.

She stared at him wide-eyed until she noticed Roberta gazing at her as though she'd forgotten to change out of her pajamas. Why, oh why, did she have on the mud-brown polyester pantsuit that made her thighs resemble the top of a turkey drumstick?

"Have a seat," Marc Edwards said. "Please, Dr. Ferrari." He motioned to the empty chair on the other side of Roberta. "We need to move through our agenda, so we can finish. On time."

Like this was her fault?

"I know everyone is very busy." He glanced at her while an almost indiscernible smile played on his lips. "I don't want to waste time going over what you missed, therefore I'm assuming you can get up to speed."

She sat down, stupefied.

Roberta passed a folder to her and whispered, "Are you all right?"

She nodded a fraction of an inch and opened her folder, then tried to sneak another glance at Marc. Their eyes met for the second time. Oh god, this was going to be awful. And yet, the excitement she felt at seeing him one more time shot through her in spite of the fact that she was doing everything she could to ignore it.

**

The minute Marc hit his front porch, he could hear the dogs going off inside. He hoped Sydney had popped over to let them out for a break. Otherwise, he might be facing a colossal corgi mess.

"Well, you can't say you aren't loved." Sydney's voice carried from the kitchen to the entry hall. She stood as Marc walked in. "They've been waiting at the door for you for the last hour. Almost like ESP."

"Hey, Syd." He hadn't expected her to be there, but he was glad someone had spent time with the dogs today. He was certainly in no mood to do much playing or talking. "How'd they do on their walk?"

"Fine." She hesitated then said, "I hope you don't mind me being over here. Lisa used to let me hang out when I needed some space from my mom's. For most people my age, one mother is too many. Two of them can drive you up the wall."

"I'm sure the dogs love the attention. And thanks again for watching them yesterday when I was in St. Louis."

She began to gather her things together. Marc felt slightly guilty over the relief he felt that she wasn't planning on hanging around. Somehow, his successful turning the tables on Gina hadn't left him with the feeling of triumph he'd thought it would, and he needed to think about that.

"So," she asked as she grabbed her last book, "does your sister have any kids?"

Ah, he hadn't told her about Betty. "My sister lives in a group home for adults with mental challenges."

"Do you have any other brothers or sisters?"

"No. Betty's it."

"At least you're not an only child like me."

There were years when he'd wished for nothing more. "She's learning how to bake pies next week."

"Let me tell you. If I ever get married—and I'm not saying I will, but if I ever do—I'm having at least three kids, and they all better like each other. Being an only child sucks." She slipped her coat on and grabbed her laptop. "Oh, the Elaine person called. She said she'd call you back. Soon." She smiled mischievously. "I dangled treats in front of the dogs, so they'd bark, and she could hear it."

He shut the door after her and chuckled all the way to the couch where he sat down and stared at his work folders spread out on top of the bookshelf against the far wall. He knew the one for the child development department was on the far left and spaced an inch further from the others. He fought the urge, but within thirty seconds, he was up off the couch to correct the spatial disparity. His compulsive tendencies had all but disappeared after his accident. Now, they were back and itching to bloom. Too many changes and too much stress.

Life wasn't a movie. Actions had consequences, and the consequence of giving Gina Ferrari her just desserts had not resulted in one molecule of satisfaction. It had, in fact, resulted in tremendous feelings of guilt on his part for hanging her out to dry like that. Everything they said about revenge being sweet was wrong. Revenge was a low, souring act. Why hadn't he gone and knocked on her door and talked to her? Because she'd made him feel like a royal chump. And now he'd made himself feel like a royal jerk.

* * * *

Gina opened her front door and swept past a confused Hairy, who had come to expect immediate attention and several treats tossed his way when she came home. Without stopping to take off her coat, she picked up the kitchen phone and punched in Rachael's number. This was a conversation that deserved the static-free, non-call-dropping realm of a landline.

"Rach, you are not going to believe this."

"My brother found another woman to go out with him?"

"Maybe, but I don't think so. That's not what I'm calling about, anyway. You are not going to believe this."

"What?"

"Marc."

"Who?"

"The guy in Rome. He's here."

"Where?"

"In Columbia."

"Ha!" Rachael howled so loud that Gina felt the need to remove the phone from her ear a good three inches.

She walked over to the kitchen cabinet and pulled out a box of snack crackers for herself, and the box of treats for Hairy. The dog began to dance.

"Say it," Rachael said with nauseating triumph. "I was right."

"Okay. You were right." She tossed Hairy a treat, then another. Why should the dog suffer because she was?

"I love the sound of those words. Could you say them again?"

"Look, he didn't specifically say Columbia, Missouri. He said he worked at Columbia. What was I supposed to think?" *Yeah*, Gina thought. *What were you supposed to think? Let's ignore the fact that you knew he screwed up prepositions, and that you were too scared to pursue exactly what he meant when he said Columbia.*

"So when are you two going out?"

"I'm never going out with him."

"You already did."

"He's the guy who's been assigned to facilitate campus-wide budget cuts. And he's probably the chancellor's spy boy, too. The first thing I'm going to recommend is that we fire him and save all of us some money. There's a budget cut for you." She tossed another treat to Hairy, who caught it in midair. Not bad. "It's just my luck he shows up here."

"What do you mean, just your luck? From where I'm sitting it seems to be what they call serendipity."

"Serendipity implies good luck. This is more like a karmic kick in the shins." She knew she had to talk fast or Rachael would interrupt. "He set me up. Everyone at that meeting was there before me because my email said eight minutes after ten. I should have been suspicious about that when I was the only name in the "To:" section, but I thought it was a tech maneuver, you know, so it seemed personalized, but really wasn't. I am incredibly stupid sometimes. So, no, I'm not dating him again."

"Did you talk to him?"

"No. I got out of there the minute the meeting was over."

"He's here for a reason," Rachael said.

"Yeah, and the reason is he's going to tell us to cut our departmental budget, which is seriously lacking any fat, to begin with."

"Things like this don't happen unless it's for a reason."

"Oh, good god. Put the crystals down and stop shaking them. I don't believe in signs. There are only facts, like the fact that every time I have fun, it comes back to blow up in my face. Only this time it's more like a nuclear explosion. If any of that gobbledygook exists, it's karma. And mine is really bad."

"First off, when have you ever let yourself have a little fun? So you meet this guy, you have the time of your life—"

"I didn't say I had the time of my life."

"Yes, you did. I saw your face when you said it, too. Maybe Aphrodite—"

"She's Greek. If we're talking Roman, it would be Venus."

"Picky, picky. That's the one thing you and my brother have in common." Rachael plunged back in. "Maybe Venus was tapping you on the shoulder when you were in Rome, and saying, hey, Gina, put some spice in your life before it's too late, and here's the man who'll do it."

"Yeah, spice like Cayenne pepper," she snorted.

"And sometimes life hands you a gift if you're smart enough to take it. Keep me posted, okay?"

She hung up the phone and made a beeline for the freezer, grabbing the chocolate marshmallow ice cream that Kimmy had insisted they buy on Saturday and then had only a teaspoon of.

Marc had seemed like such a nice, interesting person when she'd met him. Not the type of guy who'd do something like this. Then she stopped in her tracks so abruptly that even Hairy, who was following the path of the ice-cream carton as though his life depended on it, stumbled to a halt.

She pulled the spoon out of her mouth and stared blankly ahead. Look at what she'd done to him. She'd lied. She'd been deceitful on purpose. Well, not really on purpose, more like it just happened that way, but he didn't know that. What if the shoe had been on the other foot? What if Marc had been faking it and she'd fallen for his line of baloney? Well, she'd feel used and quite stupid that she hadn't seen through his masquerade. How awful. But she really hadn't meant to—she just hadn't known how to stop pretending she was an Italian once she'd started, without humiliating herself in the process. Oh god, what to do now?

***

Gina spent the rest of the week glancing nervously over her shoulder, and Roberta kept asking her if she was getting enough sleep. She met with her graduate students, both of whom she liked, one of which she worried about. The young woman was broke, had already maxed out her loans for the semester, and was working three part-time jobs to make ends meet because the small stipend she got from the department didn't cover the gap between her expenses and student loans. Nevertheless, without the it, Gina feared she would have to quit before she finished. The stipends would probably be the first item slashed in the budget, thank you very much, Marc maybe-you're-not-so-wonderful Edwards.

On Sunday morning Gina received her annual gift of water, as her pipes froze then burst in two places. She was lucky. None of the wood floors would need refinishing—both leaks were in the basement. The only damage had been to a few boxes of the kid's keepsakes, tucked away in a far corner of the basement.

An inch of water still covered the floor, and she walked in the spillage in black rubber boots, her old, elastic-waist blue jeans tucked into the tops of them. Kimmy called them her beyond mom jeans, and Gina's retort had always been that the elastic-topped denims were her dinner-was-fantastic pants. She grabbed the last wet-bottomed box and placed it on the open steps so it would stop dripping before she hauled it upstairs to dry out whatever was inside.

As she roamed around the basement, searching for other items to rescue, her thoughts went from Kimmy to Daniel to Gino, and settled on Marc Edwards and how she was going to handle this beyond-karma snafu. The second she'd convinced herself that she had nothing to be ashamed of, except lying and out-and-out deceit, the doorbell went off. She lumbered up the basement stairs and walked to the front door, bracing herself for the sudden rush of cold air against her damp clothes.

It was Marc.

"You lied to me. On purpose." His hands were shoved in the pockets of a thermal-lined wool coat, and his loose jeans, frayed at the hemline, covered the tops of brown, lace-up leather boots. Underneath his partially opened coat, she could see one of those snowflake sweaters in thick, navy wool. She'd bought a similar one for Daniel, but he'd complained that the wool was too itchy and gave it back. Instead of giving it away, she'd kept it for herself. Last winter Kimmy had talked her into donating it to the Salvation Army, proclaiming that the oversized sweater was a fashion felony. She still missed that thing.

"Is your daughter here?" he asked when he got no reply to his accusation.

"No, she isn't." She grabbed his arm and pulled him inside, then shut the door. "And how do you know I have a daughter? And how do you know where I live?"

Marc shot her a quizzical look. "I think we need to talk."

"Yes, we do," she said and swallowed. "That's a good idea."

She regretted wearing her mom jeans, almost as much as wearing her turkey-leg pantsuit at the budget meeting last Monday. At least her T-shirt with the Moms-for-Mapo ad on the front, a joke gift from Rachael, covered the elastic waistband on the jeans. Between this getup and her pantsuit, he'd probably already figured out that the woman he'd met in Rome wasn't the woman who lived in Columbia.

He followed her into the living room where she motioned for him to sit on the tan slip-covered chair, while she sat on the matching couch across from him. After a thorough sniff of Marc, Hairy jumped up next to her, his eyes glued to the stranger.

"Look," he said after the two of them settled in, "I don't quite know where to start. Suffice to say, I got the shock of my life when I saw you on the plane coming back from Rome."

She gaped at him, wide-eyed. "You were on the plane?"

"Yes, and I almost missed the flight because of you, too."

"I didn't see you."

"I was in business class."

Of course, you were, Mr. Business-Budget-Cut Man who stays in nice hotels. "Oh. Why didn't you say something to me?" Dumb question. She knew the answer.

"I was in shock. And when we got back to the States, I Googled you, and there you were, a professor at Mid-Missouri University."

She remembered what she had a right to be mad about. "You told me in perfect—no, near perfect—Italian that you worked at Columbia. In business."

"No, I told you I was going *to* Columbia to work in business, and I didn't know the Italian word for *finance* or *budget*, so I said business. Besides, it's close enough."

"You said *at*. You said you were a business professor *at* Columbia. As in New York."

"I didn't say New York."

"It was inferred. And you didn't say the word *Missouri* either, so what was I supposed to think?"

"You should have asked for clarification."

He was right about that one. She focused on the floor and said nothing.

"At least I didn't fake out that I was a real Italian for three solid days.

"I *am* Italian."

"But you don't live in Rome. That was an out-and-out lie. You're an Italian-American. And you speak English, not Italian."

"I speak both, and way better than you I might add."

"You just got done telling me my Italian was perfect."

"Near perfect. And I was being polite. Sometimes I could barely understand you."

"Well, thanks for that. And I didn't say Missouri because I thought you were Roman. Who in the hell in Rome knows about Columbia, Missouri?" Marc sighed. "Gina, you played me."

Gina felt her face warming to red. "Well, you got me back at the meeting. Congratulations."

"I did. Didn't I?" He snickered ever so slightly.

"It really wasn't funny."

"Sorry."

"No, you're not."

"Yes, I am, actually. Revenge is a rather petty act."

She stared at him, her arms folded. "I'm not the woman you met in Rome."

"I am well aware of that."

"I mean…" She stumbled over her words. "I mean…I am her, but I'm not *her*."

"She was very charming."

She wanted to tell him that she wasn't charming or sexy or any of those things she'd pretended to be for the three days they were together. It was too embarrassing to explain that she'd completely acted out of character at one of the lowest points in her life. When should she have come clean and told him the truth? When they were laughing in front of the Pantheon? After they had dinner? Or should she have dropped the bomb the next day or the day after that? When, exactly, should she have told him she was a fake?

He glanced down at the floor for a few seconds, then raised his head level with hers. "I'm a bit perplexed about where we go from here, or if we go anywhere other than a nod on the sidewalk when we're walking our respective dogs. And at meetings, of course. We need to be civil at meetings."

"You have dogs?"

"Two corgis."

"Oh." She suddenly recalled Kimmy asking her about the guy with Sydney Sheppard. "Was that you the other night with Sydney Sheppard?"

Marc stiffened. "Look, it's not like I drove across town to walk by your house. I'm not stalking you, okay? I live down the hill and around the corner."

"How do you know Sydney?"

"She's my new dog sitter. She lives across the street from where I'm staying."

"Oh." She didn't know what else to say. "Hairy isn't my dog. He's my daughter's." She paused, then blurted out the question. "Are you really a professor?"

"Of course, I am. Hey, *I* didn't lie about anything."

"If you're a professor, why aren't you teaching instead of coming here and talking about chopping budgets and using words like *shared sacrifice*? That is such a disgusting phrase."

"I'm taking a sabbatical, of sorts, from the University of New Mexico, and I'm consulting with Mid-Missouri. I'm going to write a few papers about the process of consensus building regarding budget cutbacks at state universities. It's certainly pertinent."

He crossed his legs, and Hairy growled. "I'm staying at a friend's house. Jim Kirby. Do you know him?"

"Does his wife work in the horticulture department?"

"Yes."

"It's the house with the beautiful gardens across from Syd's, right?"

"Yes." His eyes stopped at her jeans and rubber boots. "Were you in the middle of something wet, or are you preparing for the next flood?"

Gina laughed for the first time today. "One of my water pipes burst in two spots. The good news is that the leak is in the basement. The bad news is that it's Sunday, and unless I want to pay big bucks for an emergency plumber, I can't turn my water on until sometime tomorrow."

She studied his face again. He had a light coating of freckles across his cheeks, and the ends of his hair were a lighter brown than the rest of it, probably because he spent a lot of time outdoors. He looked like he wanted to say something, because his lips were pursed as though they were ready to explode.

"What?" she asked.

"I know pipes. I had a house in New Mexico, and I did a lot of work on it myself. Would you like me to take a look?"

"Sure."

He followed her downstairs and sat on the second-to-last step while he rolled up his pants and unlaced his leather boots. Hairy kept a watch on them through the open door to the basement.

"Show me where the two leaks are."

"I turned off the water to the house after I found them and marked the spot for the plumber."

"Smart."

"Yeah, well, I've been through this before." She brought him over to where the pipe was and pointed to the painter's tape she'd applied to each leak site. "Here and here."

He eyed both sides of the pipe and examined the joints. "You know, I can fix this."

"I'll be happy to pay you."

"Can you cook decent Italian, Gina Ferrari?" He grinned like a mischievous twelve-year-old. "Or do you fake that, too, and sneak in take-out when nobody's paying attention?"

"I cook." She'd be angry about that crack if it wasn't for his grin.

"I'll trade you one plumbing job for dinner. I'm tired of eating by myself."

"You're on."

He held up his finger. "Hold on. There's one more requirement."

"I'm not sleeping with you."

"I'm not asking you to."

She could feel her face getting red. "Okay, then what?"

"You have to tell me about yourself, and it has to be the truth. Not something made up."

"Deal."

An hour later, Hairy was still trotting between the door to the basement and the kitchen. Gina watched him with satisfaction, because with all that pacing, she could probably forgo his evening walk. Given the near-zero temperatures of last night, it would be a welcome respite.

She figured Hairy's non stop pacing was the result of an inner quandary for the dog. Should he watch the stranger in the basement, or keep his eye on the food? Eventually, food won out, and after a few pieces of prosciutto she tossed his way, the dog stuck by her until Marc's footsteps were heard on the stairs.

While Marc was busy washing his hands in the sink, she brought the salad and pasta over to the table.

"I hope you like this. It's pasta with prosciutto, arugula, and grape tomatoes. And of course, garlic. It's cheap, but I think it's pretty good." She pushed the bowl of grated cheese his way. "At least I think so, especially with the grated Romano."

Marc bypassed the salad and dove for the pasta, putting a forkful from his plate into his mouth. "Oh, god. My mouth is in heaven. You're making me wish more of your pipes burst this week."

"Well, that's not beyond the realm of possibilities. Hey, I have some wine in the pantry." She jumped up from the table and cast a sheepish look in Marc's direction. "It's a red, generic table wine. I don't know how good it is. It's been in there for a while."

"I'm sure it's fine."

She brought it over to the table with the corkscrew along with two glasses.

Marc watched her as she finished pouring, then picked up his glass to make a toast. "Here's to telling the truth."

Gina smiled and took her first sip.

Chapter Six

Red wine always left Gina's head achy, but this hangover was so much more. It felt like her skull and brain were rubbing against each other as they rotated in opposite directions. This morning, the mere sound of water running in the bathroom sink made her want to throw up. She picked up her toothpaste gingerly, while Hairy studied her from the bed.

"Mom." She heard Kimmy's voice downstairs then the front door close. "Jennifer's here with me, so cover up. Please."

Hairy jumped off the bed and booked it down the stairs.

"Yes," Gina whispered to herself, holding her head as she shuffled from the bathroom toward the closet. "Heaven forbid you see a body part over the age of twenty-five."

She grabbed a gray sweatshirt from her closet and zipped it halfway up over her crumpled shirt. Yesterday's jeans would have to do for the bottom part. She summoned her voice and called out, "I'm decent."

In the kitchen, she found Jennifer and Kimmy petting Hairy as though he was the anointed heir apparent. "He can do some tricks now," she told them. Last night, Marc had taught Hairy how to sit and shake in about an hour.

"Really?" Jennifer appeared genuinely surprised. "Like what?"

"Mom, you look terrible."

She ignored Kimmy's comment and smiled. "He can sit and shake."

"Wow, Dr. Ferrari. That's more than my parents ever taught him." Jennifer bent down and petted Hairy furiously. "I miss you so much, little guy."

"Mom. You look really bad. I thought you got rid of those pants."

The doorbell rang, making Gina's head throb. Hairy barked and ran in a circle, each rotation getting him closer to the door.

She zipped the sweatshirt up to her neck and thought about putting the hood up, too. "Kimmy, can you get the door?"

Marc Edwards stood on the porch, holding two large cups of coffee with steam wafting out the slits in the plastic caps.

He grinned at everyone while Hairy broke free and jumped at his legs. "Thought you could use a pick-me-up," he said, casting his eyes toward Gina.

Kimmy's eyes narrowed. "Aren't you the guy who walks those corgis?"

"Yes, I am."

"I thought so." She turned to Jennifer. "He's got dogs like the queen of England has." She turned back to Marc. "I've seen you walking them a couple of times right past our house. You stopped once. It looked like you were going to come right up our walkway, but then you kept going."

Marc focused his eyes on the cups in his hands.

"Sydney Sheppard walks them, too." Kimmy looked directly at Marc.

Gina watched the girls make a face after Sydney's name was mentioned.

"Yes," Marc said, nodding his head. "She does."

"Do you have a wife?" Jennifer asked him, her face stern and unsmiling.

"No." He turned to Gina and smiled.

"Girls, don't you have someplace to be?" Gina asked.

Kimmy's eyes went from Marc to Gina. "I'll stop by after school."

Suddenly I'm interesting, she thought, as the girls exited. She made her way to the kitchen table and sat down.

"Feeling okay?" Marc set one of the coffees in front of her.

She took it gladly, popping off the cap and taking a small, tentative sip. "No, I feel terrible. I'm almost too embarrassed to look at you." She pulled the hood of her sweatshirt up over her hair and crossed her legs.

"Like I said last night during dinner," Marc said gently, "welcome to the stew of humanity."

"You said, welcome to the club of humanity."

"See, you weren't that drunk."

"What was in that wine?" She put her hand up to her forehead, wondering if she was going to further embarrass herself with this man by making a run for the toilet.

"Wine."

"Very funny. I have no idea why it affected me that way."

"What did you eat yesterday?"

Then it hit her. "Come to think of it, nothing until dinner. I was too busy."

"And then you had five glasses. One right after the other."

"Four."

"Five. We opened another bottle, remember?"

Gina took a sip of coffee. "Were you counting?"

"That's how my mind works. I keep track of things. I'm in finance, remember? We count everything, then we run long-term predictions on the numbers. Seldom works out, though." Marc shifted on his feet and glanced at his watch. "Do you lecture today?"

"Not until two." She took another sip of the coffee and stared at her feet, noticing she had a hole in her sock and her big toe was sticking out. "I have an early-morning meeting tomorrow, at six in the morning, so I'll make sure I get some sleep tonight."

"I'll let you get to it." He stood and touched her cheek.

"Marc," she said as she put her head on the table, "exactly what did I tell you?"

"Nothing but the truth. I think." He winked. "The next time we get together I'll tell you all about me."

She picked her head up. "We didn't…do anything, did we?"

"Gina, I hope if we had you'd remember it."

He was out the door before she could summon the nerve to tell him that, given why he was here, they really shouldn't see each other again.

***

If Gina wanted to keep track of bad work days, today would rise to the top of the pile like schmaltz on chicken soup. Granted, Tuesday was never her favorite day of the week, to begin with, but this particularly Tuesday deserved the Six-Cups-of-Coffee-Just-to-Get-Me-through-It award.

The six a.m. handwashing meeting unfolded like a bad dream. Try as she might, she could not get Marty Schmidt or Barbara Goodshanks to see that teachers and caregivers in preschool and infant-toddler programs could not wear surgical gloves every minute of the day, nor could they put disinfectant on their hands every fifteen minutes. Then there was the recommendation the duo came up with that stated toddlers and preschoolers should not be allowed to touch their mouths, eyes, or noses. If these hand transgressions occurred, Barbara Goodshanks proposed that the offending child wash with antibacterial soap.

Thankfully, the woman appeared to be clueless regarding the other places toddlers tended to stick their hands.

This proposal was followed up by the introduction of a song that Barbara was working on, as an accompaniment to the hand washing policy. The problem was she couldn't find a word that rhymed with soap other than dope, which even Marty Schmidt thought wouldn't work. The lyric "don't be a dope, wash with soap" was vetoed two to one. Gina wasn't about to bring up the fact that hope rhymed with soap. If Barbara couldn't come up with that on her own, she wasn't going to help.

As for Marty, Gina made the early-morning mistake of asking if there was any coffee available. Instead of coffee, she received a sermon, masquerading as information, regarding the merits of green tea. It was all a bit much, and after the meeting, she walked to the student union, bought a large coffee, doubled her usual amount of half-and-half, and put in two packets of sugar. After she gulped that down, she went back for another and bought a doughnut to go with it.

The rest of the day was taken up with students trying to plead their way into her advanced child development class, a conference call with a colleague she was coauthoring a paper with, and a meeting in Roberta's office regarding the handwashing meeting. Given the early start to her morning, she was all too ready to head home at four in the afternoon rather than her typical five in the evening.

As she approached her driveway, she saw Kimmy sitting on the porch steps. What was her daughter doing sitting out in the cold? Not that she minded her being there. She loved her being there, and this was the second day in a row she had shown up.

Yesterday, Kimmy came over after school, stayed for dinner, and grilled her about Marc Edwards. How did she meet him, why was he over at her house this morning, her father knew about plumbing, too, and he also liked pasta with prosciutto, arugula, and tomatoes, so she should have called him for help and not relied on a stranger. The truth was, Andrew didn't know the difference between a nail and a hammer, not to mention water pipes, and he hated pasta because it had too many calories and reeked of garlic.

Gina could tell that something was not well with Kimmy the minute she turned up the driveway. Her daughter's face reeked of misery. Her long, black coat was buttoned up to her chin, and her hands were balled up in the pockets. The gloves she bought for her in Italy were probably already lost.

"Did you forget your key?" Gina asked as she started up the porch steps.

"I lost it." Kimmy stood and walked up the remainder of the steps with Gina, her lips quivering.

"Why didn't you go in the backyard and get the key under the fake rock?"

"That's the one I've been using. I lost my other one when you were in Italy."

"We'll get some more made. Do you need a ride to your father's, or can you stay a little bit?"

Kimmy brightened. "Dad's still busy at his office. He called and told me he didn't need me to make dinner. So I thought I'd come and see Hairy."

Didn't need her to make dinner? Typical Andrew. She grabbed her key out of her satchel and put it in the lock.

Whimpering at the sight of her, Hairy went right to Gina when they entered, ignoring Kimmy, who started to cry.

"I'm sorry," Gina said as she tried to get Hairy to move off her knees and onto Kimmy's.

"It's okay." Kimmy sniffed. "He was supposed to be my dog. And Jenn's. That's all."

"He is. He really is." She shut the door and hung up her coat.

Kimmy looked aghast as her eyes scanned Gina's clothing. "I thought you were going to get rid of those pants."

Gina wore her elastic-top, rust-colored, wide-wale corduroys and a long, slightly stretched-out, cream-colored turtleneck tunic over them. Both pieces had seen better days, she had to admit. But like her dinner-was-great jeans, she was incapable of parting with anything until it was ragbag quality.

"See, you think I don't need you around, but I do. Would I have walked out of the house like this if you were here?"

Kimmy burst out crying. "It's impossible to watch both you and Dad at the same time. If we all lived together like we used to..." She stopped .

Gina put her arm around her daughter. "I said that to let you know how much I miss you being around, not to make you feel guilty. I said it because I love you. How about I make you some hot chocolate while you give Hairy his dinner? Then we can talk if you want."

Kimmy brightened.

As they sat on the couch, Gina listened. Between the frenzy of her last semester of high school and playing cook and cleaning lady for Andrew, Kimmy had no time left for herself. If she wasn't saving her father from toilet rings, she was spending an inordinate amount of time propping up her friend Jennifer, whose parents were going through the divorce of all divorces. Gina wondered how Kimmy had learned this behavior, that you were responsible for everyone else's happiness.

She tucked their ancient, worn-out afghan, now smelling suspiciously like the dog, around Kimmy. "You know, you can move back anytime. You don't even have to ask. No pressure," she told her.

"Dad actually talks to me in the morning when I make his coffee. He takes me into his confidence," Kimmy said, her voice brimming with pride.

So now Kimmy was Andrew's Anna Freud, too. Wonderful. She wanted to blurt out, *does your father ever ask you how you're doing? Does he make sure you're okay?*

"That's how I know he regrets the divorce," Kimmy said.

"I don't want to see you sacrificing your academic future for—"

"My academic future isn't the issue, okay?"

"I'm sorry. I shouldn't have said it that way."

"But you did." Kimmy stood and folded up the afghan. "You know, Mom," she said, slowly, "you always worry about what other people think. Or you're worried about me or Danny or one of your grad students or Aunt Rachael or Shauntel because you think Uncle Gino should be nicer." She turned to face Gina, her arms folded. "Or you're writing some really serious paper about perfecting the outcome of the early childhood years on later intellectual development. Like being a brainiac is the ultimate goal in life. Sometimes I think you don't know how to enjoy yourself, and maybe that's why Dad really left."

She gasped and tried hard not to let it show. "I know how to have fun."

Kimmy rolled her eyes . "Right. Name one thing you did in the last year that was fun."

"I went to Italy."

"That was to save Daniel from *having* fun."

Kimmy grabbed her coat and gave Hairy one last scratch on the head. "Why do we always argue?"

She wanted to tell her daughter that it was because she was safe to pick a fight with, but she didn't. That would only start another fight. "I wish we wouldn't."

"It would help if you laid off about school."

"Point taken."

They started toward the back door. Gina fumbled for her car keys while Kimmy pulled on her coat and stuck her hands back into her pockets.

"Oh, I forgot," she said, pulling her left hand back out. "Someone left this envelope for you." She handed it to her mother. "Probably one of your grad students. Why don't you give them your number so they can text you?"

Chapter Seven

It was later than Marc thought when he pulled his Taurus wagon into the driveway, grateful to be home. The day had been brutal, and he'd spent most of it in the Nutrition and Dietetics Department. If dirty looks could kill, he'd be dead ten times over. He felt certain that the faculty were submitting strategic plans on how to pull his murder off immediately. And that woman, what was her name? Martha Schmidt. What a control freak.

Today, as he began to consider what would make his list of five things, he thought about seat heaters in cars. What a marvelous invention. Coming up with four more by the end of the day would be a piece of cake, especially if Gina responded to the note he slipped under her door earlier today. And if she responded the way he hoped, he would happily count that one thing as five and protest anyone accusing him of cheating with the numbers. Gina Ferrari, the real Gina Ferrari, was at least five things rolled into one.

He opened the front door and heard footsteps coming from the living room.

"Hey, Marc," Sydney said, as she walked up. "Hope I didn't scare you."

"No, not at all." He figured she was probably fighting with her mother's again, and that's why she was hanging out with the dogs and doing her homework over here.

Sydney took a deep breath, then started talking. "I have a psych assignment I have to finish. It's about people's first memories. Mind if I interview you? I don't know any older men. Then I'll go."

"Sure, but only if you don't refer to me as old. I can handle being old*er*, but not an old man." He settled himself on the couch, his coat still on.

Sydney walked over to the table and opened her laptop. "Is your first memory about someone or something?"

"Both. It's about my sister Betty and a toy."

"Is your first memory happy or sad?"

"Sad. And somewhat angry."

"Eww." Sydney typed his answer in. "Fantastic. Why would you say it was sad?"

"Because I got in trouble."

"Hmmm." Sydney typed some more into the form on her computer. "Why would you say it was an angry memory?"

"Because I got in trouble, and it wasn't my fault. Look, let me explain, and then you can fill in your form, okay?"

Sydney took her hands off the keyboard.

"Croak-Croak was my stuffed frog." He watched Sydney try not to crack a smile. "Don't laugh."

"Sorry."

"I had to sleep with him every night, because I was terribly afraid of the dark." He glanced up in time to see Sydney smirk again. "Hey. No making fun of me. Just because I'm an"—he made air quotes with his fingers— "older man doesn't mean I wasn't ever a kid. Okay?"

"Okay."

"Betty, my sister, must have taken the frog from under my pillow, because when I found her, she was sitting on the floor of the upstairs bathroom with Croak-Croak's little green face in her mouth." Marc blew out his breath. "I was horrified. I was sure she was going to eat him. I remember screaming louder than I ever thought I could. I tried to get Croaky out of her mouth." He stared straight ahead, his face blank. "I think my screaming only served to set my sister off more, and by the time our mother made it upstairs, the two of us were both screaming and in a fist fight to the finish. I ended up with a bloody nose, and Betty ended up with a swollen lip."

Sydney sat staring at him, her mouth open. She scanned her computer screen and asked, "Why do you think you remember this?"

Marc stuck his hands in the pockets of his khaki pants. "Besides the bloody nose? Good question. I think it was because of the injustice. I was four years old and couldn't articulate my feelings very well, but I was the one who got punished, not my sister. She almost ate my frog, and I was the one who had to sit on a chair in the corner for hitting, while my sister got peanut butter and jelly on Wonder bread fixed by the cleaning lady." He laughed and turned to look at Sydney. "Nobody made PB&J's like the cleaning lady. I mean, the jelly would ooze out the sides."

"So it was the PB&J that she got and you didn't?"

"No. To add insult to injury, my mother sat with my sister through the whole lunch. I was furious because I was missing my already perpetually minuscule share of her attention. I hated my sister for it. After that, I started to spend afternoons over at my grandmother's house. My mother would take me over there and leave me for most of the day."

Sydney frowned and focused on her computer.

He waited for Sydney to make her usual smirk. When she didn't, he began to think that his revelations had made her uncomfortable.

"Did you know that she was mentally slow then?"

Marc walked over to the sink to get a drink of water. This was the last thing he thought he'd be talking about today. "No, I didn't. It wasn't until a few years later that I realized my sister was different." He took a drink then put the glass down. "Right after I started kindergarten, I overheard my friend's mother refer to my sister as slow.

Somehow, I knew, without really knowing, that the word meant much more than Betty not being a fast runner. But I was afraid to ask my parents."

"Why?"

"Because it was a question that could get me in trouble if I asked it. I don't know how I knew, I just did."

He watched as Sydney typed his response into her computer.

"In the third grade, or maybe it was the fourth, my class did a health unit on growth and development, and a paragraph about mental retardation caught my eyes. That's what they called it back then. A few days later, I went to the public library and searched for the words in the index file. In one book, I found a picture of someone who wasn't Betty but who resembled her. And then I knew."

"Why didn't your mother tell you?"

It was Marc's turn to frown. "She couldn't deal with the fact that my sister had issues in the first place, and it made being the sibling of someone like Betty harder than it would have, had my parents been willing to acknowledge it."

Another memory came tumbling out. "When I was at school, Betty used to go into my room and mess with my stuff. She would throw everything out of order, my books, my army men, you name it. It drove me nuts. Once, I had this whole reconstruction of the landing at Normandy all set up on the floor in my room. I mean, I'd been working on it for weeks, and when I came home after school, Betty had messed it all up. She'd popped the head off every German."

"Is that why you're fussy about your folders and stuff?"

"What do you mean?"

"Well, you don't like things out of order, that's for sure. Like, you're always realigning the dog bowls, and the plates, and well...all sorts of stuff. And particularly all those folders on the shelf. I bet they're each exactly one inch apart from each other."

Marc frowned. Actually, the folders were precisely a half an inch apart. But what he was really frowning about was that he thought, after the accident, that he was over that. "My last year of high school, I put a lock on my door. My mother and father got mad at me, but they didn't take it off."

Sydney closed her laptop. "Did your mom ever talk to you about your sister?"

"No. When I was eighteen, right before I went away to college, I used the word *retarded* with my mother. I told her that she dressed my sister like a child. I said just because she was retarded didn't mean she was a little girl. I said she's a young woman, and she needs to wear clothes that fit her age. My mother slapped me across the face. We never discussed Betty again until my father had a heart attack and died. That's when she told me that she'd left the entire estate in a trust to Betty and that I was my sister's appointed guardian."

He also remembered saying to his mother, thanks for asking me if I want to be her guardian, but he didn't tell Sydney that. In truth, he wasn't ready to think about many aspects of his own behavior after he left home, like the fact that he saw his mother at his father's funeral and only twice again after that.

Sydney gathered up her books. "I don't think I'd like your mother."

Marc nodded. "Things have changed a lot since I was a kid in terms of acceptance of people with disabilities. And as I've gotten older, I understand a little more what my mother was going through." He added air quotes again when he said the word *older,* in the hopes of injecting some levity. The attempt seemed to go unnoticed.

"You're nice, Dr. Ed—"

"Marc."

"Hey, I almost forgot." She pointed with her chin toward an envelope on the counter. "Dr. Ferrari from up the street stopped by about ten minutes before you came home. She left this."

***

Gina paced from the kitchen to her entry hall, stared out the window, and then settled herself on the living room couch. Maybe he wasn't going to come. She'd asked him to in the note she'd written to him and left with Sydney. The second she got back from dropping off Kimmy, she'd written a reply and walked down to his house.

Hairy came and sat at her feet as she brooded in silence. He chomped with relish on a large rawhide bone Jennifer brought him last week, then peered up at her, belched, and wagged his too long tail. She motioned for him, and he jumped up next to her, ready for a scratch behind the ears, which she did with one hand while staring straight into space at nothing. *Fondly, Marc.* That was how he'd signed the note. No one had ever written a note to her like that. Certainly not Andrew.

Growing up around her parents, Gina assumed that fondness was a given. After she and Andrew had been married for a few years, she'd come to realize that their marriage was built on verification, not affection. To her, Andrew had meant that she was more than a North County baker's daughter, not at all like her brother, and smarter than the rest. Andrew had loved her intellectual achievements, while her father had been slightly amused. When she'd told him she was getting married, he'd shaken his head and said, "All these books and you know nothing about life." And for Andrew, she had been his one defiant act against his mother, to marry far too young, out of his faith and below his economic status.

Kimmy was right; she hadn't a clue about how to enjoy herself, except when it all came pouring out in Rome with a man she was certain she'd never see again. And now, for a reason she kept groping to find, they'd been shoved together for a second chance. But why did it all have to be so complicated?

Hairy heard him before she did, and he jumped off the couch, barking at the door before the first knock. She stood, straightened her sweater and the skirt she'd changed into, then opened the door holding Hairy by the collar.

"I got your note," Marc said.

"I know." She let go of the dog, put her arms around Marc's neck, and pulled him in.

***

If a cop in some cheesy made-for-TV detective movie asked her how the two of them got from the door to her bed, she could not have told him, even under intense TV interrogation. And, if the cop in the cheesy movie asked her for details about what happened after they got to her bed, she would have told him it was none of his business. He could arrest her for withholding information, because after sex like that, she was going to jail anyway.

She loved being naked next to him. He was warm, except for his feet, and his skin was smooth, and he smelled good. It wasn't an applied cologne smell. It was, she decided, a Marc smell.

"Marc?"

"Um-hmm."

"Are you still awake?"

"I am."

"Do you ever have trouble sleeping?" she asked, snuggling into his open arm.

"Not anymore."

"Prescription drugs or over-the-counter medication?"

Marc chuckled. "Neither." He ran the palm of his hand up and down her back, massaging her spinal column as he went. "You know you have a beautiful back."

She turned to face him. "Thank you. Now tell me what your solution is, after you tell me that my front isn't too bad either."

"Your front isn't too bad either." He laughed again.

"Okay, now tell me. What's your remedy?"

"Five things."

"Which one works the best?"

He laughed again, this time shaking his head. "I think of five things that make me happy every day."

"Sort of like saying your prayers?"

"Not the same at all. I'm not asking for help, or begging for my soul, or anyone else's for that matter. I'm thinking about what made me glad during the day, and making sure I remember it." He held her hand up to his lips and kissed each finger. "It can be simple things. Sometimes they're the best ones. The dogs make the list separately a lot of days, especially when it's been a bad one. But today it was seat heaters. A wonderful invention. Nothing like having a warm butt in late January, don't you think?"

"I don't have seat heaters."

"You should get some. And today it will be you and your note, not to mention the most fantastic sex I've had since I was in Rome with some woman who only spoke Italian. You remind me of her."

She blushed. "Thank you."

"I'm also grateful for Sydney, because she gave me your note, and walks the dogs so I don't have to come home in the middle of the day. Today, I'm overflowing with things to be grateful for."

"Sydney and Kimmy used to be best friends. Now they don't talk. I always liked her. She's a very real sort of person."

Marc agreed. "She is very likeable. And very smart in all the ways that the word implies." He kissed her fingers again. "Now you try."

"You, in all the ways that the word implies."

Marc laughed. "Thanks. That's one. Keep going."

"Okay." She turned on her side to face him and propped up her head up with her arm. "I can't think of anything else."

Marc smiled. "Gina, you're passing up happiness. What should have made you smile today, if you'd been paying attention?"

"My daughter says I don't know how to have fun."

"I disagree, but there's your second thing."

Gina looked at him questioningly.

"You have a daughter. Number two."

"Oh." She didn't want to tell him all the qualifiers that went into being thankful for her daughter today, but Marc was right. Though she and Kimmy weren't getting along, she still had a daughter, and she loved her very much. "I have a son, too."

"Number three. You're very lucky to have one of each. Many people try at least three or four times for one of each, but they don't succeed. Then their kids have to endure hearing, we were trying for a girl, or, we were trying for a boy, their entire life. Makes them feel real special."

Gina laughed. "Okay, number four is coffee, and I don't care what anyone says—it's wonderful stuff."

Marc nodded ceremoniously. "I concur, especially if the coffee comes in the form of espresso and it is sipped in front of the Pantheon with an enchanting woman. Come on, one more."

"You."

"You already said me." Marc smiled.

"Okay, sex with you."

"That was covered when you said, in all the ways that the word *you* implies. You're looking for an easy way out."

"There's no easy to this. What are we going to do? You know we can't keep seeing each other."

"Why not?"

"Because of what you're here for. You're going to rip my department apart at the seams."

"We'll go through the process of possible cuts. Ultimately, it's up to the dean of your college and your chairperson, Dr. Cooper. I'm merely helping you through the process of recommendations, and suggesting some solutions you might not have thought of."

"That doesn't make it all right."

Marc sighed. "Gina, I'm sorry. This is my job for the next year. At least I'm someone who understands academia. And I don't think it has anything to do with you and me."

She glanced at him for a moment, then she spoke. "Where did you learn to speak such bad Italian?"

"My grandmother, my father's mother. She was from a little town in Sicily called Corleone."

"You're joking."

Marc laughed. "Of course I am. My grandmother was from Mezzojuso. There's a bus that makes one trip to the town a day. If you intend to visit, you'd better make sure that your relatives are speaking to you, or you're sleeping in the town square." He stopped speaking for a few seconds, then blurted out, "My Italian is bad? You said it was near perfect."

She laughed. "I was being nice. And now I have number five."

"What? Bad Italian?"

"No, laughing."

"Touché, Gina. By George, I think you've got it. Now that I have your email, I'll send you a joke every day."

"Will you? That would be wonderful. No one's ever done anything like that for me before."

Marc cocked his head and looked at her. "It's about time someone treated you nicely."

She turned away, ignoring his last comment. "I'm sorry about faking being a Roman. Can I explain?"

"I'm listening."

"You sat down next to me and spoke Italian, and it was obvious you thought I was a native, and I thought well, this is fun, so I kept going with it. And then we had lunch together, and at that point, I just couldn't fess up and look stupid. And I thought, that's okay because I won't see him ever again after we have lunch. And then we had dinner together, and then we walked the Appian Way the next day, and somewhere in there I should have come clean, but it had gone on too long, and I couldn't tell you and look like a fool, because we only had one more day together, and I wanted it to be wonderful. I didn't want to take a chance you'd leave." She sighed long and hard. "And it was wonderful. And so I kept it up. I really didn't mean to lie to you. At all. Well, not after the first few seconds we met. And I am so sorry."

"It's okay. I think I get it now. And I'm sorry that I spied on you in the airplane and the airport."

"You did?"

"Yes. I know it sounds creepy, but I was shocked it was you."

She nodded in understanding as Marc put his arms around her, and the two of them laid side by side.

He asked quietly. "My Italian's that bad?"

Gina started to laugh. "Let's just say you could take a refresher course."

His face clouded over, and he glanced at his watch on her nightstand. "Is your daughter coming home soon?"

"She's staying at a friend's."

Chapter Eight

True to his word, Marc sent Gina a joke through her email every day, and Gina found that waking up to a good laugh with a cup of coffee was the best way to start the morning. For once, someone liked her enough to think of her every day. Somehow, it took the sting out of the fact that she'd heard nothing from Daniel for the last two weeks.

As she walked into Prichard Hall, down the hallway toward her office, Roberta Cooper called her. It roused her from thinking about this morning's email joke.

"Gina," Roberta yelled from her office door. "Have you met with him yet?" She motioned Gina into her office.

"Who?" Like she didn't know.

"Marc Edwards."

"We've run into each other." She crossed her arms and noticed that a splotch of this morning's yogurt had deposited itself on the upper part of her sweater. "How do you want me to handle this, anyway?"

"What do you mean?"

She tried not to show her agitation. "We have to suggest cuts of five percent from our already anorexic budget. Nobody wants to do this, everyone's scared about what's going to happen, and I'm the one that has to spearhead the whole discussion."

"I know."

"Please tell me. Do you want regular meetings, emails, or an anonymous suggestion box with a warning that profanity will not be tolerated? What do you want?"

"I want the people in this department to come to a consensus, or at the very least have a good feeling for what may happen via the discussion group. I don't care what form the communication takes initially, but you do have to have at least two meetings to firm things up with the staff. Whatever you do, you have to meet with Mr. Edwards."

"It's Dr. Edwards." She could see that Roberta was trying very hard not to frown.

Roberta leaned forward and whispered. "Who in the hell gave that guy a PhD?"

"I have no idea." And that was the truth.

"Do you have a problem meeting with him?" Roberta studied her face as she asked the question.

"No." She shifted on her feet.

"Because when you came into that meeting late, you acted—"

"It was embarrassing to be late. That's all." *Liar, liar pants on fire.*

"What about the handwashing committee?" Roberta asked.

"We have another meeting in two weeks, and instead of six in the morning, this one's at five thirty in the evening."

"Keep me posted. I don't want to find out that our preschool teachers are giving hugs with rubber gloves on," Roberta said.

"If Goodshanks and Schmidt have their way, there'll be no hugging whatsoever." Gina waltzed off, thinking of the date she and Marc had planned for Saturday night. If anyone saw them together, the gossip train would be so overloaded it would bend the rails. Maybe she needed to buy them disguises.

***

Instead of going out, as Marc had wanted, Gina suggested that they eat in. She offered to make dinner at her house again, while Marc insisted on buying all the ingredients for braised chicken with figs. It was a bit of a test that she'd chosen this specific recipe. Andrew hated it, while she loved it.

When Marc reached for the bottle of merlot again, Gina put her hand over her glass. "After the last time we had wine together, I decided on a hard-core rule. I have a two-glass limit. I humiliated myself with you once, and I'm not doing it again, not to mention the hangover I had."

"A little humiliation is good for the soul. Especially on a Saturday night." Marc put the wine bottle down. "Keeps us human. The words are related, *hum*iliation, *hum*an."

"No, they're not, but nice try. And I get your point."

Marc smiled. "If you're alive, it's inevitable you're going to do something stupid from time to time."

He twirled his wine glass slowly. She noted he looked particularly good in his dark-blue sweater, more the color of well-washed denim jeans than a navy pea coat. It was a loose-knit pullover, and underneath that he had on an oxford cloth blue button-down shirt.

Tell me about yourself," Gina said in a voice barely above a whisper.

"I am someone who's fully aware that he just ate the best dinner he's ever had."

"Thanks, but I meant tell me something about you. Something I don't know."

Marc sat back in his chair. "Ask."

"Your family?"

"My father died of a heart attack about ten years ago. My mother died two years ago from Alzheimer's. My sister lives in St. Louis. I'm her guardian. She has mental challenges." Marc stopped talking.

She stared straight at him. "Go on."

"There's not much else." He shrugged. "My dad was an only child, and I spent a lot of time with my Italian grandmother, his mother, growing up. That's where I learned to speak what I thought was fluent Italian." He smiled mischievously. "My sister's, name is Betty. She's one of the reasons I wanted to take this year in Columbia. It's much closer to St. Louis than Albuquerque."

Gina smiled. "I see. You said one of the reasons. Are there others?"

"My relationship ended."

"You're divorced?" This was news.

"No. We never got married, but we lived together for twenty years. It was a divorce without papers."

"Your idea?"

"Hers." Marc poured himself another glass of wine and took a generous sip. "A little over a year ago, I had a car accident. A bad one. There was black ice on the road. You know what that is?"

"I live in Missouri."

"Right. There was ice on this asphalt road outside of Albuquerque, and my car slid off into a ravine because I was going too fast and skidded when I tried to slow down. It was winter, and it was cold. Cold for New Mexico. I was in a remote part of the state, and I didn't know how badly I was hurt because I was pinned in the car and couldn't move. After a while I couldn't feel my legs, and at that point, I had to consider the possibility that if I did live, I might be paralyzed.

"I knew there was a good chance I was going to die. I was in the car until late the next morning, when a herder moving his sheep across the road spotted me. The highway patrol had to use the Jaws of Life—aptly named—to get me out of my car. Amazingly, I walked out of the hospital ER with a few bruises and not much more. Do you know how lucky I was?"

"Marc—"

"Wait. There's a point to why I'm telling you this, and parts of it aren't pretty."

She took a sip of wine to squelch her need to interrupt.

"When I thought about my life that night, it became increasingly clear that I had nothing to show for it. Maybe a few accomplishments and a few degrees, but so what? No one was going to remember me or miss me for very long. My position at the university would be filled the following semester, and I was certain that Elaine, the woman I lived with, would move on after a few months of discomfort she would misinterpret as grief."

"I laid there all night and thought about our relationship, how utilitarian it was. We were together because it was convenient. It was..." He stopped, and struggled for the right words. "We fit all the right categories. Same age, advanced degrees, liked local wines, had good table manners, both read, essentially shared the same politics, and came from families we thought we were better than. We were snobs in the same way. But really, we weren't that close emotionally. We'd come home from some sort of function, and after ten or fifteen minutes of mocking everyone, we'd go to bed."

He eyed Gina sheepishly. "I promised myself if I got out alive, paralyzed or not, I wasn't going to waste another day living my life like I was reading someone else's script. Even if I died alone, I didn't want to be the person I was. But I wasn't quite sure who I wanted to be, either."

She spoke softly. "And you made it."

"I did. But I was different. I was fascinated with everything around me. You know, simple things I hadn't taken the time to notice. I felt like a kid again. Everything was new. People noticed a change, and most of them liked me better, especially the department secretaries."

Gina settled back in her chair and twirled her wine glass.

"But Elaine didn't. It bothered her that I tried to point out all the simple things we take for granted in life. I drove her nuts. I'd take pictures all week and then pick out the most beautiful one. Then I got the dogs, which she also hated. But the last nail in the coffin was when I went on and on about the merits of water."

"Water?"

He sighed and smiled. "Don't laugh, okay? One day I let it run over my fingers to feel it, then I took a big drink of it right out of the tap and savored the stuff. Gina, coming out of that accident was like starting all over in life."

"Let me get this straight. She kicked you out because you were too happy?"

"Pretty much."

"She fell out of love with you because you weren't crabby enough?"

"She said she didn't want to live with a real-life Forrest Gump."

She started to laugh and made herself stop. "I'm sorry. I'm sorry for laughing. I mean, of all the reasons to end a relationship with someone, the fact that they're too happy never occurred to me." She thought about Andrew for one very brief second.

"What does Elaine do? Is she in academia, too?"

Marc nodded and pressed his lips together.

"What's her area?" She took the last sip of wine in her glass and rolled it around in her mouth, letting the pungent taste sink in. Marc was right. Life was too short to waste a second of it. If only she could keep that thought going for an entire week.

"Elaine is the chairperson of the Women's Studies Department."

She spat her wine out all over him, and it dripped down his chin and onto his sweater. Gina grabbed her napkin and started to mop up the mess. He smelled like soap and shaving cream and now a little bit of wine. "I'm so sorry." She managed to get the words out between bottled up snorts of laughter. "It's just so..." Her mind couldn't find the right word. Must be the wine.

"Ironic?" Marc filled in the words for her. "I know. It fits every nasty stereotype that people carp on about. I'm still a little protective of her, I guess."

Gina reached up to dab his chin as he peered into her eyes. She leaned forward an inch more and kissed him. He braced her back and she settled on his knees, straddling them between her legs.

"God," she said, coming up for air, "you are one hell of a kisser. I would have kept you around just for that, no matter how ridiculously happy you were."

Marc spoke between their kisses, holding her in his arms as he leaned her over the kitchen table. "Is that the same skirt you wore the last night we were in Rome?"

"Um-hmm."

"And the same boots?"

"Yep."

His hand went up her skirt and toyed with the top of her underwear. "Have you ever done it on a table?"

"No." Gina took a breath.

"Me neither."

"There's always a first," she said, lightly.

"Could you leave your boots on?"

"You bet."

***

Gina leaned into Marc as he kissed her fingers. She loved it when he kissed her fingers. They sat naked under the Hairy-scented crocheted afghan on the living room couch in front of a fire that Marc had made after their lovemaking on the kitchen table.

She stared into the flames then turned to face him. "I'm not who you think I am."

"Oh, this again. Who are you now? A Spaniard?"

"This isn't a joke."

"I didn't think it was the first time either."

Gina waved her hands in front of her face. "No. I mean," she leaned forward and whispered the words, "I'm a hypocrite."

Marc snorted. "Now you're a double member of the International Club of Humanity."

"I'm serious."

"So am I. Everyone's a hypocrite about something." He put down her hand and leaned closer. "What specifically are you a hypocrite about?"

"I teach other people about children and parenting and families, and I'm a failure at all three. And I lied to you. Again."

"What do you mean?" He asked, as his eyes narrowed.

"Haven't you noticed my daughter isn't around much?"

"She's a teenager."

"When I said she was staying at a friend's house the other night, it wasn't the truth. She moved out when I was in Italy trying to get her brother to come back home. Now she lives with her father. She thinks I don't need anybody but that my ex-husband does. And I only took Hairy in the hopes that she'd stop by, at least occasionally. Actually, I was hoping for every day.

"And my son ran away to Pizza University. In Naples. That's why he's really there. He's learning how to make pizzas and to get away from his father. And me, too." Her chest began to heave. "I'm a failure." In between sobs she managed to get out, "And I have a PhD."

"Well, you wouldn't be the first failure with a PhD. The country is rife with them." Marc leaned forward to wipe away the tears rolling down Gina's cheeks. "Just because your son—"

"No, no, you don't understand. He's ABD."

"ABD?"

"You know what that means." She sniffed and leaned back. "All But Dissertation."

"Of course," Marc said remembering. "Every grad student's nightmare." He was quiet for a moment then he said, "There's really such a thing as Pizza University?"

She nodded. "You can also go to barista school and become an espresso maker."

"If only I'd known."

"I don't think he'll ever finish his dissertation," she said, ignoring his joke.

"I do have to say, friends of mine that never finished live happy lives, too."

"You're in business and finance." She swallowed hard. "My son's degree is in comparative literature. Besides making pizzas, I'm sure he can have a great career making Frappuccinos, if Marty Schmidt doesn't outlaw them first."

"Who's— ooh, the woman in nutrition and dietetics. I met her this afternoon. She's scary."

Gina glanced up to see Marc hiding a smile.

"Sorry," he said, regarding his expression. "I didn't mean for you to think I find your son's choices funny, but you make great jokes, even when you're upset. It's a wonderful attribute."

"You do too."

He smiled again. "They're not as good as yours."

He got up to move the logs in the fire. Gina stared at his naked backside and for some absurd reason recalled that when she'd seen *The David* in Florence, a British woman nearby had turned to her friend and said, "Nice bum." Marc's was far better than the one Michelangelo made out of marble.

He came back to the couch, and Gina put the afghan around him, tucking it under his chin. "Do you want to talk about it some more?" he asked. "I can tell it upsets you. Look, I'm no one to offer advice when it comes to kids, but I have been someone's son."

She sniffed and tried to smile.

"Sometimes," he began, "when things appear to be bad, you have to spend a little extra time looking at all you have that's good. Do your children still talk to you?"

She hadn't thought about it that way. "Yes, but Daniel not so much."

"But he still talks to you, right?"

"Yes." She nodded.

"Then all is not lost, is it? In fact, it might be better than you think it is. Do you have a brother or sister?"

"A brother." She wasn't ready to tell him about Gino.

"That's wonderful. Do you speak to him?"

"We say lots of things to each other." Gina laughed.

"Gina, you've got something a lot of people don't. Do you have friends?" Marc asked.

"Yes." Gina thought about Rachael.

"And now you have me. I'm your friend, too. That's five."

Gina perked up. "Oh, five things, like the other night. Your count-your-blessings ritual. Did you come up with that after the accident?"

"Come to think of it, yes."

"It's not that easy, Marc. Maybe for you, but not for me."

"It is that easy. You have to decide to enjoy what life has given you, and don't focus so much on what it hasn't. You know, you named five people not five things, which is far better, if you ask me. And if you want to call it my count-your-blessings ritual, go ahead." He smiled, as though pleased. "I'm going in to see my sister tomorrow. Want to come?"

Chapter Nine

Gina and Marc left early on Sunday morning to make the two-hour drive down to St. Louis. The sun shone on the frozen landscape along the I-70. Bits of ice and snow along the roadside sparkled through the black soot layer on top, like diamonds waiting to be plucked. The sparkle matched her mood as she and Marc chatted between sips of coffee in large to-go cups. Before she knew it, he was dropping her off at Rachael's with the promise that they would meet up at Betty's group home a few hours later.

She and Rachael spent their time catching up. They talked about everything from Marc to Daniel and Kimmy and the astounding fact that Andrew was still going out with the same woman for almost a month. Though Gina tried several times to change the subject from Marc to what was up with Rachael, Rachael stubbornly found her way back to the topic of Marc. How many times did she have to state that there was no cosmic reason she met him, there was no such thing as fate, and that she had no preordained lesson to learn in life? Thank god, she'd never spilled the beans about that three-letter word she thought she heard in the Pantheon.

Soon, they were heading toward the address Marc gave them for Betty's group home, located in an older neighborhood in South St. Louis.

Gina pointed as Rachael drove past the address for the second time. "There's a parking spot. Right there."

"Where?"

"Right there." She pointed again. "Two cars down. You passed it."

"Oh." Rachael slammed on the brakes and put her car into reverse, causing Gina to lurch forward and then slam back against the seat. "Sorry." Her grin was full of mischief as she slipped her car into the narrow space along the side of the street.

Gina adjusted her skirt as she climbed out of the car. "How do I look?" she asked.

Rachael smiled. "You really like this guy, don't you?"

"It's not going anywhere."

"Hmm."

"Rach, he's in Columbia for one year to facilitate cuts in every department's budget, including mine. Then he's back to Albuquerque if he's not run out of town before that. Besides, my life is busy enough. I've got work and my kids and my papers. I don't need some man in it to feel fulfilled. Okay?" She looked away, then back at Rachael. "I really don't. And I am not falling in love with him. You can scratch that one off your list of things to bug me about, okay?"

"Whoa. Okay, but Kimmy's going to leave, even if she thinks she's staying, and someday Daniel's going to figure himself out, and he's a big boy now, anyway, so he's not coming back either. Then what? You don't want to end up like me."

Gina frowned. "And what's wrong with ending up like you?"

"Nothing. I like myself just fine, but you're not built like me. Solitary isn't what you're about. You're chicken soup. I'm a tuna sandwich."

"What?"

"One is meant to spread warmth. The other is meant to be eaten alone in front of the TV. Hopefully, there's a good movie on."

They walked together to the door of the group home and were ushered through the house to the sunroom in the back, where they found Marc seated on the couch with his sister, an open magazine between them. He smiled, laid the magazine to the side, then stood and walked toward them. Betty followed, grabbing his hand and holding it tight. She looked like a shorter and sturdier version of Marc, complete with freckles and hair color.

"Marc is my brother," she said.

Gina took a half step toward Betty and held out her hand. "I'm Gina. Nice to meet you."

"Marc is my brother."

"I'm Marc's friend."

Betty eyed Gina. "Do you have a brother?"

"Yes."

This news made Betty smile. "Is he nice?" she asked.

"Yes."

She heard Rachael chortle beside her and made a point of not glancing her way. Well, it was the truth. She could have added a lot of other attributes to the answer, like, he is a stubborn ox and he should keep his mouth shut ninety percent of the time, but the bottom line was that Gino was nice. Basically. Irritating and maddeningly so, but nice. "He owns a bakery."

"He owns a bakery?" Marc's mouth opened in surprise.

Now she'd done it. "My father started it. He just inherited it."

"You mean that you have access to cookies, cakes, and bread?"

She laughed. "Yes."

"Gina, you've been holding out on me. We have to stop by there."

"It's closed on Sundays." She looked directly at Marc when she spoke, to avoid Rachael's stare one more time.

Betty turned to Rachael. "Who are you?"

"I'm Rachael, and I have a book." She pulled a large picture book entitled *One Hundred Dog Breeds* out of her canvas tote. "I brought it for you."

Betty brightened. She took Rachael by the hand and led her to the couch. "You are my friend. I don't have a sister. Do you?"

***

Gina didn't want to drive by the bakery, but she allowed Marc to talk her into it after she secured his reassurance that they wouldn't stop the car and get out.

"What's the family specialty?" he asked as they neared Ferrari's Bakery.

"Bread and biscotti."

"Biscotti. With pine nuts?"

"Well, of course. But you can substitute almonds if the supply is low. Just so you know, pine nuts are somewhat seasonal."

She leaned over the car console and whispered, "Slow down a little. It's right around the corner. See the sign? Ferrari's Bakery. It's in red, green, and white."

"Why are we whispering?" he asked as he rounded the corner and stopped the car directly across from the bakery.

"I don't know," she whispered back, then laughed. They were in Marc's car, not hers. How would Gino ever know that she was in it? She raised her voice. "I feel like we're stalking my brother. Do you see the sign? Because if you do, we can get going."

"Yeah. It says Ferrari's Bakery."

"Okay, let's go then." She started to turn her face toward the windshield and settle back into the passenger-side seat when Marc leaned toward her and planted a kiss on her cheek, then one on her lips. Gina smiled and kissed him back. There was something strangely naughty about making out with Marc in front of the family bakery.

Something slightly sinful she'd never pulled off in high school, and she found herself enjoying every second of it.

A knock on the passenger side window made them both jump. "Gina?" The voice outside asked. "What are you doin' here?"

"Shit." She rolled down the car window. "Hey, Shauntel."

"It is you." Shauntel grinned. "What a nice surprise. And who's this?" She bent down to look.

"Uh, this is a friend of mine."

"Does he have a name?"

Marc reached over Gina and extended his hand out the window. "I'm Marc. Marc Edwards."

"Well, come on in. Gino's home." Shauntel blinked. "I was just out takin' a run, and I saw you looking at the bakery. You were coming in. Weren't you?"

"Absolutely," Marc said, his head nodding for added emphasis. "We were parking. The car."

She rolled the window up and whispered as they parked the car over a few spaces from the bakery entrance. "Oh, I can't believe this."

"Don't worry. I'll be nice."

"It's not you I'm worried about."

They trooped in through the front of the shop, Gina behind Marc. Shauntel beamed as she stood in front of the new drapes that separated the store from the back room. "Like the new curtains?" she asked Gina.

"You were right. The stripes look better than the flowers my mother had."

In the back, they could hear Gino singing. She heard opera music, an aria from *Figaro*, and Gino's loud, booming voice singing right along, each word exact and crisp. She had no idea he knew anything about opera, yet there he was belting out the lyrics with the gusto of someone who had it memorized.

"Gino," Shauntel announced with pride as they walked between the curtains, "guess who's here."

Gino turned down the music, wiped the flour off his hands, and stared at his sister. He started to say something then noticed Marc standing behind Shauntel. "Who are you?"

"He's Marc Edwards, and he's Gina's friend. Mind your manners." Shauntel smiled when she turned to address Marc. "I'm afraid to let him work out front. He's a wonderful baker, but a terrible people person." She directed her voice toward Gino. "Too grouchy."

Gino grinned and stroked his hand under his chin.

"I know what that means, Gino. I've been married to you long enough to know what that means."

Gino laughed and extended his hand toward Marc. "Nice to meet you. I was getting the bread dough ready. You know how to make bread?"

"No, but I'm trainable."

Gino grabbed one of the white knee-length aprons off the hook next to a baker's rack filled with wooden cutting boards and handed it to Marc. "Wash your hands in the sink over there and dry them off good."

He scrutinized his sister's clothing. "Gina, you look nice. Very nice. Like a woman instead of —"

"Gino." Shauntel's voice warned him.

"I was trying to compliment her."

Shauntel turned to Marc and smiled again, this time shaking her head back and forth.

"Do I get to take home what I make?" Marc asked, tying the long strings of the apron together in the front. Merriment danced in his eyes.

"If you're not more trouble than you're worth, I'll give you a free loaf," Gino told him.

Shauntel nudged Gina. "I think that's our cue for a nice cup of coffee."

***

With three loaves of warm bread nestled next to each other on the rear seat of Marc's car, they were on their way back to Columbia as soon as Gina could get her brother and Marc to quit talking together. She turned to the car window, staring into the dark night. Not even a fingernail slice of a moon was out, and it matched her mood as the sparkle off the snow had done this morning.

Marc smiled as he stole a glance in her direction. "I liked him."

"Oh god." She crossed her arms across her chest and stuck her ungloved hands in the arms of her coat. The heater was on, but it was still cold. "Why?" she asked, her voice both incredulous and disgusted.

"Well, he has a great sense of humor, he's gruff, initially resistive, slightly clannish and protective, and underneath all of that, he's very generous. If he likes you. All of which is very Italian. So, what's not to like?" He turned to her and smiled again. "And he loves his wife."

"He's lucky to have his wife."

Marc nodded. "I think he knows that. He's a man who appreciates his good fortune. Many people don't. They keep searching for the next thing, thinking it's got to be better than what they have."

"What did you mean by protective and clannish?"

"He asked me a lot of questions about you. And me."

Gina straightened. "He's not my father."

"Well, he is your older brother."

She gasped in indignation. "By five effing minutes. He's my twin. Did he tell you he was my older brother?"

Marc chuckled. "Yes."

"Oh, that's rich."

"He looks older than you."

"Well, that's what happens when you do drugs and drink too much. Do you want to know about my brother?" Gina asked, her voice rising.

"If you want to tell me," Marc said, calmly.

She swallowed hard on her indignation. "Gino—"

Marc interrupted. "Hey, that's cute by the way, Gina and Gino."

"It was my father's idea."

He put his hand over hers. Their fingers intertwined for a moment before he put his hand back on the steering wheel. "What were you going to say?"

"I was going to tell you that my brother is, no, he *was* a very bad boy. And I don't mean that in a funny way. He caused my parents a lot of heartache."

"What did he do?"

"Well, for starters he got expelled from grade school and then high school."

Marc looked incredulous.

She appreciated his reaction. "And then he got into drugs and heavy drinking. He started using, then selling, got arrested, and went to prison for a while."

"I'm sorry."

"Me, too. And now that very same brother is the one my son goes to for advice about his life, not me."

"Is Gino still into drugs?"

"No. He's a recovering addict married to Shauntel, also a recovering addict, and as far as I'm concerned, she is the only smart move that stupid ass has ever made."

"I liked her, too," Marc said.

"I don't know why she puts up with him." She swallowed. "You know." She started to speak, then stopped, and shifted away from Marc to stare out the window again.

"Hey, say it. What goes on in the car stays in the car? You know, like Vegas."

"Okay, here goes." Why did she trust this guy? Maybe she trusted him because he wasn't going to be around for long, and there was safety in that, or maybe she trusted him because he could handle her anger and not get upset himself. "I admit it's childish, but I'll tell you anyway if you won't criticize me for it. Promise?"

"Promise."

She took a deep breath and spoke. "My brother does everything wrong, and I mean really wrong, and it turns out right for him. Eventually. And now, as I told you, my son trusts him more than me."

"And you did everything right, and—"

"It didn't turn out wrong. Not exactly. I mean, I'm fine. Just fine. I'm more than fine." Gina sighed and turned to Marc. "I don't know what I'm trying to say."

"You expected more for doing everything right."

She nodded with vigor. "Yes. I can't tell you what more I expected, but yes, I guess I expected something more for doing the right things. I especially expected my son to trust me more than my brother."

"That must hurt."

"It does, and it also makes me feel small and petty because it's a very petty reaction. What did you tell him about us?"

"I told him we met in Rome." He turned to Gina and grinned. "I didn't give him any details."

"Thank you for that. What else did he ask?"

"How long we'd been seeing each other, did Kimmy know, did your son know, and what did I do for a living."

"It's none of his business."

"I think he knows that. But he's your brother, and he worries about you."

Her arms flew up, and she waved her hands in the air. "Only because he's a caveman, and he thinks since I'm divorced I should be busy finding another husband."

"Gina, you're angry."

"Of course I am," she snapped.

"Is it because of the things that your brother asked, or is it because I liked him?"

She hadn't expected that. "I'm used to keeping my life separate from my brother's. That's all."

"Maybe we should talk about something else. How about espresso?"

She said nothing for a few seconds, feeling embarrassed about her show of anger. Or was it hurt? "I'm sorry," she said, finally.

"Don't apologize. I'm glad I saw a flash of temper in you. Being good all the time gets a little boring, don't you think?"

How would she know? Except for her reckless three days in Rome, her occasional spat with Gino, and the times when she should have held her tongue with her children but didn't, when hadn't she been good as gold? Thinking about it made her want to go home and smash a stack of plates.

"You know," Marc began, "a few years ago I took a train from Frankfurt to Milan. The train from Frankfurt left on time, of course, but it got to Milan twenty minutes late. Even some of the Italians were mad, but then, they were all from the North. Anyway, I got off feeling tense, and as I walked through the termini, under a sign that said, No Smoking, were two women smoking. They were blatantly ignoring the rules. And I stopped and got their attention, then I pointed at the sign. They turned around and looked at it, then they turned back around and laughed at me. They thought I was hysterical. Later that day, after I'd gotten over being cranky, I thought about it. And I thought, three cheers for ignoring the rules. I'm not advocating smoking, but it's good to be a little bad sometimes. I think that's when I really fell in love with Italy. Sometimes you should have the guts to take the forbidden detour, no matter what people think or say."

Gina waited for Marc to speak, and when he didn't, she said, "Didn't you wanted to talk about espresso?"

"Yes, but we're almost home."

They pulled into her driveway, where a red BMW coupe was parked. "I think Kimmy is here," Gina said, eyeing the BMW.

"That's your daughter's car?"

"Are you kidding? That's her friend Jennifer's."

"Nice wheels," He spoke with sarcasm.

She sighed in disgust. "It's the most inappropriate car I've ever seen a teenager drive."

"That's for sure."

"Her parents are getting divorced," she explained. "And it's nasty. Her father bought it for her, I suspect, to poke her mother in the eye with it, and probably a little bit out of guilt. They're having a big fight about money."

Marc walked her to the door, standing there until she turned the key in the lock.

"Thanks," she said. "I had a nice time today."

"Even though I like your brother?"

She laughed. "Yes. And it was nice to meet your sister."

He cupped her face in his hands and kissed her. "Until our next cup of espresso."

And he was gone.

She opened the front door to a darkened hallway, thinking that the girls usually left the lights on all over the house. "Kimmy? Hairy? Jennifer?" Where were they?

***

After Marc said goodbye to Gina, he made a beeline home, not bothering to stop at the store for food as he had intended to earlier. Although the day had been fun, it had also been longer than he expected, and he still needed to review the folders for each department he would be meeting with in the upcoming week.

There were so many. That was one of the problems at this university. Too many departments within each college, too many programs within each department. If they combined a few, money could be saved, and heavy cuts staved off, at least for now. The school of business saw this as a challenge, but not one they liked. The English, philosophy, and language departments balked like nobody's business. But what was the alternative? The state legislature had turned down any suggestion that involved raising tuition before the board of regents had managed to finish the first sentence of their request.

And then there was Gina. He knew this was going to be hard for her. No matter how discreet they were, someone was bound to find out. He understood her ambivalence, but his desire to be with her selfishly overrode these considerations. She was real and human. It wasn't in her makeup to be false and superficial, like many people he knew.

He half expected to see Sydney Sheppard sitting on the living room couch, doing her homework, ready to rant about the latest egregious action taken by her mothers. The last one she'd told him about was that they had discussed their plans to redecorate her bedroom when she left for college— in front of her. The nerve of them. All he could think of when he listened to Sydney go on and on, was how hard it must be to raise a teenager. Then he thought about Kimmy's friend with the BMW and shook his head.

He put the bread from Gino on the kitchen counter, let the dogs out, and hung up his coat. As he passed through the dining room, he eyed the folders aligned in a perfect row across the middle of Lisa Kirby's long, streamlined teak dining room table. Yesterday he had alphabetized them from left to right and had forgotten to gather them back up before he left for St. Louis. From their position, he could tell Sydney hadn't touched them when she'd been over to feed the dogs. He hated it when his work was touched, and he would have to remind himself to gather them up when he knew she was coming over. It certainly wasn't anything she should be seeing.

His cell phone rang to the opening cords of Bizet's *Carmen*. On schedule, on the first day of every month, he changed his ringtone to something different. Change was good, even though he was acutely aware of the fact that setting a schedule for change defeated the purpose of the exercise. He felt a little guilty about the indulgence, but heck, he had no children, and Betty was well taken care of already. "Hello?"

"Marc. I was thinking about you, and I wanted to call. Hope it's not too late."

Damn, when was he going to learn to check the caller ID? "Elaine. How are you? Sorry I didn't call you back the last time you called." He'd completely forgotten about it.

"Are you sitting down?"

"No."

"Well, maybe you'd better. Darcy and Mike are getting married."

He and Elaine had known this couple almost as long as the two of them had been together. "You're kidding!"

"No, I'm not."

"I am shocked." Why, he wondered, were they getting married now? But he didn't want to ask. Somehow, it invoked the fact that he and Elaine hadn't managed to pull off what their friends were now doing.

"Any chance you could come to the wedding?"

He was speechless and relieved that Elaine couldn't see the expression on his face.

"They asked me to call and tell you they'd love for you to come."

"When is it?" He asked.

"Second weekend of April."

Did he want to go back to Albuquerque? Did he ever want to go back to Albuquerque?

He sighed. "Do you need an answer today?"

"No. I can wait."

He heard the guarded disappointment in her voice and felt guilty. Why did he feel the need to put off deciding? If he told her no right now, he could avoid another phone call. He was being a jerk, and he knew it. They'd lived together for close to two decades, and although he never wanted that life back, something nagged at him. What did they say about amputations? That years afterward, you could still feel the limb?

"I'm not entirely sure I can come." He straightened the corner of one of his folders that was leaning a half inch too much to the right. "But I'll try. Let me check to see what my schedule looks like. Hey, any nibbles on the house?"

"Not in this market. We should be very glad we bought a while ago. At least we're not underwater like a lot of people still are."

Ah, the life he led. He was privileged to have enough money so that he could afford to not give a fig about whether he was underwater, treading water, or floating. What had Syd called it the other day when they'd been talking? First world problems. "Elaine, you're glad about something. Now maybe I do need to sit down."

She laughed, which was a rarity in and of itself. "Maybe you rubbed off on me after all."

He doubted that, but it was a nice thing for her to say, considering his somewhat sarcastic dig.

"How are the dogs? Still shedding all over the place?" she asked.

Now that was more like the Elaine he used to know. He examined his pants and saw that they were well salted with hair. "Every inch is covered. In fact, I've got so much hair on me they think I'm one of them now."

"Funny."

There was an awkward moment of silence, although on Marc's end he was willing to let it lay there between them.

"You know I wouldn't have minded them so much if you'd kept them shaved, and off the couch."

How to respond to that one? "I know, and I'm sorry. Hey, I was just walking out the door to make a grocery run when you called. Can I call you in a couple of days? I'll have an answer then."

She sputtered for a fraction of a second then said, "Sure. I'm looking forward to it."

***

"Kimmy, Jennifer?" Gina kept calling everyone's name as she walked through to the kitchen, where the light above the stove seemed to be the only one on in the entire house.

"Girls, are you in here?"

"It's me, Dr. Ferrari," a voice full of emotion answered. "Just me."

"Jennifer?"

"Yeah."

"I'm turning on a few lights," Gina said. She flipped the switch to her left on the wall. The overhead light flooded the kitchen, and she located Jennifer sitting close to Hairy on the floor in the corner.

"Is Kimmy upstairs?"

"No. She's not here. She gave me a key a couple of weeks ago so I could come and see Hairy when you were at work, and I never returned it. I think she forgot I had it. I hope you don't mind." Jennifer avoided eye contact with Gina and continued to talk. "I miss him. I didn't want to have to give him to you— to Kimmy, I mean. It isn't fair, really. It's not like my parents fight any less now that they don't live together, and Hairy doesn't live with either of them." She paused for a moment and sighed. "I wish they'd quit."

Gina watched two big tears roll down Jennifer's cheeks. "I'm sorry, Jenn."

Jennifer kissed Hairy on the head and stood as though she was forcing herself to do it. "I never knew why they got married, so I asked my mother, and she told me she was pregnant. With me." She frowned, then turned to Gina. "I probably should have done the math and figured it out myself. And my dad, his girlfriend is pregnant." She snorted derisively. "I guess he couldn't wait to start a new family. You know, he can't keep a dog because they're too messy, but he can get a new kid. Like they're not going to be messy?" Jennifer laughed.

"Jenn, do you need to talk to someone? You know, like a counselor?"

"No," Jennifer said adamantly. "I'm not the one with the problem. They are. Come August, I am so out of here. I wish my grades were better. Too late for that." She turned to Gina and held the key out. "I knocked before I used the key. I only let myself in because I knew you weren't here. I wouldn't, you know, like, take anything."

"I know that, Jenn. Keep the key, okay. Then you can come see Hairy anytime you want even when I'm not here."

"Honest?"

"Honest."

"Thanks. Thanks for taking care of him, Dr. Ferrari. Maybe someday I can take him back." Jennifer threw on her leather coat and picked up her purse. Gina noted that both the coat and the purse matched and were, judging by the quality of the leather, quite expensive. What material possession didn't this kid have?

"Did you see my new car?" Jennifer asked.

"I did. Kimmy told me about it, too."

"My dad bought it for me."

"You be careful in that thing, okay?"

"I will." Jennifer started for the entry hall, then turned, and said, "I'd rather have Hairy."

Gina pulled out the kitchen chair and sat, staring at the front door as it clicked into the frame. The engine revved loud and fast as Jennifer pulled out of the driveway. What had her father been thinking? But before she could ponder on that , the phone on the wall rang.

"Mom?"

"Kimmy."

"Come get me." Kimmy started to cry. "I need your help."

Chapter Ten

After a silent ten-minute ride from her father's, Kimmy bolted into the house and peeled off her hat for Gina to see the disaster underneath.

"Oh my god." Gina put her hand over her mouth. Despite her best intentions, one glance at her daughter's neon-orange hair was too much of a shock for her to contain. Lighter orange streaks careened down the left side, and copper-colored splotches nested on the crown of her head.

"I thought it would work." Kimmy's face crumpled into tears.

All Gina could think of was that her daughter now resembled an orange version of Hairy. People always commented that dogs and their owners tended to resemble one another. Today, the saying rang true.

She turned away and pinched the inner part of her upper arm hard to keep from laughing. The situation was traumatic to Kimmy, who lacked the perspective that age brings to minor disasters. A bad dye job, a rotten haircut, a zit on your nose on the day of your big interview, all of those were survivable catastrophes compared to the other things life smacked you with. Hair grew, zits healed, and you woke up and went on with your life. This was fixable.

She turned back to face her daughter with a straight face. "What color were you trying for?"

"Blonde. You have to help me. I can't go to school like this."

Gina grabbed her coat and put it back on, then checked her watch. "Put your hat on. We're making a run to the drug store."

Three hours later, they were rinsing Kimmy's hair in the kitchen sink for the third time. Gina wondered if there was a god or minor saint who accepted quickie hair prayers. Any help would be much appreciated, she thought, as she rubbed her daughter's head with an old towel she'd plucked from the ragbag.

"Is it all out?" Kimberly asked.

"No. Color is still coming off on the towel, but not as much as the first time we dyed it. It's getting better."

Kimmy sighed. "I hope it works."

Gina moved her daughter's hair around. She couldn't see the polka dots anymore, although it was hard to tell because it was wet. Her hair appeared as though it was now the uniform color of black ink. They'd gone through two bottles of dark-brown dye before they realized they had to go to jet-black to fully cover the polka dots. Now, instead of a blonde, her daughter would resemble a Goth cheerleader, and for some strange reason, that was infinitely more acceptable to Gina.

After her hair began to dry, and it was evident that the neon-orange-splotch crisis had subsided, Gina pulled out one of the kitchen chairs and sat down. She asked the question that had been boiling up and daring to roll onto her tongue since Kimmy took her hat off. "Why did you do this?"

"Because all the Golden Girls are blondes."

"No, they weren't. One of them was a blonde. The rest of them had gray hair."

"Mom," Kimmy's voice rose in volume and pitch. "We've been through this." Her eyes filled with fresh tears as she glared at her mother.

Gina raised her hands in a beseeching manner. "I'm getting old." *And very tired.* "Refresh my memory."

"Listen to me for once, okay? Please? The cheer squad at Mid-Missouri is called the Golden Girls, as in red and *gold*, the school colors."

"Oh." Gina felt like an idiot. "You did mention that. I'm sorry."

"I went to a basketball game on Friday, and all the cheerleaders were blonde, except for the two African-American girls, and one of them was a redhead. Then I went on the internet and looked at video clips of past squads, and most of them were blondes, too."

"You thought you had a better chance if you dyed your hair?"

"Bleached."

"Hair color shouldn't matter."

"Well, obviously it does."

"It shouldn't."

"You want the truth, Mom? You may not like it, but what you look like matters in the real world."

"If cheerleading was something meaningful, it wouldn't."

Kimberly stood, pulled the towel off her head, and threw it on the table. "It may not be meaningful to you, but it is to me. You know, your free-to-be-you-and-me universe only exists in that stupid song Marlo Thomas sang that you made me listen to every day when I was three."

Actually, Kimmy was the one who'd insisted on listening to that song every day, and it had almost driven Andrew and her nuts. Gina sighed. "You're so smart. You could do almost anything you wanted. Why this?"

"Because nobody else in this fuckingly cerebral family is coordinated enough to do a jumping jack. You can't, and Dad can't. And forget Daniel. He'd stumble over his knees if they weren't attached to the middle of his legs." She crossed her arms and held them against her chest. "But I can. I own this, and I'm better at it than anyone in the family."

She made a point of ignoring the f-bomb that had shot from her daughter's lips. "When did you dye your hair?"

"Saturday morning."

"Why didn't you borrow your father's car and go to the drug store then? Or come over here right when it happened? Why didn't Jennifer take you?"

Kimmy let out a sigh of resignation. "Jen got grounded on Saturday by her mother, and Dad was gone all weekend with his car. He has a new girlfriend, and they went someplace to have fun. Maybe if you were fun…"

"He didn't tell you where he went?" Andrew should have called her if he was going to be gone. If she'd known, none of this would have happened. She wanted to throttle him. "Kimmy, you could have called me."

"I was hoping the orange and the spots would come out if I bleached it again, and it would turn into blond like it was supposed to."

From the voice at the Pantheon, she thought she'd heard, to her daughter's magical thinking. They were more alike than Kimmy would ever know. "I would have come to get you."

"I didn't want to come over here because I knew this would happen. I'd get your standard lecture about how smart I am and how I should be myself, which is a code phrase for 'be what I want you to be, Kimmy.' And I didn't want to hear it. Again." Kimmy turned away and mumbled, "You're a hypocrite to your own free-to-be-ethos bullshit. If I was free to be me, you wouldn't criticize my choices all the time." She picked her purse up off the table. "If we were still together as a family, this wouldn't have happened. Dad wouldn't be with someone else, and we would all have been together."

They drove back in silence. Kimmy sat with her arms crossed over her chest and made a point of staring out the passenger side window. She reminded Gina of herself in the car with Marc earlier today. Like mother like daughter, once again. Pouting and screaming, thinking things will happen because you want them to and hearing magical voices. Wonderful. For a second, she wondered if it was a genetic predilection or merely a learned behavior. Then again, maybe it was the interactive effects of genetic leanings and the emotional environment. She stopped her musings abruptly. Kimmy was right. Besides crazy, they were all too fuckingly cerebral.

She spied Andrew's car in the driveway and pulled up in front of his house. At least he was home now. Through his front window, she saw two heads tilting toward each other. From the back, the woman appeared to be slender, with short, light-colored hair. Andrew got lucky tonight, because if his new girlfriend wasn't there, she would walk right in and rip him a new one.

"Thanks for your help," Kimmy said, her voice sounding like she was about to cry.

"I love you, Kimmy."

"Mom, you don't even know who I am." She gave her hat an extra tug and walked inside without looking back once.

***

Marc's chin had just made contact with his chest when the knock on his front door roused him from the couch and the dogs from the carpet. God, it was way too late for Sydney. He peeked through the window, then threw the door open. There stood Gina, shivering in an old pair of sweatpants, a pair of the most worn-out Birkenstocks he'd ever seen (and he'd seen his fair share of them in Albuquerque), and a sweatshirt that was far too thin for February. He watched her lips quiver and suspected it was not solely from the cold.

"You know," she said, her voice trembling, "I'm a professional. And a grown-up. I do the right thing. Always. Well, most of the time." She hesitated, then started speaking again. "At least I try to. I'm an independent woman, goddamnit. I initiated my own divorce. But right now"—her eyes started tearing—"I need a hug."

He pulled her to him, then shut the door. They stood holding each other tight. "I needed one, too," he said, as he released her.

Gina followed him into the living room. "Lisa Kirby has very good taste."

"It's not as comfy as your house."

"Oh, you're trying to make me feel good, because I feel bad."

"No, Gina. In your house I feel like if I put my feet on something, it's all right. Here"—his arms swept the living room—"I worry a little."

Gina brightened. "I gave all the fussy stuff to Andrew when he moved out."

"Good idea. Sit down. Tell me why you needed a hug. Not that I minded giving you one in the least."

"After you dropped me off, my daughter came over. She thought she needed to be a blonde to have any chance of being a cheerleader when she goes to college. So she tried to bleach her hair this weekend, and it turned orange. With neon polka dots."

Marc burst out laughing, then made himself stop. "Sorry."

Gina brightened a fraction more. "That was my reaction. But we fixed it. Then I stupidly tried to talk to her about the mindlessness of being a cheerleader in the first place, and she got mad at me. Really mad."

"Ouch."

"Yeah, I shouldn't have done it. She said our entire family was too fuckingly cerebral, and that's what the problem is."

Marc felt his eyes widen. "That's quite the accusation."

"Yes. But I think she meant me. I should have kept my mouth shut."

"Well, at least you can be grateful that your daughter can mount a good comeback. That shows a certain amount of intelligence right there."

Gina sighed. "Should that be one of my five things tonight? I am thankful that my daughter can use the f-bomb effectively?"

He put his arm around her and squeezed. "Nobody's giving you a break, are they?"

"No, they're not." She turned to him and asked, "Why did you need a hug?"

Marc sighed. He preferred not to go into detail about Elaine with Gina, but since they were sharing, he might as well cough it up. "Elaine called. Some friends of ours are getting married, and she wants me to come back to Albuquerque for the wedding. I'm not sure if I'm ready to go back there yet." He shrugged.

"Describe her in three words, none of them negative."

"Strong-willed, orderly, verbal."

"What woman isn't verbal? Try again."

"Okay, well read."

Gina laughed.

He couldn't help but notice how beautiful she was when she laughed. "Now, you describe Andrew," he said. "Three words, none of them negative."

"Difficult."

"That's negative."

He watched her sigh and start again. "Challenging, brilliant, and, uh, well read."

"Funny."

"It's true. He's an English professor."

"Oh yeah." He yawned. "I forgot."

Gina yawned along with him. "Did you ever think at our age that life would be this muddled and unsettled?"

"No, but I didn't reflect on much before my accident, either. I just did what came next." He slapped his hands together. "I was going to bed when you knocked. In fact, I should have gone to bed two hours ago. You want to sleep with me tonight?" He watched her face contort. "No, I mean sleep with me. You know, hold each other and sleep."

She hesitated for a moment, then said, "That sounds wonderful. I really don't want to be alone tonight."

They settled against each other like two spoons in the drawer, with Albert and Victoria at the end of the bed.

"This is nice," Gina said. "You know, just being with someone." She slipped her feet over his and then pulled them back. "Your feet are like ice.

"Sorry." He started to move them away.

"No, no, keep them there. I'll warm them up."

"You don't mind?"

"Of course not." She squeezed his feet tighter between hers. "Andrew always used to complain I was like a heater."

"You're kidding."

"No."

The man was an idiot, even if he was well read. "Who would complain about that?"

"Andrew, that's who." She moved in closer. Marc could feel her body relax.

He kissed the top of her head. "I know you worry about your daughter a lot, but honestly she sounds pretty tough. You have to trust she'll find her way."

"You're right. I know you're right. But it's hard."

"Have some faith in her. She is your daughter."

The two of them were silent for a few minutes. Marc thought maybe she'd fallen asleep, when she said, "Tell me your five things."

Marc hugged her gently around the waist. He whispered, "You, you, you, you, and you."

***

Gina smelled coffee as she walked down the hallway from the bedroom toward the kitchen, but a second sniff told her it was more than that. The vapors had a richness to them that whispered, *Espresso*. She shuffled into the kitchen as Marc took the second cup off the machine and set it on the kitchen counter.

He smiled when he saw her and said, "Perfect timing."

Victoria and Albert stared at her from the rug under the teakwood dining table.

"Wow." She reached up to feel her hair then realized it was useless. There she stood, no makeup, rumpled hair, and very bad breath. And yet he smiled at her. "It smells heavenly in here. Have you been waking up to this every morning?"

Marc patted the espresso machine. "That's what I wanted to tell you on the way back from St. Louis, but we never got around to it. Wouldn't you love to have one of these?"

Gina eyed the shiny, hammered copper exterior of the espresso machine, with its levers and spigots. It was huge, and took up a lot of counter space, but then, Lisa Kirby had a big kitchen. "Is it commercial?"

"I'm sure it is. Almost as good as Tazza d'Oro." He winked. "But not quite. I think you need Roman water to pull off those masterpieces or some gelato to go along with it." He pushed the cup her way. "If I remember right, you take a sprinkling of chocolate on top of your steamed milk."

He remembered, and that made her feel suddenly uncomfortable. Why? Because she didn't remember how he took his or because he remembered such small details about her in the first place? Details that no one else had ever taken the time to notice. Heck, she was having fun. Not laughing, giddy fun, just nice-to-be-around-someone comfortable fun. It was a feeling she hadn't had enough of in her life.

Marc stood by the granite counter while Gina sat on one of the stools. "Honestly, someone named Gina Ferrari ought to have an espresso maker like this."

"It's awfully big, and it looks heavy. How can you move it?" Her eyes homed in on the top of the dining room table. "What are all these folders for?" She asked.

"Work. Would you like to walk the dogs together tonight?"

"Sure." Cup in hand, she walked over to the table for a closer inspection. "These folders are for the budget cuts, right?"

"Yes. I'm going to have another cup. You want one?"

"Uh, no, thanks. One's enough for me."

The whooshing sound from the machine filled the vacuum of silence.

"I have to be getting home." She put down her cup in the sink, gave Marc a peck on the cheek, and hastened her walk out the front door to the sidewalk.

From across the street, Sydney called good morning and grinned.

Gina waved back uncomfortably as she hurried up the hill toward home to feed Hairy. Why was it that the most fun she'd found with anyone in decades was with the budget-cuts man, also known in some corners as the asshole from New Mexico? If fate existed, and of course it did not, it was out to ruin her.

As she turned her key in the front door, she heard Kimmy's voice.

"Mom!"

"What are you doing here this early?"

"It's all breaking." She came bounding into the entry hall from the living room.

Gina stared at her daughter, not understanding.

"Where were you?" Kimmy's voice quivered. "I've been here alone with Hairy for the last hour."

"Just walking."

Kimmy scanned her appearance with a quizzical frown on her face.

"What's breaking?" she asked Kimmy.

She pulled off her dark green beret to reveal her newly dyed hair, which now resembled something a three-year-old had practiced their scissor skills on.

Gina gasped. "What happened?"

Light tears ran down Kimmy's mascara streaked cheeks. "I don't know. I was getting ready for school, and I was using my flat iron to try to get some of the bushiness out like I always do, and it started breaking off. Look." She turned around for inspection. Gina counted at least seven different levels of hair.

"Oh my god." She wished she could tell her it didn't look bad, but it did. In fact, it looked downright horrible. "I think we're going to have to shape it up. Just a bit."

"Can't we glue it somehow?" Kimmy reached into her purse to pull out a bundle of her hair that she'd wrapped in one of her father's cloth handkerchiefs.

"I don't think they have anything like glue, but we can find a first-rate hair stylist." She put her arm around her daughter. "We'll get you the cutest pixie cut they can do."

"What's a pixie?"

"A short haircut. That's what they called them when I was little."

"I don't want one."

"Have you ever seen pictures of a movie star named Audrey Hepburn?"

"Who is she?"

"She was beautiful, like you, with short, dark hair. A true fashion icon. Real cutting edge." God, she hoped she was using the right words. "Google her while I make a hair appointment for you."

"I hate short hair."

"The good thing about hair is that it grows. Go Google Audrey Hepburn."

Kimberly started up the stairs.

"Did your dad drop you off?"

"No."

"Jennifer?"

"No."

"How did you get here?"

"Hitchhiked."

Gina's heart fell through her stomach and landed at her knees. "Please don't do that again."

"I only take rides from college kids."

"No matter how mad you are at me, no matter how much we fight, please call me. I'll come and get you, or we can get you an account with a car service, and I'll make sure I have my cell phone with me at all times from now on." She made a mental note to remember to charge the thing every night. "If you don't ever hitchhike again, I won't ever bug you about being a cheerleader again. Deal?"

"Deal." Kimmy's eyes were steady and her face calm. "You won't tell Dad I hitchhiked, will you?"

"If you do it again, I will. I'm serious."

"Do I have to go to school?"

"No. I don't have to go in until one. Let's get you out of this hair mess."

***

As it turned out, Gina didn't get to her office until three in the afternoon due to today's Hair Disaster, The Sequel, as she had come to think of it. She canceled her office appointment with her graduate students, rescheduling them for later in the week. Both students seemed more relieved than upset.

Roberta Cooper, as usual, managed to stick her head out of her office when Gina was walking down the hallway, wanting a report after the handwashing committee later in the day. She was somewhat glad Roberta had yelled it down the hallway, because if she hadn't, Gina would never have remembered the meeting.

She sat at her office desk and tried again to reach Andrew on his cell phone and on his office phone. He wasn't picking up. "Andrew," she said, talking into both voice mails and feeling like a stuck record. "It's Gina. Please call." He knew her office and cell phone numbers. She knew his schedule. He never taught after three, and it was now four in the afternoon. It was her fifth phone message. How many did it take to get him to call?

The answer came, as her cell phone rang.

"Let's see, seven messages, Gina? That's a record. It must be about Kimmy or Daniel, because they're the only things you ever cared that much about."

Was it seven? She thought it was five. Maybe he was counting the emails, too. "Andrew, when you leave for the weekend, I need to know because I don't want Kimmy left alone."

"Relax. She'll be in college next year."

She could barely make out his words. "This phone connection is really bad."

"I said, she'll be in college next year," Andrew yelled into the phone.

"Well, she's not this year," she yelled back. "You left her without a car the entire weekend, and you didn't tell me she was alone. You can't leave her alone like that."

"She's not going to burn down the house."

Minus the crackling noise, silence ruled both ends of the conversation for the next few seconds.

Gina rose and left her office to walk outside, where the reception was always crystal clear. She pushed open the door to the building so hard it banged against the outside wall.

"She's at the age when it's hard for her to call and ask for help." She spoke in a calmer voice. "She's trying to be independent, but her judgment isn't entirely up to snuff yet. This weekend she tried to bleach her hair, and it was a disaster. Did you notice her hair when I dropped her off last night?"

"Hair? Are you talking about that dog again?"

What an idiot. "No. I'm talking about the stuff that grows on your head, not the dog. Ask her about it. You need to tell me when you leave so I can work it out with her if she needs to go somewhere and get something."

"Oh. Now it's my fault your daughter doesn't call you? Should I blame you for Daniel not calling me? I probably should, come to think of it."

Andrew had always known how to get her goat, and this time she bit. "Your constant criticism is what drove him away. And that's not what I meant, anyway. I merely meant that I want to know when Kimmy is alone, in case something happens."

"Calm down."

"If you stay over at your girlfriend's—"

"My girlfriend's?"

"Yes. Your girlfriend's. Kimmy told me you were dating someone, and if you stay over at your girlfriend's or go away—"

"That's what's bothering you, isn't it? That I have someone, and you don't. That I'm moving on, and you aren't."

Why did he have to sound so triumphant? "I could give a rat's ass if you are dating or not. I'm calling about our daughter being left alone without transportation. I want her safe. I want you to tell her to call me, or at the very least, leave enough money for a cab, in case something happens."

"She's almost eighteen."

"She doesn't have her own car, and she's still in high school. If you're gone for a whole weekend, let me know."

"Trying to live vicariously?" he said.

She'd had enough. "Listen up, you sanctimonious ass. I don't care if you date a goat. Just make sure that when you leave for the weekend, our daughter isn't left in a precarious situation with no transportation. Try once, Andrew, to think of someone other than yourself."

She ended the call and noticed out of the corner of her eye that two undergraduate students she recognized from one of her classes were staring at her like she was a train wreck. She turned and walked back into the building to get ready for her handwashing-policy meeting. Oh joy.

***

The early evening handwashing meeting had been worse than the morning one was. Despite the subzero temperatures, Gina felt relieved to be walking home across campus, for a chance to clear her head.

Neither she nor Marty could get Barbra Goodshanks to move off her insistence that the infant-toddler caregivers needed to wear protective gloves throughout the day. "I'm merely recommending it, not mandating it," Barbara kept telling them. Recommendations had a way of eventually becoming mandates. When Barbara looked at children, all she saw were germs.

Then there was the strange, friendly overture from Marty. After the meeting, she'd suggested to Gina they should get together sometime soon over coffee. Coffee? In all honesty, Marty Schmidt was the last person she wanted to spend any additional time with.

The hardest part of the meeting was listening to the discussion between Barbara and Marty about Marc and what he was doing to them. Gina knew for a fact that Marc wasn't doing anything other than facilitating discussions about how each department might make the cuts that the university, not Marc, was demanding. Unfortunately, one of the ideas being floated was to merge Nutrition with Public Health, because many parts of the curriculum overlapped. It made sense to merge, but someone wasn't going to come out on the right side of it. She suspected it was Nutrition, as Public Health got more grants and therefore had more clout. Nevertheless, Marc was the one they were blaming.

So far, no one around the college knew about the two of them. But Columbia was a small town. It was bound to get out sooner or later, and when it got out, was she capable of tolerating that kind of judgment? She was literally sleeping with the enemy, an enemy who was leaving sooner rather than later. And yet, there was no one else she'd rather spend her time with.

It was scary to feel this way, this vulnerable. Life with Andrew had always been controlled and organized. Even if it was passionless, it was predictably passionless. There was never much emotion to the marriage apart from a slow, simmering disdain that eventually managed to boil over and end in divorce.

She shifted the strap of her briefcase across her body and trudged toward home. Today, after Kimmy, Andrew, and the handwashing committee, feeding Hairy and a hot bath seemed like heaven. Sometimes life was too complicated to hope for anything more than peace at the end of the day. After she fed Hairy, she'd give Marc a call. Maybe he wanted a hot bath, too.

Chapter Eleven

Today was Valentine's Day, and for once, Gina was looking forward to it. She heard her door knocker rap several times, and she thought about the fact that six weeks ago, a knock at eight in the morning would have more than likely spelled some pending teenage disaster. But since Marc had come to town, there was always the possibility that it meant a few moments of delightful conversation and a laugh or two along with her morning coffee.

They had managed to spend at least part of the day together every day since she'd crawled into his bed, wrapped herself in his arms, and slept better than she had in months. Yes, she was attracted to him sexually, but he was, despite her enormous fears and misgivings, becoming the person she depended on most. With Marc, she could relax, and that was more dangerous than fantastic sex. In fact, it was all too comfortable. He was leaving in a year. If she was smart, she'd end this before she got hurt, but it was way too late for that. She was head over heels in love for the first time in her life.

She saw the top of his head in the plate glass window of her door as she went to open it.

"Happy Valentine's Day." He beamed as she opened the door. Next to him stood a box, with a big red bow on the top, that went from his toes to his knees.

She gulped. She'd gotten him a card, one she'd run out to get after a two-hour Skype conference with the coauthor of a paper she was writing. And she hadn't expected anything more than a card from him either. Andrew had trained her well. Her romantic life had never been filled with that type of thing, and she had come not to expect, much less hope for, a gift. She could count on one hand the number of times Andrew had remembered her on Valentine's Day, and if she added it to the times either of them had remembered their anniversary, she'd come up with a smaller number than six. At least he'd always remembered the kids' birthdays—she had to give him that.

He hoisted the oversized box up and followed her into the kitchen, where he plunked it down on her table, grinning like a schoolboy. "Open it."

She pulled the wrapping paper back to see the picture on the front of the box. "An espresso maker?"

"Just like Lisa's."

"It's so big. And expensive. It's too much. Really."

"You want me to set it up?"

"Um, I have to shower and get ready for work, but sure, go ahead."

"By the time you're done, we should have espresso. Like in Rome."

Gina ran upstairs to change, glad for a moment to escape Marc's cheer. Why did he buy that? The thing was huge. He really should have asked her first. She hadn't gotten him anything, not even a box of chocolates.

She turned the shower on, as the lights in the bathroom went out.

"Gina, where are your breakers?" Marc called up the stairs.

"Breakers?" she shouted down.

"Yeah, I plugged in the espresso machine, and all the lights down here went off."

Shit. The wiring in the house was ancient. "On the wall next to the washing machine in the basement."

After her shower, she came downstairs. There was Marc, standing in her kitchen with two cups in his hand. "You look beautiful," he said, beaming as he handed her a cup of espresso. "I'd have steamed some milk, but you don't have any. Oh, and to use this machine, all the lights have to be off. Otherwise, you'll keep blowing the fuses."

Great. Just great. "Thanks." She was wearing a black, pleated skirt, a simple red sweater, and a pair of black tights that matched the flats perfectly. That, Kimmy informed her, was how you made your legs look long, if you weren't agreeable to wearing heels.

She handed him the card she'd gotten at the Circle K. "I'm sorry. It's not much. I don't think you're going to find an espresso maker in there."

Marc laughed. "Gina, I didn't give you this machine to get a gift back. I admit it's a bit over the top—"

"It's so big."

"I got you this because of what it means. This is how I met you in Rome. If I could bring you Rome, I would, but I think the Italians would have something to say about that."

If I could bring you Rome. God, that sounded like some cheesy rom-com movie, the kind she and Kimmy used to watch together, the lowbrow nature of which used to drive Andrew nuts. Oh well, it was Valentine's Day, and people said stuff like that to each other today. But that's not how real love ever happened. And why, she asked herself, was she in such a bad mood?

Marc opened his card. On the front was a staged photograph where two Pugs squared off over a bone. Each stood an equal distance from the object of their desire. The inside read, *If it was the last bone on earth, I'd let you have the big half. Happy Valentine's Day*. He beamed as he read it. "It's perfect. Thank you."

But it wasn't perfect. She'd spent two minutes picking it out last night from a thinned collection of cards at the closest convenience store she could find. She wasn't used to romance.

He leaned over and kissed her cheek. "Hey, you want to walk the dogs tonight after work?"

At night it would be dark, and no one would see them together. "I'd love to."

***

Late in the afternoon, as Gina returned home from work, she noticed that the lights were on inside the house. From the porch, she could see Kimmy snuggled with Hairy on the couch, watching television. Although they'd talked on the phone several times, she hadn't come over since the morning of the second part of the hair disaster.

Her daughter looked beautiful with her new haircut. She was beginning to think Rachael was right about it all. Kimmy was fine. Maybe if Daniel had bucked them more, he wouldn't have felt the need to declare himself a separate entity by bolting to Pizza University. He would have charted his own course from the beginning. And, she reminded herself, if it had led him to the very same place he was now at, she would have to be okay with it.

"Happy Valentine's Day." Kimmy produced a red, shiny, heart-shaped box of chocolates from behind her back.

"For me?" Gina was incredulous.

"Open it," Kimmy said, with an eagerness only someone her age could exude.

Gina put her satchel down and sat on the entry-hall bench. Kimmy sat next to her and watched. Without taking her coat off, she opened the box. "This is so thoughtful."

"They're from Dad."

She sincerely doubted that. "Here, you have first pick."

Without a second's hesitation, Kimmy plucked out a square, dark-chocolate caramel. "Everyone loves my hair," she managed to get out between chews. "It was such a great idea. A few girls on the cheer squad told me they were making appointments to get the same cut. Do you believe it? Me, Kimberly Francesca Ellison, setting a trend. Hey, do you know where there's some vintage clothing stores? Audrey Hepburn was amazing. I never knew she was the star of *Breakfast at Tiffany's*. But her hair was longer in that movie. Like you said, the good thing about hair is that it grows. You know, Mom, sometimes, you're really okay."

Those words beat the espresso maker and the chocolates hands down. "Thanks," Gina said.

Kimmy smiled. "I didn't want you to be by yourself on Valentine's Day."

"Are you worried about me?" Gina asked.

"A little."

She looked at her daughter straight in the face. "Kimmy, who really bought the chocolates?"

"Me."

Gina put her arm around Kimmy and gave her a hug.

"Where did you get that espresso maker?" Kimmy asked, as she walked into the kitchen.

Gina felt her cheeks turn red.

"Is that a Valentine's Day present from someone?"

"Yes."

"The corgi guy?" Kimmy frowned.

"Yes."

"Sydney told me last week that you walk down there. A lot."

"I didn't know you and Sydney talked anymore."

"We don't. At least I try not to."

Gina changed the subject. "It was nice of Jenn to take you to get the chocolates. How is she?"

"She's fine, but Dad's new girlfriend is the one who took me."

"Oh."

"Yeah, the whole way to the store she kept talking about how chocolate should be for the holidays and how empty the calories were, like I'm three or something and can't read the back of a label. I know it doesn't contain vitamins C, D, and E, but it sure does make you feel better.

Then she bought a box of it for Dad and reminded me again that gifts like this were only for holidays."

"What did you say the name of your father's girlfriend was?"

"I didn't. It's Martha, but I refer to her as Maleficent. I don't remember what her last name is, and I really don't care."

This couldn't be. "Does she ever go by Marty?"

"Yeah. Dad calls her Martha, but she said I could call her Marty. She's really pushy, Mom."

Gina tried hard to keep her face straight. She may not believe in fate, but she was beginning to believe in karma.

"I think she teaches classes about food." Kimmy helped herself to another chocolate-covered caramel. "I don't get why he's dating her. She's always, you know, telling Dad what to eat and what to wear. Stuff like that." She made a face. "She's not like you at all, so I don't think it will last any more than another week. I'm telling you, Mom, you could get him back if you'd just jump in there and act like you're interested."

"Staying for dinner?"

"No. I'm going to Jennifer's, but I'd love a ride."

"Her father's or mother's?"

"Mother's. She can't stay at her dad's anymore. He says she's too messy. I think it's because of his new girlfriend. So now he takes Jenn out to eat." Kimmy laughed. "And she orders the most expensive things on the menu every time they go, even if she doesn't like what it is."

Gina didn't laugh along.

"Thanks again for saving my hair." Kimmy touched the top of her head. "It was a stupid thing to do."

Gina frowned. "Stupid?"

"You know, bleaching it. I guess that's part of why I started a fight with you, and I've been trying to find a way to apologize ever since. It's hard to admit when you screw up and you need your mother to bail you out. I am almost eighteen, you know."

Gina nodded as she grabbed her keys and put her coat back on.

"Besides." Kimmy perked up. "It'll be at least shoulder length again by the time I try out for the Golden Girls cheer squad."

She bit her tongue. Why wreck the moment? "Think we can keep this not arguing thing going?"

"Maybe."

Gina laughed. "That's almost a yes."

"Mom, it's also the truth."

***

After dropping Kimmy off at Jennifer's, Gina hurried home and made it back through the kitchen door in time hear a knock on the front.

"Ready?" Marc stood with his dogs under the light, all bundled up with a thick down coat, a scarf, and a pair of gray flannel earmuffs. The earmuffs were a new addition, and the gray brought out the blue in his eyes. She took a long look at him.

They fell into their walk together like a couple who knew their routine so well they didn't have to talk about where they were going. They let all three dogs lead the way.

"You're not going to believe who my husband— I mean my ex-husband—is dating."

"Who?"

"Marty Schmidt. The woman in Nutrition."

Marc roared. "Does he have a death-by-nagging wish?"

Gina shook her head. "No. But I do think they deserve each other." She stopped then started again. "You know, I don't even think Marty deserves Andrew. She may be overly directive, but it's with the best of intentions."

"Yeah, you know what they say about the best of intentions."

"Right. Anyone else give you a Valentine's Day card?" Gina asked, partly joking.

He laughed. "Betty sent me one in the mail yesterday."

"Oh, that's nice." She watched his breath in the cold night air as he spoke.

"Yeah, it had candy hearts on it. Don't tell Marty Schmidt, but I ate them this morning for breakfast without thinking twice." He paused then said, "I started with the College of Education today. There's nothing like a bunch of teachers to give you a good dressing down, especially when they've turned into professors and you're trying to take money away from them. I think I'm going to be the most hated man on campus by the time this is over."

Gina agreed with his last sentence one hundred percent but said nothing. "Thanks again for the espresso maker."

"You're welcome, but it's a bit selfish of a gift. Now we can have espresso whether we're at your house or mine. As long as we turn the lights off before we use it." Marc's face lit up. "Before I forget, guess what your pal Rachael has been doing?"

"What?"

"She's been going to Betty's group home and reading to the residents. They love it. According to the house supervisor, Betty calls her *my Rachael*."

She hadn't talked to Rachael in a while, so this was news, and somehow it bugged her that he knew, and she didn't.

"I'm sure she'll be calling you." His cell phone went off to Beethoven's "Ode to Joy," and he paused on the sidewalk to answer it.

Gina starred with her mouth open. Why that ringtone? Did she talk in her sleep? Had she told him what happened in the Pantheon and just forgot? No, of course not. She'd made a point of not telling anyone for fear they'd think she was a nutjob. Marc liked classical music and changed his ringtone often. It was nothing more than that.

She watched him engage in a conversation that made him laugh with whoever was on the other end.

"Your brother said to tell you hi. And to wish you Happy Valentine's Day," he said, as he slipped the phone into his coat pocket.

"You were talking to Gino?"

"Yeah, he called to tell me how nice it was to see me last Sunday and to wish us Happy Valentine's Day."

Gina pursed her lips. "How did he get your number?"

"I gave it to him. He called when I was down there seeing Betty, and I stopped by. At his invitation." She watched as he cocked his head at her. "Gina, I think he's happy you and I are seeing each other. And I think he'd like to be a small part of your life."

"And when did you download that ringtone?"

"Today. It felt like Valentine's Day music to me. I usually change it on the first day of every month, but today, I thought 'Ode to Joy' was just perfect. That's how you make me feel."

She said nothing and kept walking.

Marc came to a halt and turned to her. "I feel like you're angry about something, but I haven't a clue as to what. You have something against 'Ode to Joy?'"

"No, of course not," she said with a terseness that betrayed her. "But in all honesty, it's not my favorite. I think joy— I mean, I think 'Ode to Joy' is highly overrated." She glanced at Hairy, who had stopped sniffing something stuck to the sidewalk and was now gazing up at her. "Tomorrow morning I'm holding my first meeting about the budget cuts, and tonight I've got a satchel full of anonymous concerns and suggestions to go through before the meeting. This isn't going to be pretty. People are upset, and I feel terrible."

"I understand that." The smile on his face disappeared.

"And right or wrong, they blame you," she told him.

He nodded in agreement. "If I hadn't come here, this would still be happening."

Her lips formed a flat line. "I think we all know that."

"Then what are you implying, Gina?"

"Nothing, really. These are people's careers you're messing with."

"I'm trying to find a way to make it more inclusive for the people involved, and I hope less painful, if that's possible. I don't know if it will work, but that's what I'm trying to find out."

"Oh, I see. We get to vote someone off the island ourselves, right? Make us the bad guys. Get us fighting amongst ourselves, then we lose sight of who's really behind all of this."

"I am looking for a way to make the process more inclusive, more of a consensus, and therefore, less painful."

"I'm sure you'll get a few publications out of it." She cringed inside from the hurt on Marc's face. "This could get nasty if somebody saw me with you, if they knew we were involved."

"Why do you care what people think?" His corgis, tired of standing, sat on the sidewalk on either side of him and stared up at Gina.

"I don't, and I resent you saying that."

"Gina, are you trying to start a fight with me?"

"Of course not."

"Are you mad because your brother and I are friends?"

"No, but as long as we're talking, I'd like it if you don't tell him what I do, or what we do together. And I don't know why you even bothered to ask that."

"Because you're angry. We got along so well in Rome."

"That wasn't real life. This is. People are going to lose their jobs. And I don't want—"

She kept her eyes focused on Hairy.

"You don't want to be seen with me." The anger in his voice was palpable. "You want to know what *I* think?"

"I think I'm going to know whether I want to or not, so go ahead. Speak."

"I think you're scared. Not just about what other people think, which in all honesty, I get. Sort of. I see the potential conflict of interest you're worried about. But I think you're afraid to be in love."

"You think I'm in love with you?"

"Yes." He stopped and looked at the dogs, then back up at her. "At least I hope you are. Love is about letting go of your armor. It's about taking a chance on your feelings, not your head. And that makes you vulnerable. To really love someone, you have to give up some control. And I think that's hard for you."

"I love. I love my children."

"You're their parent. You're the one in control. And you're upset with both of them right now because you're losing that control."

"Is this what you talk to my brother about when you have your little get-togethers? How messed up his sister is?"

He shook his head. "No. He doesn't think you're messed up, by the way. He thinks you've been hurt. By him and your ex-husband."

"I am not your psych case, and I am not Gino's psych case either. In fact, *he's* the psych case, not me. And I can't reinforce enough to you that in the future, I'd appreciate it if you two don't talk about me when you get together. And the same with Rachael."

"I'll make a note of that."

"Please do."

They stood there for a few seconds, each of them staring at the other then turning away quickly, only to steal another painful glance.

Finally, Gina said, "I have to go." She took off up the hill and yelled over her shoulder, "Happy Valentine's Day."

***

Marc had a theory that phones rang only when you didn't want to answer them, and by the time he'd located his cell phone in between the couch cushions, he'd missed the call.

How immature could he get? It had been years since he'd lost his temper. Gina did that to him. She brought out all his emotions and all his fears about not being loveable, nor worth anyone's time.

That ringtone needed to be changed, pronto. "Ode to Joy" was the antithesis of this Valentine's Day. Then again, maybe he'd keep it as a reminder that life didn't always get you what you wanted, and that you still needed to find a way to live with what you were handed. "What a bunch of shit," he said to himself, regarding his last thought.

He checked the caller ID. It was Elaine. A part of him wanted to call her right back, and another part of him was relieved he'd missed her. It gave him some time to collect himself and calm down.

The dogs trailed behind him as he walked through the kitchen, hoping for a treat that did not materialize. "Hey, you two," he said. "Get used to the fact that you don't always get what you want, and it'll save you a lot of disappointment." He settled onto the couch and called Elaine.

"Happy Valentine's Day," Elaine said, as she answered his call.

"Same to you." He put his stocking feet up on the teakwood coffee table.

"Marc, you are not going to believe this, but we got an offer on the house."

Finally, something good. "How much?"

"The asking price."

"Let's take it." One more step out of his old life, but to where?

"Hold on." Elaine sounded a note of caution. "That's the good news."

"What's the bad news?"

"Well, it's good news and bad news."

"Don't tell me. They want a new kitchen."

"No. Of course not. Our kitchen is wonderful. Why would you say that?"

Marc could tell by the innocent tone of her question that she had no idea what he was digging at. After they had spent thousands of dollars remodeling their kitchen, installing a commercial grade gas stove and three warming drawers next to it, Elaine didn't want to use it. In fact, she even complained when he cooked because she didn't want it to get greasy.

"So, what's the bad news?"

"They don't want to close until the beginning of April."

"I can live with that. What's the good part of the good-bad news?"

"That's the weekend of Mike and Darcy's wedding. I'm hoping you'll be here."

Two birds with one stone. "I'll probably come a couple of days early, so I can get my stuffed packed up and put it in storage when we sign the papers." What else did he have to do these days? Then he remembered Betty and felt terrible. He made a mental note to ask Sydney to watch the dogs. She was fighting with her parents again. This time over the reuse of paper products prior to recycling them. Even though April was a month away, he knew she'd jump at the chance to have a legitimate excuse to get away from them for a while.

"And you're staying here," Elaine said firmly.

Why not? It was his home too, at least for two more weeks. But then again, maybe not such a good idea. "I think a hotel might be better. Then I can get some work done and not keep you up."

"Whatever you want."

He detected not a shred of bitterness or disappointment in her voice when they said goodbye. What a relief that they'd finally gotten to that point. He walked back through the kitchen and into the laundry room, pulling a handful of dog treats out of the bag. Dividing them equally, he let Al and Vickie eat from his outstretched palms as he squatted on the floor. Not everyone had to be disappointed today.

Elaine's news managed to take his mind off Gina, at least for a few minutes, and he was grateful for the break. He had to admit it: he was in love with Gina. He also had to admit that he liked her more than anyone he'd met in a long time. Loving someone and liking them didn't always go hand in hand, but it had with Gina, and now the two of them had gone and had a fight over a stupid song by Beethoven. But it was much more than that, and he knew it. Now that he had calmed down a bit, he was left with simply feeling sad. Maybe tomorrow he'd call her. But would she pick up?

Start counting, he told himself fiercely. Today, especially today, he refused to use the dogs as two separate things to be grateful for. Today he was thankful for the fact that his house in Albuquerque sold, number one. Number two, that Elaine was being reasonable. Perhaps their separation was not only good for him but for her as well. Number three was that he could look at himself in the mirror and like who he saw, someone who tried to get it right and often got it wrong, but never on purpose. Number four stopped him short. Without the dogs, he didn't know if he could make it to five. He cast around for two more things. Lisa Kirby's espresso maker most certainly wouldn't cut it tonight, nor would the one he bought for Gina. That gift was a bomb. Number four was that he could handle being alone, and if that was what life ultimately gave him, he knew he'd be okay. And number five? He looked at his pants legs. Dog hair? Yes, without dog hair, he might still be with Elaine, and being alone was better than hiding in a relationship that was the emotional equivalent of a coma.

Chapter Twelve

"My grandmother used to tell me that if I sat and watched TV all day, my eyes would freeze, and I'd need an operation to unglue them." Sydney grabbed her coat and zipped it up, casting Marc an I-know-what-you're-doing-and-you-shouldn't-be-doing-it look.

He was all too aware that he'd spent the last few days on the couch, doing absolutely nothing. Last night, he'd drunk the three beers in the fridge and promised himself that he wouldn't buy anymore. There was something about drinking alone that didn't sit right with him.

"And did you believe her when she said that?" Marc asked. Even he could detect a note of sullenness in his voice, and he was slightly embarrassed. He was supposed to be the grown-up, not his almost eighteen-year-old dog walker. He took a whiff of himself. Yeah, he needed to clean up, literally and figuratively.

"Of course not. But she made her point."

"And so have you." He stretched his arms and made himself get up from the couch, knowing he could have sat there all day. "Thanks for walking the dogs."

"No problem, boss, but I think you could use some exercise yourself." Sydney cocked her head. "All I did was take them around the block, and they looked at me like they'd been cheated when we turned for home. Maybe we could do another turn around, you know, you and me, and the dogs." She went over to the coatrack, grabbed his parka, and threw it at him.

"Okay, okay." He caught his coat in midair and smiled. "Boss."

They each took one dog and watched as the two corgis struggled to be the one in the lead. It made for a fast-paced walk, and in no time they'd reached the end of the street, where they either had to go up the hill toward Gina's or continue on the downward slope.

"Up or down?" Sydney asked.

"Down."

"Figured. No Dr. Ferrari, huh?"

"So, your grandma," Marc began, steering the conversation away from Gina.

"Yeah? What about her?"

"Which one was she? Your mom's mother, or your father's?"

"Oh. My father's. She died about five years ago. I really liked her." She was silent for a few minutes, then she said, "I don't understand how nice people can have such messed-up children. Or how messed-up parents can end up with nice children. But it happens both ways."

"It's a mystery for eternity, I guess."

"Like, take Dr. Ferrari."

Oh, let's not. Marc knew she'd bring the conversation around to Gina.

"She's really nice," Sydney continued. "I mean, you know she's nice, right? You're going out with her. Right?"

"And?"

"Her daughter acts like a ditz, and she doesn't have to. She's really smart. But ever since her parents got divorced, she could care less about school and college. And her parents are professors, and her brother—"

"He quit school."

"You're shi—uh, you're kidding me. Eww. I bet Kimmy's parents are blown away."

"I don't think they're happy about it," Marc said, flatly.

"Well, at least I bet he doesn't want to be a cheerleader when he grows up."

"Is that what Gina's daughter wants to be?"

"That and a fashion queen. Total waste of brains."

"Syd, people find their way through many different paths."

"And some people never do."

He nodded, and smiled. "And some people never do."

"And some people need to get over themselves," Sydney said.

He noted that she looked at him about five seconds too long after she spoke. "Is there a message behind that sentence?"

"Look, I'm only eighteen, and I'm no expert at romance, and— "

"This is true."

"And personally, I don't know if I ever want to be an expert. I want a career and to marry someone really nice, who likes my mothers. And I want to have more than one kid."

"So your point is, Ms. Sydney?"

"My point is…well, like I said I'm not an expert but—"

"That has been established."

"And it's also been established that you don't like advice."

Not from an eighteen-year-old self-confessed novice in the romance department. But Marc left that thought unsaid. "Okay, Ann Landers, I'm listening."

"Kimmy's dad is a real pompous jerk. Everyone thinks so, including my mothers, who had to put up with him from time to time when Kimmy and I were, uh, hanging around. And he was kinda rude to Dr. Ferrari in front of other people. A lot. No one was surprised when they got a divorce. So maybe she's scared of being with someone."

Marc nodded, silently marveling at her insights.

"All I'm saying is, if you want to be with Dr. Ferrari, go up there and make whatever happened right and stop sitting in front of the TV. Your eyes might freeze. Oh, and by the way, those beer bottles in your trash are recyclable."

***

Gina paced the floor while Hairy sat on the couch, his head following her from one end of the living room to the other. It had been two days since her fight with Marc, and she missed him. Horribly. This morning she glanced at the espresso maker but couldn't bring herself to use it, nor could she bring herself to move the thing, either. See what you could have had, it whispered. Someone to make you espresso every morning, someone to laugh with, someone to treat you like a real human being.

Marc had called her twice, but she hadn't picked up the phone. This morning, in her inbox, there was a joke email from him, the title of which read, "Thinking of you. Hope you're well."

"Well, I'm not well," she said out loud to Hairy. "In fact, I'm downright shitty. For once I'm going to make myself not care what other people think." But she did.

The first departmental budget meeting, the day after Valentine's Day, had been horrendous, even though she'd baked three dozen biscotti and brought in special coffee. Everyone was upset and cursing the chancellor, the state legislator, and of course, Marc. Kill the messenger. It wasn't fair, but to many, it felt good.

My private life is my business, she told herself. It's time to start worrying about what I think, and I think he's wonderful. "If they want to blame someone for this budget disaster, they can blame the legislature for being cheap, and the chancellor for being a weasel. And maybe Roberta for some of her bad budget decisions, too. But not Marc." She looked at Hairy, who stared straight back at her. "And I really don't care if Gino likes him, either."

Hairy cocked his head and wagged his tail.

"Sorry, pal, but I may be gone for a while. In fact, if things go well, I may not be back until tomorrow morning. Make yourself comfortable on the couch, and don't lick the afghan too much." She ran her fingers through her hair, grabbed her coat off the hook in the hallway, and set off down the hill.

Rachael's words flooded her mind as she formed her hands into fists and stuffed them into her coat pockets. Saint Gina. It was time to give it up. Her own children had been telling her that in one way or another for months. She killed everyone with kindness and with a superior, condescending rendition of maturity. It's just that for so many years, she had to be so good to make up for Gino and to make certain no one thought of her in the ways they thought of him.

Halfway down the hill, she saw a lone figure making his way up her side of the street. He, too, had his hands thrust in his pockets, and when the man passed under the streetlight, she saw it was Marc.

"You know," Marc said when they both came to a halt in each other's arms. "I think this is halfway between our two houses. Get it?"

"No."

"We're meeting each other halfway."

She burst out laughing and hugged him harder. "I missed you. And I'm sorry. I…I have a bit of a temper."

"And I have a sarcastic mouth. And I missed you, too, and I'm sorry."

"I missed you terribly," Gina said.

"I missed you horrifically."

"I missed you gigantically."

"I missed you…uh, colossally. You know, like the Colossus we saw in the Metropolitan museum, in Rome." He smiled and said, "I'm running on empty here, Gina."

She smiled back at him. "You know, I'd be all for keeping this up if it wasn't freezing."

"Should we flip a coin over whose house we recommence at?" Marc asked. He reached into the pocket of his jeans and pulled out a quarter. "You know, give luck and fate some credence?"

She shook her head as she took his hand and started down the hill toward his house. "I think we should focus on the facts. There's far less possibility of a Kimberly-Jennifer interruption at your place. And tonight, I want you all to myself."

***

They heard the sirens at six in the morning. Gina sat up in bed next to Marc, and glanced at the clock. It was time to get up anyway, as she had Hairy to feed and let out. She swung her feet down and stepped on one of the corgis, who let out an indignant noise of disgruntlement somewhere between a yelp and a growl.

"Sorry, sorry," she muttered, trying to wring the sleep out of her voice. The dogs were put out with her for taking up their space on the bed. Last night, she'd received the evil eye from them both before they begrudgingly settled down on the floor.

Marc stirred next to her and groped for her hand.

"Did you hear those sirens?" She grabbed her sweater and pulled it over her naked body, hoping it covered her rear end when she stood. "That sounds like a five-alarm fire."

Marc sat up. "Yeah, it does. And it sounds close." He reached down to grab his jeans and underwear. He threw his T-shirt and sweater on as Gina struggled with her bra and pants. "Do you know where my shoes and socks are?"

"By the couch with mine. Remember we were playing foots—"

"Oh yeah." She yawned, then walked over to his side of the bed and kissed him gingerly. "I'd kiss you more but—"

"I get it. Come on, let's check the sirens out."

"Oh no!" Gina's face contorted in frustration.

"What?"

"I left my cell phone at home last night." She wondered if Kimmy had been trying to reach her. Ever since she'd promised to keep her cell phone with her, her daughter had been texting her regularly and even attaching pictures. This, without her even having to ask.

"Let's drive and go get it, check out the sirens, and then double back here for some espresso."

"Sounds good. I have to let Hairy out and feed him, anyway."

They threw their jackets on and climbed into Marc's wagon, turning left and driving up the hill to her street. She saw the fire trucks, their bright headlights shining in the subdued morning light. Her neighbors were gathered on the sidewalk to watch the smoke, still wafting up from what was left of the roof on her house.

"Oh god, that's my house!" she screamed, and she was out of the car before Marc eased it up to the curb. And then she remembered who was in the house. "Hairy!"

She started to run across the street but was stopped by a fireman.

"Ma'am, are you the owner?"

"Yes!"

"You can't go in there," he said, touching her arm.

"I have a dog," she said to the fireman while staring at the remains of what had held everything she owned.

"There wasn't a dog in there."

"Did you check all the rooms?"

"Yes, we did."

"The basement?"

"Yes."

"Upstairs? Did you check upstairs?"

She felt a hand on her shoulder and turned into Marc's arms. "It's okay. I have him. One of your neighbors heard him barking and broke in your back door." Marc held up his hand and she could see he was holding a leash. "He said Hairy ran right out."

She pulled away from Marc as she felt the dog's too big tail brush against her pants leg. Hairy wagged at the sight of her, and as she bent down to hug him, he wiggled out of Marc's grasp to lick her face.

Another fireman, who had overheard their conversation, approached them. "He got out in the nick of time, too. He'd have died from smoke inhalation. You're probably going to want to take him to the vet and get him checked out as soon as you can."

Gina took the leash from Marc and held it tightly as the fireman walked off to speak to the rest of the crew. She stared at the ruins. The front windows were broken out and the blackened porch roof looked as if it could fall any second. She was afraid to see the back. Where would she and Hairy go? She could probably stay with Marc until that was figured out. Thank god Kimmy's stuff was over at Andrew's, and for the first time, she was relieved Kimmy was there, too.

Marc, who had been at her side a moment ago, was over by one of the fire trucks, talking to the police and one of the firemen. They would talk then look at her then talk again. From the looks on their faces, she could tell it wasn't good. The house may be a mess, but everyone was safe. They broke off their conversation when they caught her staring. Marc and one of the policemen walked over to where she was standing.

"Do they know what caused the fire?" she asked Marc.

"Something electrical. It started in the kitchen. That's all they know so far."

She and Andrew had been meaning to rewire that house since the day they'd moved in . She felt horrible and irresponsible. But thank god, no one was in there when it happened.

"Gina," Marc said to her quietly, and as evenly as possible. "Your neighbor said he'd take Hairy for the day. The police have some...some bad news. Let's go over to the police car. They need to speak to you privately."

***

Gina rushed through the glass doors of the emergency room, her winter jacket zipped up over her crumpled day-old clothing. She pushed her way toward the information desk with Marc two steps behind her.

Marty Schmidt, who sat in the front row of chairs close to the reception desk, stood and beckoned to them, giving Marc a quick once over. She blinked, then turned to Gina when she spoke. "She's going to be okay, but she's in surgery right now."

"Surgery?" Gina said.

"She's okay," Marty repeated. "You look very pale. I think you should sit down."

Gina felt Marc's hand on her shoulder as he gently pushed her into the seat next to Marty.

Marty reached forward and picked a stray thread off the sleeve of Gina's jacket. "She broke both of her arms, and her wrists are fractured. They'll have to be pinned for a quite a while. That's what they're doing in surgery right now. Besides that, she's bruised and scratched up, but nothing else is broken. At least nothing that we know about."

Gina gasped, then caught her breath in a small choke.

"Put your head between your knees," Marc instructed.

She did as she was told, grateful in part to avoid eye contact with Marty, who kept glancing in horror at Marc.

"And keep it there until you can feel some blood in your head," Marc added. "I'm going to get you some water. Don't sit up until I get back." He stuck his head down to her level and stared into her eyes. "I mean it."

Irritation was a welcome emotion. "Okay, okay." She watched him pull his cell phone out as he walked away. Another wave of nausea rolled through her, and she swallowed, her head still down as instructed. "Is there more you can tell me?" she asked Marty.

"You know about Kimberly's friend, right?"

"Yes. The firemen told me."

"She didn't suffer. She died on the way to the hospital and never regained consciousness. It's something you might want to tell Kimberly when she wakes up. You know, to give her some comfort." Marty took a deep breath and continued. "According to the police, they think Kimmy's friend was texting and ran a red light. That's all I know, except that Kimmy should be out of surgery soon. Andy asked me to stay here and wait, in case the police located you. He's going to let me know when she's out of surgery."

"They said she'd be okay?"

"Gina, it's just two broken arms and two fractured wrists." A horrified look came over Marty's face. "I'm sorry. I didn't mean that's not serious."

Gina could hear the pained tone in her voice as she stumbled to say the right thing. She tried lifting her head, then put it back down. "I know. What you meant is, she's alive."

"Yes. She's alive." She could hear Marty breathe out a huge sigh of relief. "This is a horrible way for you to find out that I've been dating Andy. I'm sorry."

"I've known since Valentine's Day."

"Oh. Of course. Kimmy told you." Marty was quiet for a moment, then she said, "We couldn't find you. We tried to call, but you didn't answer your landline or your cell phone. Consequently, this morning I went by your house and saw it smoking. That's when I called 911. Oh, and your dog…Kimberly's dog, I mean, he's with—"

"I know." Gina kept her head down.

"They can't find Jennifer's parents, either. Do you know how to contact them?"

Gina had trouble speaking through her tears, which dripped onto her shoes, leaving small, clear splotches where the dust was. "I don't know either of them well enough to have their phone numbers." Why did that make her feel so irresponsible? Kimmy was almost eighteen, a senior in high school, and she'd only been close friends with Jennifer for the last six months. It wasn't like she was organizing carpools with everyone's parents anymore.

"The police said her driver's license listed an address they no longer live at, and the neighbors didn't know where they moved to," Marty told her. "I guess we'll have to wait until Kimberly gets out of surgery for the contact information ."

Marc came back with two bottles of water. He handed one to Marty, who took it from him as though it might be poison. The other he unscrewed and kept. After Gina sat up, he handed her the bottle in his hand and put his arm around her.

Marty studied him with narrowed eyes.

"Okay. They know you're here now," Marc told her. "I told them at the desk when I went to get the water. When you're ready, walk over to the desk, and they'll let you in." He pointed to a door against the wall next to the information desk where a security guard stood. "I'll wait here until your brother comes."

"My brother?"

"I called him. He's on his way. And you're all staying with me tonight."

"That's not a good I—" Gina started to protest, then she remembered. She didn't have a house anymore.

"Has Dr. Schmidt told you the rest of what happened?" Marc asked, tilting his head toward Marty.

"You mean, Jennifer?"

He nodded silently.

"There's a little bit more." Marty volunteered quietly. "Jennifer ran into another car, I think they call it T-boning, and the man she hit is in critical condition.

"Does Kimmy know about Jennifer?" Gina asked.

Marty shook her head. "I don't know."

Marc got up to make another phone call. While he was out of earshot, Marty turned to her and asked, "Are you seeing him?"

"Sort of."

"Is that where you were—I'm sorry. That's none of my business."

Gina said nothing. She was relieved Marc didn't offer to go into the surgical waiting room with her. As she walked toward the door that would let her into the emergency surgical waiting room, she looked over her shoulder and saw that he was seated next to Marty, politely putting up with the stolen glances she directed his way. The hospital security guard opened the door, and she walked down the hallway into the waiting room. Andrew glanced at her and smiled slightly but said nothing.

She acknowledged his silent greeting with a nearly imperceptible nod. It was the most she could do without falling apart, and she didn't want to cry in front of Andrew. They were distant with each other now and had been years before they divorced. She didn't want to seek comfort from him, but there were many questions she wanted to ask. Questions about when the accident happened, and where it happened, and was it somehow connected to her house burning down? Instead, she picked up a copy of the hospital's AARP magazine and flipped through it, hoping he didn't notice she was wiping her eyes every few minutes.

"Where were you?" Andrew asked, finally.

"At a friend's."

"At a friend's?" He stared at her, his eyes narrowing, then he looked away. "Next time, take your cell phone. To your friend's."

An hour and a half later, a man in greenish-blue scrubs came through the door and settled his gaze on the two of them. "Mr. and Mrs. Ellison?" he asked.

"Dr. Ellison," Andrew corrected. He turned, waiting for Gina to add her own editing, but she declined. She could care less. Correcting the doctor only put off what she wanted to know.

"Our daughter?" She stood and gave her partially unzipped coat a tug at the bottom, so that it slid over her hips. Andrew gave her a withering glare.

"She's out of surgery and doing fine. She's going to need help, though, and a lot of it. Both arms are in bent casts that extend from the joints in her fingers to four inches above her elbow. She won't be able to dress, bathe, or toilet without help. Eating, of course, is going to be a problem, too."

Andrew cringed. "How long will she be like that?"

"We'll put her in a smaller cast, one that goes from the palm of her hand to below her elbows in about a month, when we remove the pins. Then she'll have more independent functioning. She'll need a bit of physical therapy after the second casts come off. But she has youth on her side, so I strongly suspect she'll heal quickly." He spoke with them for a few more minutes, answering questions and giving them more information about Kimmy's postsurgical care. "Unless there is some complication, and I doubt that there will be, they'll be releasing her tomorrow," the doctor told them. "I'll have the nurse come in to give you the discharge details for tomorrow."

"Can we see her?" Gina asked.

"Of course. One of the nurses will come and get you shortly."

She turned to Andrew as the doctor took his leave. "Does she know about Jennifer?"

"No." Andrew waited until the doctor was well beyond earshot. "I can't do this."

"I understand. I'll tell her about Jennifer. You don't have to."

"No. What I meant was that I've got tests and a paper to submit, and I have to be back east for an important meeting. A very important meeting. She'll have to live with you."

"Andrew, I don't have a house."

"Right." He threw up his hands. "Fine. Then you two can stay at mine, but with my schedule, I can't do any of this."

"What is *this*?"

"I can't take care of Kimmy. It's up to you."

Up to you. That was the way it had been since the day they were married, and up-to-you had been compounded by the birth of each child. Her head swelled with anger that she forced herself to squelch. She wanted to scream at him, then smack him across the face, but she wouldn't. This was about taking care of Kimmy, not about exposing Andrew's innate self-centeredness to the world.

"Okay," she said. "Fine. But you'll have to tell her that."

By the time they sat with Kimmy in the recovery room and Gina told her daughter about Jennifer, it was mid-afternoon. Between sobs, Kimmy explained that they had been at the house to see Hairy, and that they'd gone out for some milk to steam for the lattes they were making with the new machine. Of course, the espresso machine. The way it was blowing fuses, it had more than likely caused the fire.

Andrew excused himself the minute the nursing staff told them they were moving Kimmy to a room on the third floor. After Gina made sure she was settled in, and the sedative brought her some much-needed sleep, she went to look for Marc in the lobby. She found him standing by the entrance of a small meeting room off the waiting area.

"Your brother's here," he whispered, and pointed with his chin into the room. "He's with Jennifer's father."

She peered in and spied Gino comforting Jennifer's father, who had collapsed onto one of the small sofas against the wall.

"Gino told the staff he was family," Marc explained, "so they let him have Kimmy's phone. He scrolled through Kimmy's contacts and found both of their numbers. They still can't find her mother, though." He glanced at Gino and Jennifer's father, then spoke again. "Did you know that your brother and Shauntel do crisis counseling with the families of people who've overdosed?"

"No. Of course not."

"He has extensive training in crisis intervention. Shauntel, too. Oh, and I called Roberta Cooper."

"You called Roberta?"

"Yeah, I explained the situation. She said she's got your classes covered for the next week."

Part of her felt relieved she didn't have to make the phone calls, while another part cringed. Between Roberta, Marty, and Andrew, everyone would now know about Marc and her. Then, too, there was the part of her that was disgusted she was reacting to something that petty, given the circumstances.

Gino walked out with Jennifer's father, ignoring her and Marc as though they weren't standing six inches away. When Jennifer's father was securely in the hands of a woman Gina strongly suspected was the hospital social worker, he made his way back to them, just as Marty approached them, too.

"I gave Andrew the keys to my car this morning," Marty said. "He left without me. By accident, I'm sure. He's not thinking very well right now. Can I get a ride with one of you?"

"I'll take you home," Marc volunteered.

Gina looked away from Marty when Marc offered. If she had to take in another emotional reaction to anyone or anything today, she was going to melt into a large puddle and pray that the hospital carpeting would absorb her.

"Who are you?" Gino asked Marty.

"I'm Marty Schmidt, Andy's, uh, girlfriend." Marty looked uncomfortable when she said the word girlfriend.

"Andy?" Gino looked at her questioningly.

"Andrew." Marty waited politely, still looking at Gino, expecting him to complete his half of the introduction. "And you are?" she finally asked.

"Gino. Her brother." He cocked his head in Gina's direction.

"You're Kimberly's uncle. Nice to meet you," Marty said, extending her hand. "Sorry it's under these circumstances."

Gina watched Marty's head jerk back ever so slightly as she took in her brother's tattoos, unconcealed for the world to see via his rolled-up sleeves. As he raised his hand to shake hers, he looked Marty squarely in the eyes, appraising her as though she was his bread flour supply for Monday morning's baking.

"You okay?" he asked Gina, turning abruptly away from Marty.

"No. Of course I'm not okay." In spite of everyone around her, she spat the words out, strangely grateful she had someone she didn't have to be calm and polite with.

"Good. You still have your wits about you. The fire department wants a word. I told them we'd meet at your house in thirty minutes." He turned to Marc and said, "We'll see you tonight."

***

Gina glanced over at Gino as he steered his truck out of the hospital parking lot and on to Stadium Road. He'd insisted on taking charge.

"Rule number one," he explained, "never let someone who is emotionally traumatized drive. Remember that, okay?"

"Marc drove."

"Good. I don't want you driving for the next twenty-four hours. I'll get your car and drive it down to Marc's, as soon as you show me where he lives. I know it's close."

Her head throbbed, and her chest felt sore. Telling Kimmy about Jennifer was one of the most difficult things she'd ever done. Her daughter's sobs had been uncontrollable, and Gina felt pain and relief when they gave her something that made her sleep.

Kimmy would be all right, she kept telling herself over and over, as though it were a meditation mantra. She would mend but the loss of her friend would be a devastating event to get over. She stopped and revised her thinking. The right words were get through, not over. Her death was something that would stick with Kimmy for the rest of her life, and the thought of Jennifer made silent tears stream down Gina's face again.

She turned to stare at her brother, who scanned the road for cross traffic. He pressed on the brake in anticipation that the two kids on skateboards wouldn't bother to look before they rolled across the street. They didn't. She wanted to pull down the window and yell. Didn't they know they had parents who would miss them if they died?

"Thanks for coming up here," she said in an almost whisper.

He reached over and squeezed her hand. "I'd say anytime, but I really don't want this to happen again."

A firetruck was waiting outside the remains of her home. The entire roof, minus the porch, had collapsed into the house, but the garage appeared unaffected. The shock of seeing it again made her crumble.

Gino helped her out of his truck, then went next door to get Hairy from her neighbors while she talked to the firemen. No, they told her, she couldn't go inside. Yes, they told her, the house would more than likely be condemned. Did she have insurance? She needed to call them, immediately. The cause of the fire? The espresso maker shorted out and caused an electrical fire within the walls. This confirmed what Kimmy had told her. Her daughter had been dying to try that espresso maker out ever since she'd set her eyes upon it. Oh god. If she'd been at home where she was supposed to be and not with Marc, none of this would have happened. She'd have her home, and her daughter would have her friend. Who did she think she was? A twenty-something college student with no responsibilities?

Gino joined her with Hairy when she was done talking to the firemen. He grinned cautiously. "This is one ugly pooch, Gina," he said.

The dog wagged his tail uncontrollably when he saw her. Gina, scratched his behind without thinking, too lost in her thoughts to be fully conscious of what had become an automatic gesture.

"Did they tell you when Kimmy would be awake?" Gino asked.

"They said she should be out all night, and they'd call me if she woke up before that and wanted me."

"And Andrew?"

She looked at her brother and shook her head.

"Come on then," Gino said. "Let's get to Marc's."

***

In addition to the aroma emanating from Lisa Kirby's espresso maker, Gina woke to the sound of two male voices in annoyingly genial conversation. She wandered down the hallway with Hairy, still in her clothes from two days before. To her well-worn ensemble, she had added her brother's black hoodie, which he'd lent her yesterday.

It hit her when she reached under the bed for her Birkenstocks that this was all she had. Who knew what was salvageable in the house, if anything? Last night, when they'd arrived at Marc's, she'd collapsed, grateful to have reached a level of exhaustion that prevented her from processing all that the day had wrought. Now, as she ran her fingers through her hair, she realized she needed a shower, a good tooth brushing, and some deodorant, all of which she no longer had. Then she remembered Kimmy, and none of it mattered. She had to get back to the hospital.

Gino and Marc quit talking the second she entered the kitchen, and Marc pushed a latte, the way she liked it, toward her. Something angry and growing inside Gina overruled her manners and stopped her from saying thank you.

"You okay?" Marc asked. She watched him scan her face with concern.

"Yes," she told him, stiffly.

They resumed their conversation as though she wasn't there, and she stared at the two of them silently until the caffeine kicked in. "So you two are BFFs now?"

"What's a BFF?" Gino asked.

"Yes," Marc answered her. "And how are you?"

"I told you. I'm fine." Gina glared at him. This morning of all mornings she didn't feel like answering his questions, especially when she remembered that he'd taken it upon himself to call Roberta, and Gino. Who did he think he was? Her husband?

"What's a BFF?" Gino asked again. "That could mean lots of things. Some of them insulting."

"It means best friends forever," Marc told him. He turned toward Gina. "Your brother has been giving me baking lessons when I'm down in St. Louis, visiting Betty. So far, I've mastered biscotti. We are now on to Italian breads."

"He's got a lot to learn," Gino said. Her brother's hands spread out as he spoke.

"Lovely. Yes, brother dear. Just give away the family recipes." She turned to Marc. "First Rachael, and now Gino. Anybody else in my family you want to make friends with?"

His mouth fell open along with her brother's. "Hairy?" A tone of cautious humor coated Marc's one-word reply.

She ignored his comeback.

"Look," Marc said, turning serious. "Both Rachael and Gino are good people."

"Thank you," Gino said, beaming.

"Yes, I know that. They're my family."

She caught her brother's eyebrows as they shot up, and his espresso spilled over the rim of his cup.

"Not to mention Shauntel," Marc added. "And you don't normally find a whole family of nice people. There's usually at least one stinker in the bunch, but not with all of you."

"You haven't met her ex-husband," Gino volunteered.

This wasn't joke time. Laughing about anything felt obscene.

"Speaking of Andrew," Gino kept talking, "he called this morning on Kimmy's cell phone, which his girlfriend must have told him I have. He was looking for you. He said he wasn't wild about Hairy being at the house, and could you find somewhere else to put him? I hope you don't mind that I stepped in, but I told him that without the dog you weren't coming with Kimmy, and he'd have to make arrangements for taking care of her on his own."

Gina almost dropped her cup. Her instinct was to protest anything her brother did, but his response to Andrew had been near perfect. Reluctantly, she nodded in acknowledgment.

"After brief consideration, very brief I might add," Gino continued, "he relented. But he asked me to tell you that you'll have to have the carpets professionally cleaned when you move back out, and to keep the dog off the couch."

"Is he going to be staying there, too?" Marc asked.

"He's going to his girlfriend's," Gino told him. He cocked his head and frowned. "That woman kept trying to start a conversation with me about trans fats last night, when you were filling out paperwork. It was very strange, given the circumstances."

"She's not a bad person," Gina told him. "Just a bit—"

Marc broke in. "The first time I met her, I felt like I was in food church."

He glanced at Gina for affirmation, but she gave him none.

"The first time you met her," Gina told him, "you were talking about chopping up her department, so I'm sure she was a bit terse." Why had she said that? Because it was true. In part.

"We need to go," she said to Gino. "I have to stop by the house and get some things."

Gino looked at her strangely. "Nothing is salvageable. Remember when the fire department told you that yesterday? They have what's left of the house taped off."

Marc looked at Gino. "Do they have any idea how the fire started?"

"The espresso maker," Gina said, looking at Marc straight in the eyes. "It shorted out the wiring and started a fire in the wall."

"But you were at my house."

"The girls were over seeing Hairy."

"Oh."

"What am I going to do?" Gina asked her brother.

"I think Lisa left some clothes here," Marc said. "I'm sure she wouldn't mind you borrowing them for a day or two."

Gina stared at him in angry disbelief. "Lisa is about thirty pounds lighter and three sizes smaller than me."

His eyes popped with embarrassment.

She jumped off the stool and grabbed her car keys. "Gino, can I meet you out in my car? I need a few minutes alone with Marc. You have my keys, right?"

"Yeah." Her brother stood and grabbed his coat off the back of the chair. "Thanks for letting us stay here," he said to Marc. "I owe you for last night." Gino turned to make a face at her then made his way toward the door.

"Yes, thank you. For everything." She uttered those words as though they had been coated in unsweetened chocolate then thrust her arms through her coat, giving the zipper an officious pull before she reached for the bottom of her coat and tugged it down over her hips.

Marc's eyes widened. "Call me if you need help. Or anything. Anything at all."

"My life is a mess, and if I wouldn't have been down here last night, it wouldn't be. My daughter's friend wouldn't be dead, my daughter wouldn't be in the hospital right now, and my house wouldn't have burned down from that stupid espresso maker you bought for me, if I'd been where I was supposed to be. The girls started messing with that machine. I should have removed it the minute it blew the fuse. Too many things have fallen apart because of you and me, Marc. This isn't Rome. My daughter needs me. I can't do this right now. I can't see you anymore."

He nodded as he listened and said nothing.

She clipped the borrowed leash to Hairy's collar and made her way out the door to her car, her legs shaking all the way.

Her brother sat in the driver's seat.

"Gino, I can drive."

"No, you can't."

"Get out! It's my car!" she screamed.

He unbuckled his seat belt, opened the driver's side door, and walked to the other side of the car. The second her brother's seat belt snapped into place, Gina started the car's engine. She searched her rearview mirror, began to pull out of the driveway, then hit the brake hard. "Well," she said, turning to Gino. "Aren't you going to berate me for being rude?"

"No."

"Don't you think I was?"

"Yes. Very."

"You've all been having one big party in St. Louis." She could hear herself screaming. "And nobody asked me." She knew she was doing it, but she couldn't have stopped if she wanted to. "Why not bring Daniel home and get him in on it?"

She put the car in park and laid her head on the steering wheel, crying in big convulsive gasps.

"Gina, let me drive."

She ignored him and continued to sob.

"Sis, turn the car off and give me the keys.".

Gino got out of the car again without saying a word, walked around to the driver's side door, and opened it, indicating to Gina that she should exit from behind the wheel.

She shut the engine down, handed him the keys without looking, and felt a soft tug on her arm as Gino pulled her out.

"I am so goddamn tired of being the grown-up in the room." Her crying turned into yelling. "This time, I want to be the one who gets to lose it. Not you, not Kimmy, and not goddamn Andrew." She broke free from her brother and turned around to kick the car door hard with her foot, once, then twice, ending with a third kick. She would have done it five times, except for the fact that her foot was throbbing, and right now she hated five of anything almost as much as she hated the word joy.

"Done?"

"Yes."

"Feel better?"

"No. Well, sort of."

"Okay, let's go get your daughter."

***

Marc heard a knock on his front door so tepid that when he went to open it and saw Sydney Sheppard standing there, he was more than surprised but less than shocked. Her signature knock was strong and sharp. That's how he always knew it was her, but then again, how many people in this town bothered to knock on his door in the first place?

"Can I come in?"

He made note of the fact that when she spoke, her eyes were focused on picking at the cuticle on her left index finger.

"Of course. We can sit in the living room." He had all his folders spread on the kitchen table, and he didn't want her to go in there and start looking at them.

She followed him, appearing even more uncomfortable than she had when standing outside his door. Something was up, because this was not the girl who'd made herself at home in a matter of seconds. He motioned for her to sit down on the couch while he situated himself on the brown leather chair across from it, the teakwood coffee table between them.

Sydney stared then busied herself with petting Albert and Victoria.

So, it's up to me to begin, he thought. "Are you okay?" he asked. God, how many times had he asked that question today?

"Yeah. I mean no. But it's not like I'm going to off myself. Don't worry, okay? I just...I just need to tell you something."

"Okay, tell me."

"Where do you want me to start?" Sydney asked.

Teenagers. He was totally out of his element. "At the point so that when you're done, I'll understand what you're trying to tell me." *I think that's called the beginning, Syd.*

Sydney breathed in, but said nothing.

"You know what happened to Kimmy and her friend last night, don't you?" he asked.

"That's why I'm here," she said, staring at the floor. "I feel horrible because of all the times I've wished the worse for Jennifer, and everyone at school knows it. I even booby-trapped her locker with catsup. And once I managed to attach a sign to her back that said, 'Say hi if you think my ass is big.'"

Marc tried hard to keep his eyes from widening as he listened. He wanted to ask her how she'd managed to pull the sign prank off, but thought better of it.

"And another time, I—" Sydney stopped mid sentence. "Let's just say that the list goes on and on. I wished the worse things ever on Jennifer, and now it's happened." She choked up. "I feel horrible. I'm a horrible person," she said, then started sobbing.

Marc moved to the kitchen and came back with a roll of paper towels. He thrust them at her face, stopping one inch from her nose.

Sydney took the roll of towels, ripping off the first one and wiping her eyes with it.

"Kimmy is staying at her father's house because of the fire," he said, sitting back down. "You know her house bur—"

"I know. I saw it." She nodded nervously. "I smelled it too. They got the dog out, right?"

Marc nodded. "If you want to go see her, I'll take you by. She's at her father's."

"No. Absolutely not."

"Kimmy's uncle, Gino, told me the funeral for Jennifer is in a few days. Maybe your mom can take you."

"I don't want her to go with me. Either one of them. That's why I'm here." She wiped her eyes, blew her nose and sat straighter.

No more tears. Relief flooded Marc's entire being.

"A lot of the moms don't like my mother. My real mom. They don't even know my other one."

"I'm sorry, Syd. Some people are still prejudiced."

Sydney stared at him like he was the village idiot. "Oh, it's not because she's a lesbian," she said. "Heck, this is a college town. It's because she's a nude model. She doesn't wear a bra, either."

He wasn't about to touch that one.

She looked up at him. "She never baked cookies for events when I was in grade school, either. She bought them at the quick stop. A lot of the other mothers got bent out of shape about that. You know, natural ingredients and all that sort of stuff."

Sweet Jesus. "You want me to take you?"

She smiled halfway. "Yes."

"Okay, but ask your mothers first."

"I'll go ask right now." She stood and walked toward the front door, then turned around.

"Do you want another paper towel?" Marc asked, as he followed her to the door.

"Um, not to hurt your feelings, but my face is a little raw from them already. Thanks, though. You would have made a great dad."

Chapter Thirteen

Kimmy was released from the hospital in the late morning. Gina and her brother took her to Andrew's condo after Gina picked the key up from his department secretary. He'd thoroughly cleaned out all of his clothes and personal items, as though he'd made a getaway in the dark of night. Now, his condo resembled an Airbnb, more than a personal residence.

Her daughter looked as though she'd spent the last ten months shut away indoors. The only color left on her face were the dark circles under her eyes, which matched her recently dyed jet-black hair. Gina didn't know if the circles were from the accident or from crying. All she was certain of was that now was not the time to tell her about the fire. They could do that later.

While Gino made a run to the store with a list of items that filled three pieces of legal paper, Gina and Kimberly had their first conversation since she was in the recovery room. As they talked about the upcoming funeral, it became clear that while Andrew had told Kimmy that she was moving into his condo to take care of her, he had not told her that that he was moving out. She sat in the chair next to the couch and quietly explained the situation to a once-again sobbing Kimberly.

"I thought we'd all be together again." she'd sobbed. "I thought maybe it was the one good thing to come out of the accident, that we'd be a family. Maybe if I talk to him, or if you talk to him…maybe if you tell him you need him, he'll come back and be with us."

Her daughter's world had been blown apart in so many ways during the past year, Gina felt she didn't need to add to it by being openly hostile toward Andrew. Nevertheless, she was going to kill that weasel.

As for the next few days, if Gina could have fast-forwarded through it, she would have. Besides fielding questions from her department and grad students using Andrew's landline, and getting a new cell phone that was so complicated she hadn't a clue how to use half the features, she also met with the insurance adjustor several times.

The decision to condemn her house rather than pay to rebuild it had been made during the first five minutes of the initial inspection. Nothing she said could dissuade the adjustors. She would get a payout check, as well as one to reimburse her for her possessions after she filed a loss claim. Still, she hadn't been able to bring herself to tell Kimmy about the fire. She'd decided, again, to put it off for a few more days. It was enough that she had to explain to her where her father was, and that they were never going to be together under one roof again.

With everything going on, she'd forgotten to contact Daniel, and she felt terrible when his email appeared in her inbox, after figuring out how to access it on Andrew's desktop computer. He told her he'd heard from Uncle Gino about Kimmy's broken bones, Jennifer, and the fire. Most of all, he was concerned about how his sister was and how she was taking the death of her friend.

Gina stayed up late until one in the morning, writing a well-crafted response that left her feeling cathartic by the time she hit the send button . For the first time, when she put it in written words to Daniel, she realized that with two broken arms, Kimmy's plans for cheerleading were more than likely both literally and figuratively crushed.

Saturday brought Jennifer's funeral, a horrible, sobering event. She, Gino, Andrew, and Marty navigated Kimmy through it, helping her to negotiate the cemetery hills and shielding her from the naïve yet thoughtless comments that tended to pop out of people's mouths in such circumstances.

It seemed as though the entire high school had turned out for the funeral. There they were, kids with their whole lives in front of them, paying their respects to a classmate who passed away before most of them fully comprehended the finality of death. Gina shuddered at that thought more than she shuddered at the animosity on display between Jennifer's parents.

Marc was there with Sydney Sheppard. She glanced over at them once to see Sydney holding onto Marc's arm as though she had stitched herself to it. The two of them hung back on the edges, then walked forward at the end to pay their respects to Jennifer's parents. Sydney kept stealing glances at Kimmy but kept her distance.

Their small group returned to Andrew's condo, where they all gathered somewhat uncomfortably together—Marty, eager to meet and please everyone; Gino, hoping to avoid Andrew; Andrew, as usual, oblivious to much of anything other than himself; and Kimmy, angry and hurt over everything that had happened, including her father moving in with Marty Schmidt.

Marty held the door open, then followed them inside.

"I'm glad that's over," Andrew said, as he gave Marty a peck on the cheek. He sat on the couch and loosened his tie. Hairy jumped up next to him and began to sniff his suit jacket, poking his nose up and down Andrew's arm. "While you're living here, can you please try to keep that dog off my couch? Please?" His voice went out to anyone within earshot.

Gina ignored him, along with everyone else. She didn't care if Hairy peed on the couch, much less jumped on it. The dog was the best medicine her daughter had. She turned in time to see Marty flashing Andrew a warning look, the kind a mother gives to her child in a restaurant when they've put their elbows on the table or belched particularly loud. It seemed to subdue him immediately.

Hairy shifted his focus from Andrew to her daughter when Kimmy sat down gingerly next to the dog. Today, there was more color in her face, although the black A-line dress she wore still matched the circles under her eyes. Hairy seemed to understand that with Kimmy's arms in casts, getting petted by her was next to impossible. He snuggled into her side and licked her face. Andrew turned away in disgust.

Gina wore a dark pair of pants and a loose, cream-colored blouse that Shauntel, who had joined them yesterday, brought up with her from St. Louis, along with a few other clothing items she'd graciously picked up. Those things, in addition to the clothing she wore to Marc's the night of the fire, was all she had. While she was overwhelmed with the loss of her possessions, there was also something frighteningly freeing about it all, too.

Soon, they would all be joined by Rachael, who was staying through the end of the week, while Gino and Shauntel were leaving after lunch today.

"I made some fava bean soup last night for us to eat, and there's bread in the oven," Shauntel said, walking out of the kitchen and looking directly at Andrew. "Your sister is due to arrive any minute, if you'd like to stay and have dinner with us."

While Marty's eyes brightened at the prospect, Andrew stood to leave. "I have work to do." He leaned over Kimmy and kissed the top of her head, giving Hairy yet another dirty look. "I'm going to be very busy this week. I'm preparing for an important meeting I have back east, but I will call you," he said to his daughter.

Kimmy sniffed and turned away.

"He's going to Boston." Marty volunteered the information with a certain amount of pride. She turned to

Gina and spoke softly in her ear. "Can we meet a week from Monday? In the morning?"

"How early?" Gina winced inside as she prepared to hear six a.m.

"Eight. The faculty lounge in the student union. Just the two of us. I think we need to talk." And with that, she and Andrew took their leave. Kimmy's narrowed eyes followed them to the door until it shut.

Rachael arrived minutes after her brother left, in time for a lunch that Kimmy refused to partake in, even though all four adults present were happy to help her.

Directly after lunch, Gina walked her brother out to his truck while Shauntel said her goodbyes to Kimmy. "Where have the last few days gone?" Gina asked him.

"Why ask that? Do you want them back or something?" Gino asked her.

"Are you kidding? No, but I am going to miss you," Gina whispered the words to avoid her throat catching.

"I'm sure you'll recover from the shock." Gino grinned. He stood with one foot on his truck, the other on the street in front of Andrew's condo. Hairy made a slow circle around his vehicle taking in the unfamiliar smells then lifted his leg on the front left tire. Gino watched and shook his head. "What a dog."

"I put your sweatshirt behind the driver's seat. I washed it." She cocked her head and smiled. "Just so you know."

"You could have kept it. It's not like you have much to wear right now."

She shook her head. "I have a couple of things, thanks to your wife. Besides, it's yours. I don't know what I would have done without you these past few days." She reached up and hugged her brother hard. After a few seconds, she felt him hugging back, first in a hesitating way and then equally as hard. She let go and said, "Wow. What would Mamma say if she could see us now?"

He laughed. "She'd probably take your temperature." He grabbed his sweatshirt out of the back of the cab and put it on. "Don't forget the meals in the refrigerator. Each one is prepared and ready to go. The baked ziti is for today; the chicken cacciatore is for tomorrow."

"And serve it with the romaine?"

"Yes. It's cleaned and in a bag."

"And the soup?"

"Saturday. Take the bread out of the freezer in the morning and let it thaw naturally. No microwave. If you have questions, call us." He stopped for a moment and scanned her face. "If you need me to come back up, you tell me, okay? Don't keep quiet about asking like you usually do. All it takes is for someone to be nice to you, and you're out the door. And be nice to Marc. He's a good guy, Gina." He studied her as though he wanted to say more, but didn't.

Gina shook her head. "You're beginning to sound like Papa. The next thing you'll tell me is to get my head out of my books."

"No. It's not the books I worry about. But that reminds me." He handed her a bag that he grabbed off the passenger seat. "These are Mamma's diaries. I asked Shauntel to get them down from the attic and bring them up. Thought you'd like them."

"You didn't have to do all of this. The food, and now the diaries."

"I know." Gino kissed her forehead. "She wrote in Italian, so I can't read them. But tell me if there's anything interesting, besides the obvious."

"The obvious?"

He paused a second to stare at the diaries. "That I broke her heart."

***

Marc could not recall a time in his recent past when he had been as glad to get home as he had been today. Between the tears and the hateful stares that passed between the dead girl's parents, he'd had enough of funerals to last him a lifetime. He decided right there and then to opt for cremation and an ice-cream party. It was his sincere hope that there would be someone around to honor those wishes.

"You okay?" he asked Sydney as the two of them got out of the car.

Sydney sniffed. "It's weird going to the funeral of someone I said I hated. And now she'll never know I really didn't. And I didn't know that until she passed away. It doesn't make me feel good about the person I am."

"It took courage to go," Marc told her. "You know that, right?"

"I didn't want to. Not with everyone there." She sighed and crossed her arms against her chest. "I always thought I was this crusader against mean girls. Jennifer might have said things about the way I look and the way I dress and how much I weigh, but I made fun about how stupid I thought she was. It's just a different way of being mean and feeling like you're superior, when the truth is that no one is any better than anyone else."

Marc thought about all the adults he knew who had never figured that out. "Do you want to talk to Kimmy?"

She gave him an uneasy nod. "Yes, but not right now. Not for a while. I need to think about what I want to say first. She may not want to talk to me."

He watched Sydney's foot grind back and forth on the sidewalk and knew she was about to step over the line and ask a question she shouldn't.

"Um, you're not seeing Dr. Ferrari anymore, are you? Not that it's any of my business," she added quickly.

"Not that it's any of your business is right, Ms. Sheppard."   His cell phone went off, and he pulled it out of his pocket—the chancellor's office. At least he'd finally learned to check the caller ID. Well, it was a good way to end his conversation with Sydney. He silently pointed to his phone, waved goodbye, and went inside.

***

Gina refreshed Rachael's mug of peppermint tea, then poured what was left into hers. The two of them had been chatting for the last hour sitting at Andrew's glass-topped kitchen table, while Gina gleefully ignored the fact that he'd asked her to use coasters on it. Her eyes wandered around the kitchen and settled again on the tabletop, which, she noted, made the entire kitchen look cold and sterile. Of course, left to his own making, Andrew would render a living space antiseptically barren. She reminded herself guiltily that the person she was now criticizing had generously given her a place to live rent-free, then she remembered she was staying in his condo to take care of Kimmy so he didn't have to. Her guilt dissipated as quickly as it had emerged.

"Have you talked to Marc?" Rachael took another sip of mint tea and waited for Gina to answer.

"No. Rach, no offense, but it feels weird to be talking about him with my ex-husband's sister in my ex-husband's house." She hoped this would make Rachael stop and change the subject.

"You told me all about him at the airport."

"That was before you knew him."

"Got it. Well, have you talked to him?"

Gina nodded. "Yes. I said I couldn't see him anymore."

"He could help you. I'm sure he'd love to." Rachael took a sip of her tea. "Go see him."

"I saw him at the funeral. I didn't talk to him."

"Why? It wasn't his fault that the espresso machine sparked the fire."

"Lower your voice." Gina jerked her chin toward the living room and mouthed the word, Kimmy. "He was with an old friend of Kimmy's that she doesn't want to talk to right now, either. It would have been...I don't know. Uncomfortable."

"I see. But he did help you. He called Gino and me."

Gina made a face. "And I thanked him. You know, none of this would have happened if I wouldn't have been at his house that night."

"Gina, you can't blame yourself for this."

"And..." She stopped and looked through the archway toward the living room, making sure Kimmy was far away enough not to hear. "And Kimmy is holding out for the possibility that somehow Andrew and I are going to reconcile."

"You need to talk to her."

Gina sighed. "I'm going to. It's just that so many things have happened to her I don't want to load on anymore. Seeing Marc right now isn't a good idea. It just adds to the problem."

Rachael ignored her comment and continued. "Marc doesn't let a lot of things get to him, and he's always searching for the positive points in life. It's like he refuses not to see something good in every day."

"He told you about his five things?" Gina rolled her eyes.

"What are you talking about?" Rachael frowned. "I was referring to his attitude when he's with his sister at the group home."

"Nothing. Just nothing." She waved her hands dismissively.

"But that's another good thing about him. Whatever sort of list it is, with most people it's ten things. He's concise and to the point about everything." Rachael paused then asked again, "What five things?"

"Forget it, okay?"

Rachael took another sip of tea. "You know, Gina, if you don't watch out you're going to end up being a martyr in a polyester pantsuit."

"That hurt. And I don't even own a polyester pantsuit anymore. They all burned up."

"Probably melted," Rachael said.

She shook her head in mock disgust then picked up her tea and sipped it.

"Where's the fun in your life? Where's the joy?"

Gina's voice rose in response. "My daughter's friend died, and my daughter's arms are in casts past her elbows." She looked around to make sure Kimmy didn't hear, then lowered her voice. "My house and everything in it has been reduced to ashes. How much fun am I supposed to have? And could you not use the word *joy*? I hate that word."

"Pretty soon those casts are coming off Kimmy's arms, then she's off to college, whether it's here in Columbia or not. She's eighteen and she's leaving you for people she thinks are far more interesting than her parents. And Danny's already gone." Rachael lowered her voice. "With Kimmy's broken arms and wrists, I think she'll have to find something other than cheerleading as a career to annoy you with. Gina, it's time to launch yourself, not just your kids."

Gina stared mutely ahead.

Rachael got up from the table and disappeared into the guest bedroom, reappearing with a large plastic bag. She plopped it down gently on the floor next to Gina, then she leaned to the right, and glanced into the living room where Kimmy sat stretched out in Andrew's recliner.

"What is this?" Gina asked.

Rachael put a finger to her lips and whispered, "Open it."

Inside were her black leather boots, the ones she'd worn in Rome and a few other memorable times with Marc here in Columbia. "Where'd you get these? I thought they were lost in the fire."

Rachael glanced toward the living room again. "Kimmy was wearing them in the car with Jennifer. She didn't want you to know because you told her she couldn't borrow them. She gave them to Gino in the hospital, and he handed them off to me."

Of all the things to survive the fire, why these?

Rachael picked up her cup, looking somewhat amused. "Those were your Rome boots, right?"

She nodded.

"Maybe it's a message. Let go of the past. Embrace the future."

"Maybe it's karma and not the good kind. I lost everything in that fire. Everything familiar in my life for the last twenty years and some things from my childhood. And I can't yell or scream or be angry because, like we already talked about, Kimmy feels bad enough already, and I haven't even told her about the house yet."

"I think you should tell her soon. Heck, with Instagram and Facebook and email and texting, she's bound to find out from someone else."

"You're right. I don't know how in the hell I'm going to do it, but I have to, and soon."

Gina picked the boots up out of the bag and examined them, trying to find something light or funny or sarcastic to say, but she couldn't. Nothing came to her, so she put them back in the bag, and stuck them in the cabinet under the sink. "Can we not talk about Marc anymore?"

"Sure." Rachael nodded. "Whatever you want."

"Ever again?"

Rachael looked at her skeptically. "Okay."

They were silent for a good ten minutes. Rachael read the newspaper while Gina tried to focus on her grad student's thesis outline. She took a sip of her now lukewarm tea and put her mug down softly, staring at the tea leaves in the bottom and wishing she could read them. It was a bunch of hooey, but some guidance right about now sounded wonderful. If she could hear voices in the Pantheon, why couldn't she read tea leaves?

"Maybe I should go and see him."

Rachael put down her newspaper. "Are you talking about Marc?"

"Yes."

"I think you should at least talk to him," Rachael said.

"None of this would have happened if I hadn't been there that night."

"I know. You said that already." Rachael started at her. "From what you've told me about Kimmy's friend, something was more than likely to happen, sooner or later."

Gina shook her head emphatically. "Something's always going to happen when you're that age, but to most kids, for some reason or another, it doesn't. Every one of us has at least one tale to tell where we could have died or been arrested or hurt ourselves badly, but it didn't happen. I should have been there for those girls, so it didn't happen to them. And I wasn't." Gina took a breath and readied another rebuttal when she heard Kimmy yell from the living room.

"Mom. I'm stuck in Dad's chair, and I can't get out. Can you help me? I have to go to the bathroom. Bad."

She eyed Rachael as they both stood. "I really have the time to get involved with someone right now, don't I?"

* * * *

Gina was grateful to be back at work on Monday, even though her department inbox was loaded with returned forms, each detailing the positive and negative aspects of the suggestions offered at the initial budget meeting weeks ago. She was receiving concerned glances from many of her colleagues, and it was difficult to ferret out whether this was from what had happened to her house and her daughter, or whether they knew about Marc. Or maybe they had heard that Marty Schmidt was now living with her recently divorced ex-husband. She didn't stop to ask. As for Roberta, she never said a word to Gina or questioned her about Marc calling that day from the emergency room. She only encouraged her to forge on, and said they could talk later after her life settled down. In spite of Roberta's arm-twisting reputation, she knew when to give people space, too.

The morning after Jennifer's funeral, she heeded Rachael's advice and told Kimmy about the house fire. When she asked her how it started and Gina told her, she decompensated into a pool of tears. What could Gina do but hand her tissues and tell her that at least Hairy was okay. She also told her that, in part, it was her fault, too. The entire house should have been rewired at least five years ago. Like many things in life, including getting a divorce, it was something she and Andrew had put off doing, but that wasn't something she was about to share with her daughter, now or ever.

Marty called on Wednesday to invite them all to her town home for dinner on Sunday before Rachael headed back to St. Louis and, she added with emphasis, before Andrew took off for his *very* important meeting in Boston. Gina accepted for everyone, although Kimmy made a face when she told her.

When Sunday finally rolled around, it turned out to be a glorious, early spring day, complete with sunshine and a warm wind that promised summer. Rachael and Gina decided to give Hairy a spin around campus before helping Kimmy into the car for dinner at Marty's.

"So prep me for meeting Martha," Rachael started up. "Am I going to get a trans fat lecture, like your brother?" she asked, as she walked alongside Gina and Hairy.

"I don't think so," Gina told her. At least she hoped not.

"What's she like?"

"She's attractive in a polished sort of way, and she's very smart, and she's very…well, whatever she thinks, she thinks it's right."

"Oh, she's a pushy bitch, huh?"

"Ah, I wouldn't use that word. She's into healthy eating, and she thinks everyone else should be." Why in the hell was she defending Marty Schmidt?

"So she's the food police?" Rachael asked, petulantly.

"You know Rach, it's okay if you end up liking her. That doesn't mean you can't like me, too."

"I know, but the fact that she likes Andrew makes me suspicious already."

Gina smiled. "She's under a lot of pressure. The university wants to move nutrition and dietetics into public health. People may lose their jobs, and if they keep their jobs, they'll be melded into a big department."

"And this is Marc's—"

"Doing," Gina finished Rachael sentence, wondering why Rachael always had to bring it back to Marc.

"Well, who hired Marc?" Rachael asked.

"The chancellor."

"But everybody still blames Marc?" Rachael asked, a smirk suddenly appearing.

"He's the visible presence. And I thought we weren't going to talk about him."

"Hmm." Rachael's eyes suddenly widened, and she stopped walking. "This Martha isn't the Martha whose emails you used to forward to me about the fat content of chocolate, is she?"

Oh god. "Why would you think that?"

"Holy shit. I can tell by the look on your face that she is." She threw back her head and laughed.

"She didn't do it this year." Gina refrained from telling her about the handwashing committee.

Rachael glared. "I reserve the right to pick up dessert on the way back. Something packed with chocolate, sugar, and dairy fat. Lots of dairy fat. Oozing with dairy fat. Artery-clogging dairy fat."

"Deal."

***

"Gina," Marty threw the door of her town home. "I'm so glad you came. And you, too, Rachael." She extended her hand as though she was already part of the family. "You and Andy look so very much alike."

Gina watched Rachael's eyebrows shoot up two inches.

"Please, come in." Marty gestured.

Kimmy dragged a good twenty feet behind them, her arms bent in their casts, her face unsmiling, and her head down. "Kimberly," Marty said, "I'm so glad you could make it, too. I've made up a number of smoothies for you, so you can easily eat with us using a straw."

Kimmy glared at Marty, until she saw Gina glaring at her. "Thanks." She grunted out the word, then went to look for her father.

Somehow, they all made it through dinner with minimal overt discomfort. Rachael carried the ball and put on her best manners, inquiring about her brother's latest publications. Once Andrew got going about himself, the issue of table conversation was quickly resolved.

Gina glanced over at Marty, who had on a deep-red sweater that hugged her trim midsection and a pair of black, pencil-legged pants. She radiated happiness, but the glow didn't come from makeup, or from the sweater that complemented her skin tone. Marty was in love with Andrew, and as strange as it sounded, Gina felt happy for them. A contented Andrew meant a better father for both of her children. At least she hoped.

"You've already had two servings of those." Marty commandeered the platter of eggplant as it was making its way around the table toward Andrew. She smiled at him like an indulgent schoolmarm.

"But it's so good." Andrew gazed at Marty like he wanted to lick her.

Rachael rolled her eyes.

"Have some more salad and chew it before you swallow. That way you won't be so hungry. You eat your food too fast, Andy. It takes at least fifteen minutes before your brain gets the message that you're satiated." She smiled at the women assembled. "I'm trying to get him to lose ten pounds. For his health." She turned to Kimmy. "How is that smoothie? I made strawberry-banana and mango, too. In case you don't like the apricot, but your father told me it was your favorite fruit."

Kimmy sighed. "It's my brother's favorite."

Marty's face clouded over. "Oh. I'll have to make a note of that."

Andrew cut in. "We walk every morning."

"Two miles," Marty said.

"Three on the weekend," Andrew added, then went back to chewing.

"You need to seek balance in every meal." Marty stated to no one in particular. "Vegetables, protein, fruit, and a small portion of carbs." She turned to Andrew. "Very small."

"Sometimes I like popcorn for dinner," Rachael said out loud. "With a big diet root beer."

"I made a wonderful tofu cheesecake," Marty said, smiling.

"Why don't you call it a tofu cake? It doesn't have any cheese in it, does it?" Rachael asked.

"It gives one the idea that it's a dessert," Marty answered.

"So would saying tofu *cake*," Rachael batted back.

"Texturally they are identical." Marty bristled.

Andrew glared at his sister. "It tastes like cheesecake. That's why they call it tofu cheesecake."

Kimmy made a loud sucking sound with the straw, then turned to her mother and beamed mischievously.

Marty shifted her focus from Rachael to Gina. "I simply love Kimberly's hair. She told me you came up with the idea. It's different. Artsy. Avant-garde. You seldom see such individualism in young women Kimberly's age. They all want it long and blond. Like a Barbie doll."

Gina watched her daughter blanch. Kimmy glanced at her with pleading eyes that begged her not to say anything.

"She does look pretty. And sophisticated," Gina said, smiling at Kimmy.

"Iconic," Marty added.

Rachael broke in. "Iconic and sophisticated."

All three women eyed each other.

"Well," Rachael continued, "we may not agree on the name of the dessert, but we can all agree on Kimberly."

Smiles broke out across the table. It occurred to Gina that with three women in her corner, her daughter might make it through this late adolescent mess called *launching* and come out the other end in reasonable shape. Rachael could listen to Kimmy's complaints about her, and maybe sometime in the future, when Kimmy got used to the idea that she and Andrew weren't ever getting back together, Marty could help her, too. Maybe with career advice. Marty would never hesitate to volunteer her opinion about anything to anyone, including Kimmy. And maybe if that kind of message came from someone other than herself, her daughter would listen.

Andrew looked from his sister to Gina then to Marty, with a puzzled expression seldom seen on his face, because whatever Andrew thought, he was certain of it in a matter of seconds. Clearly, he didn't understand the pack that had been formed. It was as though he had walked in on advanced Latin when he should have taken the class for beginners.

Chapter Fourteen

How had it gotten to the end of April, Marc wondered as he sat across from Stuart Webber in the chancellor's office, with an oversized and over carved, walnut desk between them. As he waited for Stuart to finish scanning the summary report, he gazed around the wood-paneled room and noticed a set of blueprints spread out on a long legal table against the wall. What could they be planning to build in this fiscal climate?

The chancellor put down the report and smiled, his teeth gleaming like highly polished veneer over particle board. "Looks good. Very good."

"All the finished reports are here," Marc told him. "Some of the departments are struggling with their choices, but what has been turned in so far appears as though everyone gave a great deal of thought as to how the cuts were to be implemented. It's been a painful process."

"Any trends?"

"Unfortunately, yes." Marc leaned forward about a fraction of an inch. "In many departments, although not all of them, the cuts came in adjunct pay and positions. It troubles me because I wonder where the future teaching staff will be coming from."

"Anything else?"

"Yes. There was a trend to eliminate teaching assistantships, which of course, as you know, will result in more borrowing on the part of graduate students to finish their degrees and less hands-on experience."

"Maybe they can get those kids to volunteer. For free."

His chin jerked back involuntarily. "There was a great deal of resistance to raising the copay on faculty health insurance." He was quiet for a moment before saying, "I see you're contemplating a new building on campus."

Stuart's eyes gleamed as they turned to gaze upon the blueprints. "Yes. Well, it's not a new building. It's an addition. We're planning on adding twenty new positions in the coming year, and I'll need more space to house them."

"To what department?"

"Administration."

"So admin isn't cutting five percent?"

Stuart Webber snorted. "Good god, no."

"I thought you said across the board."

"I meant everybody else." He spoke with a light dusting of briskness to his voice, paused, and rearranged his words. "Everyone else has to, but admin can't. Hell, we're getting more and more students every year, especially out-of-state and foreign students. That's where the real money is. With more students, we need more admin."

"So you're enrolling more students and enlarging the administrative staff, but asking the teaching end of the university to cut their budgets and therefore their staff?"

"Whoa, there. I didn't ask them to do anything but cut their budgets. If they cut staff, well, that's their decision, not mine."

Marc swallowed hard. He'd provided the perfect cover for this. "Is there anything else you need from me today?"

"No. Don't think so. Just the rest of the reports when you've got them."

"Of course. That won't be for a few weeks."

As he rose to leave, he opened his mouth to tell Chancellor Stuart Webber what he could do with his addition to the administration building then decided against it. Some things were best put in writing after they marinated a bit in a cold fridge. Besides, he had a sister to see, a plane to Albuquerque to catch, and a wedding to attend.

***

The past week had been hard. After Gino, Shauntel, and Rachael went back to St. Louis, Gina and Kimmy were left to themselves, and Gina was left to brood on her own in a house that wasn't hers and that she would never quite feel comfortable in. She found her thoughts returning to Marc when she'd hear something funny on the television or at work or when she read an article or book she liked. There was no one to share any of those thoughts and observations with, as her daughter often didn't get the things people in Gina's age group found interesting or funny. It didn't matter. What mattered was that Kimmy was doing reasonably well keeping up with her schoolwork, and her counselor felt she would graduate on time with the rest of her class in spite of her lengthy absence.

On Saturday night, after Kimmy went to bed early for once, complaining that her arms underneath her casts hurt and itched like crazy, Gina pulled on her coat, grabbed her car keys, and set off toward Marc's, blocking the part of her mind that kept murmuring, *What in the hell do you think you're doing?* She passed by her burned-down house and willed herself not to look. By the time her car drove down the hill and turned the corner, her feelings of loneliness increased.

She wanted to apologize and tell him that it didn't matter that he was the asshole from New Mexico and that it wasn't his fault that his stupidly large, overly tooled, and incredibly intricate espresso maker was implicated in the house fire. Most of all, she didn't care that her brother liked him. In fact, she was happy he did. What she wanted, what she needed, was to feel him, have him put his arms around her, cry on his shoulder, and fall asleep nested next to him.

The dogs barked when she rang the bell, but no one came to open it. She tried again and waited, thinking that at least the corgis were getting their lungs exercised. Well, he was probably out having a good time with someone.

By the time she turned around and was two feet from her car, the front door opened. Sydney Sheppard stood in the archway.

"Dr. Ferrari?"

"Hi, Sydney."

"Are you here to see Marc?"

The corgis ran out the door, stopping at the front gate. Gina bent down to pet them through the fence. "Yes. He isn't here, is he?"

"He's still at his girlfriend's in New Mexico. He's not coming back until late on Monday. Hold on." She shut the door and reappeared in a few seconds. "Here's the number at her house." She waved a small white piece of paper at Gina. "His cell phone number is on there, too, if you need it."

"No. I'm fine." She continued to scratch the corgis through the fence for no reason other than she didn't want to go back to the condo and think about the fact that Marc was visiting the woman he used to live with.

"The dogs know you well, don't they?" Sydney called from the door.

"I used to walk my dog—well, he's really Kimberly's dog— with Marc's."

"I know. Sorry about your house."

"Thanks." She looked up and smiled. "Do you know what your plans are for college?"

"I'm going to the best school I can get a scholarship at that's also the furthest away from here."

"Good for you."

"I should know pretty soon."

"Come by before you leave. I'd love to know what your plans are." Gina watched confusion form on Sydney's face. "Oh. I just realized. I don't have a place for you to come by anymore."

"Where are you staying?" Sydney asked.

"At Kimmy's father's."

"Oh. I'm sure Kimberly likes that. Do you want me to tell Marc you stopped by? I'm keeping a list of all the women who come by this weekend. I can add you at the top."

What an odd thing to say. Gina forced a smile she was certain appeared more like a grimace. "No. That's all right." She shooed the dogs toward the door and got back in her car, remembering what her brother told her about letting people who are upset drive.

***

Mark and Elaine walked out of Mike and Darcy's wedding reception at the Albuquerque University Club together. His arm steered a slightly tipsy Elaine safely off the curb and into the parking lot. They were both dressed formally, and it made Marc think back to the fact that the last time he'd worn a suit was at his mother's funeral two years ago, right before the car accident that changed his life.

The early evening air hinted that a slight chill was beginning to set in, and Elaine wrapped the woven shawl she'd carried with her all day around her shoulders. Marc adjusted it in the back for her so that it laid flat. It was a Pavlovian response, attending to her. No one was perfect when it came to the end of relationships.

"It was lovely, don't you think?" Elaine asked Marc.

"Yes, it was a...lovely wedding." He hesitated before he uttered the word *lovely*. Elaine and her friends used it to describe practically everything, and it both irritated and amused him. "I particularly liked the open bar at the reception. Now that was lovely."

She glanced at him dubiously and rolled her eyes.

The low-lying mountains surrounding Albuquerque looked plum purple in the setting sun. They were on the short list of things he would miss about living here. St. Louis, where he'd gotten a job, was all green and brick. The sky felt closed in, and the mosquitos were the size of grasshoppers. But, he reminded himself, his life would be more real and far more honest. He knew the difference now.

This trip back would be his last. Closure was important to him. More than he cared to admit, he liked things in his life to be neat and tidy. Loose ends were not for him, but they were a part of life he'd come to respect and understand. Life was far more gray than black and white, as were feelings of ambivalence.

"After all these years," he said to Elaine, "I don't quite understand why they felt the need to marry. Do you?"

"Health insurance." She reached over and picked something off the sleeve of his suit coat. "Dog hair," she said, holding it up to show him before she let the wind take it.

They laughed and leaned against his rental car, both suddenly as quiet as they were on their first date.

Elaine turned to him and smiled. "So this is it? We just say goodbye, and you get in your car and drive away to the airport, and we'll never see each other again?" She threw up her long thin arms in exasperation.

Marc took a deep breath. "Elaine, this is what you wanted, and we both agreed it was for the best."

"What if I've changed my mind?" She looked at him long and hard, then her shoulders began to deflate. "But you haven't changed yours, have you?"

"Right before I came here this weekend, I was offered a job with Jesuit University in St. Louis, and I'm lucky to have it. My things will be out of storage and on a moving van headed there in about two months." He cleared his throat. "And I know how you feel about St. Louis. Besides, the flat you found here is perfect for you."

After they'd signed the papers for the sale of their house, Elaine had taken him to the vacant flat she'd put an offer on. It was near the old market district in Albuquerque, and it had hardwood floors, solid wood, lightly stained cabinets, granite countertops, and stainless-steel appliances. All the essential kitchen must-haves for today's well-heeled urban dweller in a kitchen she'd more than likely never use. The flat was in the new, right part of town with good restaurants, frequented by individuals who did interesting things and had lots of cats, but no children.

Marc knew she would love the fact that there was no yard, front or back. There was nothing to take care of, not a single molecule of life dependent on her for attention. Her designated parking was in the garage across the street, and her only worry would be if an unauthorized vehicle parked in the space belonging to her. Knowing Elaine, she would worry about that a lot.

"Will we stay in touch? Will I ever see you again?"

Marc smiled. "Of course. If I have anything to say about it." He put his arm around her shoulder and gave her a gentle squeeze. He felt as though he could snap her in two. "We lived together for twenty years. I didn't want to go your way, and you didn't want to go mine, but that certainly doesn't mean I don't care about what happens to you."

There was nothing that had worked in favor of keeping them together. No children, no business partnership, and few shared interests, although he had always been willing to participate in whatever she wanted him to. In all the years they lived together, Elaine had gone to visit Betty with him once, and if the truth be known, Elaine's sister liked him more than her. She told him, after a few glasses of wine, that she found Elaine to be an insufferable snob, and her children groaned every time she visited. It was something he hoped Elaine never found out because she would be crushed. Maybe, in the future, as they all became older and wiser, she and her sister would become closer. It was possible. Look at what had happened between Betty and him.

"By the way," he said, "did you notice how Mike Cleary was looking at you?"

"No."

"He asked me if we were really broken up. I think he wants to date you." He detected a minimal spark in her eyes and crossed his toes for good luck.

"If you hadn't had that accident, we could have kept going."

"And gotten those dogs and insisted on living each day like it was my first and last. I can't go back to who I was. I don't work like that anymore."

He didn't want her to hurt. He didn't want her to go home and feel the way she did right now. "Let's make a deal," he said, searching his pants pocket for his rental car key. "We'll plan on calling each other the first day of every month. Like clockwork. I'll check in on you, then you check in on me, and we'll keep going like that. Okay?"

"Okay." She stared at him wide-eyed. "Promise?"

"Promise. We won't lose touch, even if you end up with Mike Cleary."

She smiled at his comment.

"Oh, by the way he asked me for your number, and I gave it to him." This time he smiled, because actually, Mike Cleary hadn't asked for her number, but he was going to give Mike a call at the airport and give it to him anyway.

She reached up and kissed him on the cheek. "Whoever gets you next is a very lucky woman."

"I wish you'd convince her of that."

"So there is someone?"

"Not really. Not anymore. Just someone I wanted, but she didn't want me." He corrected himself. "She didn't want me enough."

"Well, she's an idiot."

"I don't think I'll be passing her that bit of information." Marc opened the driver's side door, leaned forward, and hugged Elaine again, this time a little harder. "But thanks for your vote of confidence." When he released her, he said, "Actually, she's very smart. Sometimes things don't work out the way we want them to."

Elaine chuckled. "Yes, I know all about that."

***

After days of watching Kimmy lay on Andrew's couch, staring blankly at the television, Gina took a gamble and intervened. She had a plan that she thought might work to get her involved in something and on her feet again. Quietly walking into the living room, she turned off the TV.

Kimmy looked up, irritated. "Hey, I was watching that."

No, you weren't. "Hope you don't mind, but I have something I really need your help with."

Kimmy's eyes narrowed. She cocked her head in curiosity. "What?"

"You know, when the house burned up, so did my clothes."

"I'm sorry, Mom."

"Forget it, okay? You always told me that my clothes needed to be burned, anyway, and maybe that's one of the good things that came out of it." She watched her daughter's eyes go from narrow to wide, in curiosity. "So I have a request, and it directly involves you."

Kimmy swung her legs off the couch. "I'll do anything. What do you need?"

"I need you to help me shop for clothes."

"Are you serious?"

"Yes."

"When?"

Gina grabbed her purse and keys. "Now. I'm really tired of washing out my stuff every night."

With her arms in those casts, Gina had no idea that Kimmy could mobilize herself that quickly. They both piled into the Ford Focus, and in a matter of thirty minutes, they found themselves in the department store with an armload of clothes to try on, each of them having picked out several items.

"No. No and no." Kimmy sat on a chair in the dressing room and shook her head at Gina as she held up three turtlenecks she'd plucked from the bargain table.

"But they're on sale."

"Mom, they're on sale because nobody wants them. You're way too short, and your face is too full for any kind of collar that's high on the neck. You look good in bright primary colors, or plain black and white, if it's accessorized correctly. Not pastels or anything with an orange tone, and these turtlenecks are all pastels."

How had she missed this about her daughter? She stared at Kimmy like she was seeing her for the first time. "Look, instead of me picking stuff out, why don't you just do all of it. Then you can explain to me why you think it looks good, or maybe why it doesn't."

"You'll really listen to me? You won't argue?"

"No, I won't argue, but I have one request."

"What?"

"Don't pick out anything I have to iron."

"Okay, but no polyester. Maybe poly-cotton, but only if it looks like cotton."

"Deal."

"How do you feel about dry-clean only?" Kimmy asked.

"I don't want a whole wardrobe of it."

"And you'll listen to me?"

"I'll even pay you."

"Really?" Kimmy's eyes bulged. "Starting when?"

"Starting now." Gina held up her hand like she was taking an oath. "I confess I need help big time."

"Okay. The first step is admitting you need help." Kimmy launched herself off the dressing room chair and moved the curtain aside with her right bent arm. "I'll ask a salesperson to carry in all my selections, and then I'll tell you why they work on you. Don't move until I get back." She stuck her head back in and smiled the way she used to. "This is going to be so much fun."

Gina swore she could hear her daughter singing.

***

As Gina had agreed to several days ago, on Monday morning, not a minute before or after eight o'clock, she met with Marty in the faculty lounge across from the College of Human and Environmental Sciences. They stood together while a student waiter loped over to wipe off the table they'd chosen.

"You missed a spot." Marty leaned over the table and pointed to a microscopic-sized dot the young man had failed to clean. "Right there." She paused for a moment and pointed out another one. "And there."

The two of them settled their briefcases around the table for two as the young waiter hightailed it as far away from them as he could get.

"Gina, I wanted to give you this." Marty reached down into her case and pulled out a manila folder. Inside was a loose leaf document entitled, *Handwashing-Policy Recommendations. Joint Committee, Mid-Missouri University, Departments of Public Health, Child Development, and Nutrition and Dietetics.*

"Oh god, I am so sorry. With everything that's been going on, I forgot to submit my suggestions."

"Completely understandable," Marty replied.

"I dropped the ball. Again, my apologies," she repeated. "Did Barbara email us a copy? If she did, I must confess, I haven't seen it."

"She didn't. This got handed to me by an office assistant in Public Health. Apparently, Barbara dropped it off with the department secretary when she resigned."

"Resigned?"

"Yes. You haven't been around to hear the gossip. Remember I told you she wasn't happy with Public Health and Nutrition merging? Well, she cashed in her sick days, of which there were many, and split. Her colleagues, or her former colleagues I should say, are scrambling to fill in her classes. No one can find her, and she deleted her grade books. Fortunately, a grad student in one of her classes kept a copy herself, but in the other classes, they are in big trouble. I suspect Barbara has gone around the bend. Oh, and this was all told to me in confidence, of course."

"Of course."

They sat in silence as the waiter put two glasses of water on the table and passed out the menus.

When they were alone again, Marty leaned forward and said, "Gina, she completely rewrote the recommendations. I'm so glad I caught them before they went in. She has every caregiver wearing gloves twenty-four seven. It's over the top. Even for me." She pushed the document toward Gina. "All I have is this hard copy. Fix it the way you want it, and we can scan it and send it in."

"Don't you want to see it when I'm done?"

"No. I trust you. Besides, it's due on Friday, and I'm meeting Andy in Boston." She smiled and said, "We're spending the weekend."

Gina smiled. She and Marty Schmidt had come a long way.

"I'm under the impression that you're not seeing the man from New Mexico anymore, is that right?"

He has a name, Marty. "Things got too complicated."

"Well, that's probably for the best. You look wonderful, by the way." Marty crinkled her nose. "Is that a new outfit?"

This morning, Kimmy helped her pick out a pair of straight, black trousers, a wrap blouse with a geometric print, and a boxy, short jacket that contrasted with the pants, and played up the colors in the blouse. These were but a few of the coordinating separates her daughter had made her buy the other day, while explaining to her why these pieces worked with her body type. Gina had to admit it made a difference.

"Kimmy helped me buy this," Gina said. "I've hired her to be my personal shopper." She took a drink of water. "I'm amazed at how she can look at me and figure out this fashion stuff. It's quite a skill. One she most certainly didn't inherit from me."

"Do you think—" Marty's eyes narrowed. She stopped and started again. "Would you mind if I asked her to do that with me?" Before Gina could answer her, Marty said, "Gina, I don't want you to think that I'm trying to insert myself into your daughter's life. I don't have children. I'm never going to have them. I know she's your daughter, but I'm, well, I'm sticking around, and I'd like to have a relationship with Kimmy." She held up her hands, her palms out and facing Gina. "I'm not trying for mother-daughter. More like friends."

Gina watched Marty's face contort as she tried to navigate her way through family relationships, and not step on anybody's toes. It was, she realized, tough to be the other woman, the pseudo-stepmother.

"Honestly, anything that will keep Kimmy's mind off what's happened is a very good thing." She cocked her head and smiled. "I'm glad you want to get to know my children."

"Thank you." Marty breathed a huge sigh of relief. "I hope you don't mind, but I love Andy with all my heart. He can be a real jerk, but then we sit down and negotiate a compromise." She laughed nervously. "I'm sure you know. You have to put your foot down and point out to him the fallacy in his stance. He needs some direction. Some structure. But the sex is fantastic." She laughed again. This time a slight blush appeared on her cheeks. "Well, I'm sure you know that too."

Thank god she'd swallowed her water before Marty spoke.

***

Spring was no longer around the corner. It had arrived, and with it came the worried looks of many college students around campus, who suddenly realized that the end of the semester was closer than they cared to think. Marc saw it on their faces as he walked home from the College of Engineering and Applied Sciences.

The meetings hadn't gone too badly today. Only a few dirty looks and lots of calculations. This group loved math, statistics, and measures of accuracy.

Every day he walked past the remains of Gina's house, thinking back to the evenings they spent together in her warm and comfortable living room, talking and holding each other. He hoped she and her daughter were all right. He made a point of not asking Gino or Rachael about her, as it seemed rude and intrusive. But whenever they brought her up, he listened and smiled encouragingly for more. And there was little that they gave him, as both Rachael and Gino were protective of both her and her daughter.

He met Sydney walking up the hill with the dogs, as he was going down it. She changed course and fell into step with him, having no choice but what the corgis wanted to do anyway.

"I haven't seen much of you lately," he said, in a good-natured manner. "You slip in and out before I'm home from work. How have you been?"

"Okay. I guess. Sorry I'm walking the dogs a little late today. I stayed after school and helped one of the teachers plan part of the graduation. I'm the valedictorian."

"Syd, that's fantastic. Congratulations. Your mom must be so proud." He thought back to his senior year in high school and how he slid by, eager to find any fun he could out of his house and knowing his parents would pay for college anyway. So, why should he work?

"We use the word *mom* in the plural, remember? And yeah, they're both super excited."

He watched her eyes brighten a fraction. "Like I said, you haven't been around much. Did I say something that offended you?"

"Uh, no."

By this time, they had reached the bottom of the hill and were turning the corner. Marc took the dog's leashes from her and started for his front door, only to find Sydney right behind him.

"Can I come in?"

"Sure. What's up?" He unclipped Victoria and Albert from their leashes and sat down in the living room chair.

Sydney sat on the couch directly opposite him and picked at the cuticle on her left index finger. "Look," she said, finally fixing her gaze on him. "I haven't been avoiding you. Well, I have, but not because of anything you did or said."

"You've been busy." Marc offered her a way out.

"Yes." She shook her head back and forth. "No."

"No?"

"No, that's not the truth."

"Okay, what is the truth?"

"You've always been honest with me, so I have to be honest with you. I lied. Well, no," she added quickly. "I didn't tell you something. Technically, that's not a lie. It's withholding information."

Maybe she should consider the law as a career. "About?"

"When you were gone to New Mexico, Dr. Ferrari came by, and I didn't tell you on purpose."

"Okay. Well, that was a while ago, and so many other things have happened it doesn't matter all that much anymore, but I appreciate your honesty." He had no idea why Gina had stopped by, because she certainly hadn't returned any of his emails.

"I was angry that she ditched you. I didn't think you deserved that."

"Syd, I thought you were upset about my asking you about her daughter. I thought that's why you've been avoiding me." *Gentle, gentle*, he cautioned himself.

"No. But yeah, sort of. I mean that didn't help, but mostly I felt bad about not telling you about Dr. Ferrari. So, the truth is sort of what you think and not what you think."

"Okay, tell me what I need to know so I know the whole truth."

Sydney took a deep breath. "Kimmy Ellison and I used to be best friends."

"I knew that."

"We studied for everything together, and we'd tutor each other on subjects the other one was better in. We were the smartest girls in our class, the Brainiacs of Hickman High. In a college town, that's a big accomplishment, given how neurotic everyone's parents are about achievement and grades. We were proud to be nerds. And then she ditched me and went stupid."

"Stupid?" *How does someone go stupid?* he wondered.

"Yeah, stupid. She quit caring about being on the honor roll and being the smartest, and she started caring about stupid clothes and stupid cheerleading and being popular."

"That must have hurt."

"Like I said, don't call the teen suicide hotline."

"But it hurt."

"Yes. She didn't want to be my friend anymore. I'm not pretty or skinny, and I don't have nice clothes." Sydney's eyes started to water. "I don't want nice clothes, either. They're expensive and stupid."

Her emotions betray her, Marc thought. Then he saw the tears welling up in her eyes. *Don't cry on me*, Marc thought. *Please don't cry. I hate it when girls cry.* "When did this happen?"

"The beginning of our junior year."

"Hmmm." Marc rubbed his chin and thought of Freud. What would Sigmund do? He couldn't help thinking something funny, though the situation certainly wasn't. Now he knew why Gina pinched her upper arm to the point of bruising it. "So, this friend breakup, it happened around the time that her parents started getting divorced?"

"Pretty much."

"Hmm." He cleared his throat. "Don't you think that had something to do with it? Maybe more than it had anything to do with you?"

"Maybe."

"Like we talked about a while ago, people find their way by many different paths. I'm sorry you got hurt in this. Do you want to go see Kimmy?"

"Yeah, I do. I want to tell her I'm sorry about Jennifer and her house and the accident, but I'm afraid she won't want to see me, and it'll be weird."

Marc nodded. "Do you want me to talk to Dr. Ferrari or her brother before you go over there? You know, test the waters?"

Sydney stiffened at the thought. "No. I'd be too embarrassed. It's something I need to do on my own. I'm a big girl."

He noted that Sydney still looked uncomfortable. "Something else?"

"I wanted to apologize for messing with your folders. I kept moving them out of alignment."

"Oh, I thought they looked different every once in a while. I shouldn't have left them out. That was very irresponsible on my part." He scrunched up his face. "Did you look in them?"

"No. That's an invasion of privacy."

This kid had lawyer written all over her, Marc thought. And woe betide to anyone who crossed her path.

"You know why I did it?" she asked him.

"Because you were angry?"

She gazed at him like he was the village idiot for the second time in three weeks. God, teenagers could be rough on your ego. Then again, maybe he *was* the village idiot.

"I did it because you're kind of OCD about them," Sydney said. "They have to be just so, like somehow you haven't gotten over your sister messing with your stuff, and whenever you leave and come back they're the first thing you look at. No offense, it's kind of weird. Not that it excuses what I did."

Maybe a career in psychology. He looked at her and tried very hard not to smile. "No, it doesn't excuse what you did, but it has given me something to think about." Truthfully, he was amazed at how insightful she was.

He started walking to the door, hoping she'd take the hint, which she did. He shut the door behind her, but within seconds he heard her signature sharp knock. "You okay?" he asked, opening the door for what he hoped would be the last time today.

"I forgot to tell you what else I said to Dr. Ferrari when she came here."

"What did you say?"

"I said I'd add her to the list of all the other women that had come by to see you."

Marc burst out laughing.

Sydney looked a tad put out over his reaction. "Well, I didn't want her to think that you were unpopular. Even my mothers think you're good looking for your age, not that they'd be into you or anything."

"Thanks for defending me." He hesitated, then in an awkward and cautious move, he gave her a hug.

Sydney hung on like she was a koala bear and he was a tree.

***

"Mom, you'll never believe who called me today," Kimmy said. She was spread out on Andrew's leather couch, a light afghan over her legs, and Hairy on her feet.

Gina sat in the adjoining recliner reading through the handwashing policy. Barbara Goodshanks had left them with a mess, and thanks to Marty's warning, she had a chance to fix it.

"Who called?" She glanced up from the paper, grateful for the break.

"Martha. From the airport, she and Dad were waiting for their plane. You know, if I put a pencil in my mouth, I can swipe my cell phone with the eraser end and answer calls. I figured that out. I can do it with Dad's desktop, too." Kimmy's pride was visible.

"That's clever. I'm amazed at how quickly you've figured out a way around your casts."

Kimmy sniffed. "Mom, I have to blow my nose. Can you do it?"

Gina jumped off the chair and grabbed a tissue. She walked over to her daughter and said, "Blow." wiping her nose as she had when she was a little girl.

"I'll be glad when this is over," Kimmy said.

"I'll bet." Gina settled back down in the chair. "What did Marty want?"

"She said she really liked the outfit you wore when the two of you met, and she wanted to know if she could hire me to be her fashion consultant."

"Wow. That's a compliment. What did you say?"

"I said yes, of course. Do you think I should print up business cards, or do you think it's too early in my career?"

"I think it's a good idea. Maybe Rachael can help you. She's good at that stuff." She put down the handwashing-policy paper. "How did you learn to put outfits together like that?"

"Jennifer and I used to try on clothes after cheerleading." Kimmy smiled. "We'd try on all kinds of stuff, you know, clothes we'd never wear, and then figure out why something looked good or why it didn't. Then we'd go to the mall to people watch and talk about who looked good and who didn't and why they didn't. You know, anyone can look good if they try."

"Oh," Gina said, with great care. "I was just wondering." She hadn't a clue the girls had been doing any of that. Given their ongoing battle, Kimmy wouldn't have told her, and she wondered what else Danny and her daughter felt the need to keep from her. She'd been so blinded by her own expectations for them she'd nearly missed who they really were.

Kimmy continued. "We were never mean. Well, sometimes we were. Just a little. Most of the time we weren't, though. A lot of girls in high school are."

"Are what?" Gina asked, only half listening.

"Mean. Does that ever change?"

How to answer that one? She took a deep breath and thought before she spoke. "Most people grow up as they get older, but some people never do. They sort of stay stuck in high school. I don't think that will happen to you, though. I think you're already on the road to growing up."

"Jenn would be proud. She'd be proud that since I can't cheerlead anymore, I'm starting a business."

Gina smiled and waited for more to come out.

"I guess you're glad," Kimmy said.

"That you're good at fashion? I'm amazed, given who your mother is."

"I meant you're probably glad that my professional cheerleading plans are gone. Aren't you?"

She chose her words carefully, knowing that a part of Kimmy wanted to fight. She'd been inside all day, pacing around the condo like a penned in colt. On Wednesday, she'd be going back to school with a personal aide until her bent casts came off, and they were replaced with smaller ones that ended below her elbows. Gina was fairly certain that the anticipation of returning to school was adding to her behavior. "I'm glad that you're alive, and in one piece, and that when those casts come off you can get back to your life. If you want to be a Rams cheerleader, go for it."

"The Rams left St. Louis. You didn't know that, did you?"

"No, I didn't. Wait a minute, where'd the Cardinals go?"

Kimmy shook her head. "Phoenix. Years ago."

"Oh. We still have the baseball team?"

"Mom...you're absolutely pathetic. No offense. I love you and all, but how could you grow up in St. Louis and not know if the Cardinals left or stayed?"

It was pathetic, she had to admit. "Anyway, I want you to know that I'll respect your choices no matter what they may be. Including cheerleading."

"What about that guy you were seeing?"

"Have you been talking to your aunt?"

"No. Well, maybe a little, but when Aunt Rachael was here we talked mostly about Dad."

Gina's ears perked up. "Oh."

"She told me that I needed to let go of the idea that you and Dad would get back together and that both of you would be happier if you were with other people."

Gina nodded. "Or alone. How do you feel about what your aunt said to you?"

"Stupid. Stupid for thinking what I thought. And sad. I miss us, our family, but I think I'm the only one who does. Danny doesn't. I talked to him about it, too. Aunt Rachael made the call for me on her plan, so don't worry—you're not going to get hit with the bill for an international call."

"That was nice of her." She hesitated then asked, "How is your brother?"

"He's fine, Mom. He's a little curious why he doesn't hear from you much."

"I'm trying to convey my respect by giving your brother some space."

"He thinks you're mad."

"I'm not mad at him."

"Every time we talk about Daniel you get this look in your eyes, like you have right now. It's the same one you got when I told you I was staying with Dad for college."

"Kimmy, I never get angry at either one of you. Hurt, yes, but angry, no."

"Hurt's worse than angry when you're somebody's kid. And come on, Mom. You get angry at us. You just don't want to admit it, because…like, you think you have to be this perfect PhD parent. You were mad at Danny. And you were mad at me, too."

Gina took a deep breath and let it out. "I was frustrated."

"That's kind of like calling fighting a disagreement. That's what Dad and Martha do."

Gina crinkled her forehead. "They're fighting already?"

"No. When Martha took me to get your Valentine's Day candy, besides a lecture about sugar"—Kimmy made a face of slight disgust—"she told me she and Dad never fight. They disagree and then they develop a—"

"Compromise?" Gina guessed. Marty had been using that word a lot lately.

"How'd you know?"

"Oh, I figured."

"Yeah, she made a big deal out of letting me know this, like she and Dad are some evolutionary couple. Desserts would only be for the holidays, was their first negotiated solution." Kimmy rolled her eyes. "I mean, compromise. But right before the accident, I opened the trunk of Dad's car, and he had a jumbo-sized bag of Milky Ways and a box of Tasty Cakes stashed in there."

"Oh my." Gina discretely squeezed her upper arm hard with her fingers to keep from laughing. Between Kimmy's hair debacles and tales of the evolutionary couple, those bruises were going to be permanent. But it felt good to laugh again.

"So should I call him?" Gina asked.

"Dad?"

"No, your brother."

"I'd email him," Kimmy told her. "It's less intrusive. But don't mention that I said anything. Ask him how he's doing and tell him what you're up to."

"Good idea."

Gina picked up the handwashing policy again and started to highlight the parts she wanted taken out. At the rate she was going, she'd be needing another highlighter in about half an hour, tops.

"You know," Kimmy spoke quietly, as though her words were treading on private property. "I've been talking to Uncle Gino, too. He told me that Dr. Edwards is applying for jobs in St. Louis."

This was news, but not completely surprising. "He has a sister there."

"He and Uncle Gino are friends. Uncle Gino says he drives down to St. Louis about every weekend to see his sister, and sometimes he brings the dogs. Aunt Rachael likes him too, and she doesn't like anybody. Neither does Uncle Gino for that matter, except you and me and Danny. And Shauntel. And now the corgi guy. So there must be something nice about him."

Gina squeezed her eyes closed, then opened them. "Kimmy, I don't want to talk about this."

"Okay. But, Mom, you look good now, with your new clothes. You know, if you wanted him back, we could work up a special outfit."

"Relationships shouldn't be based on looks."

"Yes, you've told me that. A lot. I was just offering to help. You don't even have to pay me."

Gina heard her voice rise. "Well, thank you for the offer, but my personal life is not open to discussion."

"So, we can talk about me but not about you."

"Pretty much."

"That's not fair."

"You're right; it's not. I'm your mother, and you're my daughter. This isn't a democracy."

"I'm almost eighteen."

"I believe there is a teen on the end of eight."

Kimmy sighed. "Okay. Be that way. But we could work up a great outfit. I know you have a meeting with him coming up."

Gina put the hand washing policy down. "How do you know that? Aunt Rachael?"

"Well, yeah."

They were silent after that. Gina finished ten more pages, at which point she needed a new highlighter, and Kimmy watched TV while Hairy licked her face. When she glanced up, she noticed that her daughter looked miserable. Her thoughts had probably drifted back to Jennifer, the accident, and the fire.

"Mom?"

"Yes."

"This is all my fault."

"The fire? No. That's not all your fault. That house should have been rewired years ago."

"I was talking about the fact that you aren't dating the corgi guy anymore. It's because of me and the accident, and the fact that I was upset about you and Dad and the divorce. That's why you broke up with him, isn't it? Because of me."

"There were other things in the way, too, and sometimes things are more important than...falling in love."

She watched out of the corner of her eye as Kimmy scrutinized her. "I'd like to make it up to you. I could make you look hot," Kimmy said.

"Not too hot. I'm not twenty-three, okay?" She put the document aside again, knowing that at the rate she was going, it would take a full week of sheer drudgery to get through Barbara Goodshanks's vision of a preschool, which horrifically mimicked a laboratory clean room. "But if I was to look hot at a meeting— not so hot that I look like I'm headed for a Saturday night date, but hot enough to make him realize that maybe he's missed me—what would I wear? I'm curious."

"When's the meeting?"

"In a couple of weeks. And I'm not saying I'm going to do it, because I think he may be getting back together with his old girlfriend in New Mexico."

"Mom, trust me. I'll have it all picked out."

***

After mulling it over, Gina emailed Daniel and, much to her surprise, got a reply the next day. He was busy, he told her. Very busy. Pizza was serious business, and he wanted to learn it all and learn it well. That was Daniel. He'd also been touring vineyards in and around Campania with Gina's uncle. From the tone of his email, she could tell that his flight to Naples was no lark but a well-planned move. He had a goal. He was planning something. What it was, she didn't know, but she had a feeling in the pit of her stomach that his plans involved Gino. Missing from his email was any inquiry about Andrew. Well, that was for the two of them to work out. Or not.

Daniel's writing, in a simple email, was beyond amazing. The words he used when he described Naples made Gina feel as though she was right there with him. It reminded her that when he was five, and she'd read him *Wind in the Willows,* he'd begged her to say the passages one more time, because they were too beautiful not to hear again. *Oh, Danny,* she wondered, *what have you gone and done to yourself because of your messed-up parents?*

It was hard to raise a boy that smart. He was so good with words, any words, and now Italian ones. Had they pushed him too much, or had they not pushed enough to round him out? It had been all too easy to mold him into what they assumed he wanted to be, which was like them. But if they were those kind of parents, who could explain the intrepid, stubborn, and wonderful daughter they'd brought into the world? Gina felt like an enormous failure, not because her children hadn't turned out the way she wanted them to, but because she had disrespected them in the first place by expecting them to be exactly what she wanted. She hit the send icon and sat silently, staring at the computer screen.

Her thoughts scooted from her children to the child development department to her extended family and to Marc. Always back to Marc. The man was like the word game she kept deleting and then downloading one more time onto her Kindle, always promising herself that this time would be the last time she ever wasted her time playing it.

Since he'd moved on to other departments around the university, she'd heard very little scuttlebutt. She knew Rachael ran into Marc on the weekends when they both visited Betty's group home, but Rachael wasn't giving away any information, and she wasn't asking. The two of them still had their final meeting to discuss the department's budget conclusions, but that was no big deal. No big deal at all. Not even a medium deal, and with her daughter's help, she'd make sure she looked fantastic.

Later in the day, Marty called and asked if she and Andrew could drop by the condo after dinner and bring dessert. Dessert? Since it wasn't a holiday, Gina suspected something had to be up. and though she correctly picked up the scent of change, she was by no means ready for what unfolded. And if she wasn't ready, she could only imagine what her daughter was going through right now.

"Let's all toast Andrew." A beaming Marty picked up Kimmy's champagne glass, and held it for her.

The four of them, Kimmy, Martha, Andrew, and Gina stood around the sparkling clean, spot free glass table, scrubbed minutes before Andrew and Marty waltzed through the door with a tofu cheesecake and a bottle of champagne. Hairy lurked under the table hoping something good would hit the floor. Gina wanted to tell him not to waste his time.

"Here's to your new position, Andy," Marty said, beaming with pride.

"To Andrew." Gina lifted her glass and caught Kimmy glaring in her direction.

Marty took a sip from her own glass then helped Kimmy, whose face looked more like she'd imbibed castor oil. Nevertheless, she wasn't about to give up a chance to taste alcohol, even if Marty was delivering it.

While it wasn't Harvard, his new position at a small liberal arts college in Boston put Andrew well within reach of rubbing elbows with those whose elbows he felt were worthy of rubbing. He wore an expression that reminded Gina of a little boy who had won the Missouri statewide spelling bee, and he and Marty would be leaving after the semester ended in May. It was a quick departure. Then again, Gina bet Andrew had been planning something like this since their divorce, or maybe even before, though he'd covered his bases with Kimmy staying in Columbia to take care of him just in case. Meeting Marty and leaving with her was a perfect getaway for Andrew. He had everything he needed now to make his departure smooth as silk.

Andrew's smile became bigger, if that was possible, as he poured another glass and lifted it in a gesture that told Gina he was intent on drinking the entire thing.

"Andy." Marty smiled at him like she was the little spelling champ's mother. "Think of the calories."

Kimmy's face was a mix of hurt and anger, and Gina wasn't sure which emotion ruled the other. It didn't matter. Her father wouldn't notice either one.

"Will you be moving there on a permanent basis, too?" Gina asked Marty.

"I've taken a job with the college, too. My grant goes with me, and that sealed the deal. They couldn't say no."

"Who could say no to Martha?" Andrew asked, beaming.

Gina smiled to herself as Marty and Andrew looked at each other like they were better than a partnership of cake and icing. For everyone, there is someone, she thought, until she looked at her daughter.

The minute Andrew and Marty said their goodbyes and Gina shut the door, Kimmy began to cry. Gina pulled out a tissue from the almost empty box and held it in her hand, ready for the flash flood of tears.

"He said I should stay here so we could spend some time together, you know, and make up for all the years he was working so hard and we didn't. And now he's going," Kimmy sniffed between sobs. "He didn't ask me. He didn't even mention he was thinking about it. And I registered for college here." Her voice cracked and more tears careened down her face. "And now she's going with him."

"I don't think you can blame Marty for this," Gina said, her voice close to a whisper.

"Why not? She shows up with her stupid tea and tofu, and it's Andy this and Andy that, and suddenly my father is moving halfway across the country. You think that was his idea?"

"Yes."

Kimmy's eyes blazed. "I don't want to talk about this with you. If you hadn't gotten divorced, none of this would have hap—" Kimmy stopped herself, looking slightly horrified. "I'm sorry, Mom."

Gina put the box of tissues on the side table. She folded her arms and scrolled through her mind for possible topics to change the subject with. "How's your business coming? Get any takers?"

"Aunt Rachael said she'd be in for a makeover the next time I was in St. Louis. I don't know when that will be. And Uncle Gino said Shauntel couldn't afford it, but I think I'll ask her myself."

"Very good idea," Gina said. "And remember: I need a semi-hot outfit for my meeting early next week."

Kimmy rose in an awkward motion from the couch. "I can't wait until I get new casts."

They walked into the bedroom, and Gina pulled open the closet.

"Here's what I was thinking." She showed Kimmy a pair of black pants and a white blouse with detail around the collar and cuffs.

"Not black and white again." Kimmy walked over to closet and stood next to Gina. "It's almost April. Ditch the black. Put some color on. Lighten up your pallet, but don't go pastel."

"I don't have anything pastel, remember?"

"Right. Those colors are your no-no's. In fact, they're your nevers." She pointed with her nose toward a royal-blue silk blouse. "Pull that out."

Gina pulled out the blouse and held it under her chin,surveying herself in the mirror. It really was a good color for her.

"Something like that with those linen pants would look better. And don't tuck it in. There are slits on the side for a reason."

"But the linen pants are black. You said—"

"Nothing is written in stone," Kimmy said with authority.

She loved watching her daughter get all fired up. It was so much better than wasting tears on her father.

"I meant that rule in regard to what you wear close to your face." Kimmy walked back over to the closet. "Hey, how about this floral dress we bought? Pull that one out."

"That one?" Gina pulled out the dress and gave it a once over.

"Yeah, you can wear a jacket with it so it's not so revealing but still hot."

"What jacket?"

"Any of them but the black one. The dress is a floral, so pick one that complements it, and by that I don't mean an exact match."

Complement, don't match, no black. Good lord, this was a lot of work. "What am I going to do when you're not around?" she asked Kimmy.

"Well, seeing that I'm not going out of state for college next year, and I won't be living with Dad either, you don't have to worry about it, do you?"

She willed herself not to wince at the bitterness in Kimmy's voice. "Eventually, you'll go away."

"By that time, you'll have mastered dressing."

"Maybe."

"I'll write it all down for you like they do on the TV shows. Don't worry."

"Maybe you'll write a book someday."

"It's been done."

"Yes, but not by you. You'd put your own twist on it."

She watched Kimmy's eyes widen in surprise. "You think I'm that good?"

"Yes, I really do." And much to Gina's surprise, she did. Then she went one better. "And when those casts come off, if you want to go back to cheerleading, we'll find the best physical therapist around."

Kimmy smiled, but with a hint of sad wistfulness. "No, Mom, I think that ship has sailed."

"Are you sure about that?"

"Yes," she said, then turned away.

Time to change the subject once again. "When are you going shopping with Marty? You're still going to do that, aren't you?"

"Yes." Kimmy's eyes narrowed a fraction of an inch. "And soon."

Chapter Fifteen

Some things never change, Gina thought, as she walked down the hallway toward her office, only to be stopped by Roberta Cooper rolling around on her chair and sticking her head out the door.

"Have you given any thought to your summer course load?" Roberta asked.

Gina leaned against the doorframe. "Well, I was going to tell you tomorrow when we have our meeting scheduled, but since you asked, I might as well right now. I won't be teaching any classes because I'm taking the summer off."

Roberta's eyes widened. "That's a first."

"As soon as Kimmy's last set of casts come off, I'm getting her out of Columbia and taking her to Italy. It's her high school graduation present. We're going to see her brother and my uncle in Naples. I won't be back until the fall semester starts in August."

"Any ideas about who's going to teach your classes?"

"I was going to suggest that you give them to one of the adjuncts."

Roberta cleared her throat. "Rumors are afloat that Marty Schmidt is leaving Nutrition before it merges with Public Health and that she's leaving with your ex-husband."

She nodded in affirmation. "For once the rumor mill is correct."

Roberta's eyes widened again. "Rumor also has it that Barbara Goodshanks had an emotional meltdown and vanished."

"I've heard something similar." She wasn't about to add to that bit of campus news.

"Did that affect the handwashing-policy paper?"

"Marty and I got a hold of it before it was turned in. We fixed it. I wrote the entire thing as recommendations and best practices, not mandates. Marty agreed."

"Good." Roberta gave her an approving nod.

"And the budget-cut priorities?"

"I'm meeting with Dr. Edwards later today at the chancellor's office to review them. You'll have a copy of the report emailed to you after that."

"Wonderful. Make sure the copy you send me is dated after you turn it into the chancellor's office. I don't want any hint of my hands being on it before that. You look nice, by the way."

"Thank you."

"The way that dress looks under that jacket is very classy." Gina watched Roberta scrutinize her face. "But you don't seem happy."

Gina straightened. "Roberta, this semester I've been the dreaded member of the faculty, I've been forced to develop policies for caregivers and young children that I find petty, unnecessary, and less than child-focused. My house burned down, my daughter was in an accident, and her best friend died. Andrew promised Kimmy that they'd spend next year together, but now he's leaving, and I have to clean that mess up, too. The only good thing about it all is that Daniel ditching his PhD program looks trivial when lined up against everything else. If he wants to make pizzas for the rest of his life, so be it."

"You haven't had much fun lately, have you?"

"That's one way to put it. Add that to the fact that I'm having lunch with Andrew in thirty minutes, and I'd say all in all it's been a supremely miserable semester." *Except for Marc, and even that went bad.*

She turned to go, then stopped, and turned back. "When I come back in August, I'm saying no to anything other than my classes, my research, and my grad students— if they can still afford to be here, that is. Don't think about putting me on another committee next year. Because," she said, halfway out the door, "I won't show up."

* * * *

Today, Marc put aside his writing for thirty minutes and treated himself to Lisa Kirby's backyard. It was one of those spring days where the sunshine made you feel hopeful. He sat on the bench in the middle of the boxwood maze, soaking up spring. The corgis avoided the maze and sat outside the entrance to it, waiting for him. It confused them, and he thought the lack of an open visual field probably frustrated them as well. The maze was a place for privacy, and for once he welcomed it, because he had so much to think about.

His position at Jesuit University would start in August. It was a pay cut, but so what? His sister was there, and he had friends who were not Elaine's but his own, even if they were Gina's family. He'd also found a place to live that took dogs. That was four things. He needed five. He could use Vickie and Al as one thing, but listing them at all, either separately or together, was beginning to feel like an old, lazy habit. The purpose of five things was not to get lazy about relishing life, but to discover new aspects that made every day worth living.

He still wasn't over wanting Gina to be on the list. That was the real problem. He left room for her every day then had to scramble at night to find something else. If she hadn't needed him after the fire, she was not very likely to need him now, and he'd emailed her so many times without a single reply.

Today he would see her when she turned in her report, but that was business, and it would take just a few minutes, unless he could find some way to convince her to go and have coffee with him. He wouldn't mention espresso, seeing that the history of that drink between them was now far too loaded. Maybe going out for ice cream was a better idea. That would remind her of gelato, which would remind her of Rome, and hopefully remind her of when they were together and happy. And then, who knew?

Gino said his sister was scared. That's all he would say, and Marc had an ironclad rule about not pumping him for information. Gino was protective, and Marc appreciated that. He had a sister he was quite protective of, too.

Then he thought of number five. Life had to get bad so it could get better and you could appreciate it again. But right now he wasn't ready to do that, because letting go meant giving up the hope that somehow he and Gina might find a way to each other again, after everything that had happened.

He could hear the dogs barking and going wild inside the house, which meant someone was at the door. Probably Sydney. She was the one friend he'd made the whole time he'd been in Columbia, although Syd's mothers had taken to asking him over for dinner since they knew he'd resigned his position and would be leaving soon.

He hightailed it back into the house and to the front door where his hunch was proven correct. Sydney Sheppard stood there, her arms crossed against her chest.

"Syd, I'm sorry. I forgot to tell you I don't need you to walk the dogs today."

"Can I come in anyway?"

"Sure." He shut the door and they both walked into the living room, each assuming his and her usual place. "What's up?"

A smile spread across her face. "I got accepted at George University. In St. Louis. And I think I'm going there because they gave me the biggest scholarship."

"That's wonderful, and a very smart choice. Good for you. Hey, you know I'm going to be living there. In St. Louis."

"Really?"

"I got a job at the Jesuit University there. That way, I'll be close to my sister."

"Oh." Sydney sat on the couch and moved her mouth as though she was going to speak, but didn't.

"Cat got your tongue?" he asked then wondered why adults always said stupid stuff like that to young people.

"Do you think, since I'm going to be there, and you're going to be there, do you think sometimes, I don't mean all the time, because I will have a life, but do you think sometimes I might, you know, like come over and walk the dogs?"

"I was going to ask you that."

"Really?"

"Really. I look forward to it." He watched Sydney's mouth start to quiver and her eyes start to water. Oh god, he thought, not again. He walked quickly to the kitchen.

From the living room, he heard her voice, cracked and quivering. "Please, not the paper towels, okay?"

"Okay." He searched the kitchen for something else to use, then darted down the hallway to the bathroom and grabbed a roll of toilet paper. "Better?" he asked.

"Much," she nodded. "You're definitely getting the hang of it."

His phone rang as he handed the roll to her. It was the number from Betty's group home, and by the tone of the caregiver's voice, he knew immediately it wasn't good news.

***

Gina vowed to herself that if Andrew misbehaved, she would not order the Katy Station onion rings he loved to mooch. Yes, it was petty, but that way she could avoid having to watch him eat food he'd given her a lecture about five minutes prior to putting it in his mouth without wanting to see him choke on it.

Escorted by the hostess, she slid into the side of the booth opposite Andrew and laid her purse on the table. This time there was no newspaper present for him to hide behind. Perhaps he was making progress after all.

"I'm guessing you called this meeting to tie up all the details." Andrew spoke in a brisk manner. "Just so you know, I'm putting the condo on the market, but only after you and Kimmy have found other accommodations and no hurry on that."

"Thank you."

"It was Martha's idea. But I will be taking the couch, and my glass table when we leave. The rest of the furniture you're welcome to sort through." He grinned. "Marty has a much better bed."

Gina didn't know if she wanted to slap him or gag. "I wanted to talk to you about Kimmy."

He stared at her. "What about her?"

"You convinced her to stay in Columbia and go to school here, so she could spend some time with you. And now, without any warning, you're leaving. She's heartbroken."

"She can come and visit."

"That's not the point."

The expression on his face told her to brace herself for an onslaught of defensiveness. "You are not going to make me feel guilty for advancing my career. I've waited a long time for this, and I finally found a woman who supports me." Andrew took a drink from his water goblet then continued. "I raised two children, one of them disgustingly ungrateful. I invested all that money in sending Daniel to school so he could make pizzas?"

"He had a full scholarship."

"It still cost me money. As far as Kimberly is concerned, she will have to understand that any plans we made are superseded by my career and Martha's. Things change. The only person you can count on is yourself, and the sooner she grows up and accepts that, the better her life will be. Had I known that fact years ago, I could have saved myself a lot of grief. I'm getting married, by the way."

"Oh my god." Gina's mouth fell open, more because of the manner in which Andrew had absolved himself of any responsibility regarding his daughter than of his announcement of marriage. "I guess congratulations are in order."

"Thank you."

"She is perfect for you, in so many ways. Really."

"For once we agree on something."

"Look, you need to talk to Kimmy yourself. She'll be heartbroken and won't understand this if she hears this from anyone but you."

He fumbled with his napkin, then picked up his menu, hiding half of his face behind it. Gina noted it was an improvement over completely disappearing behind the newspaper and silently attributed the change to Marty.

"Andrew, she's your daughter. Someday you're going to want that relationship."

He lowered the menu four inches and stared at her over the top of it. For a split second, she caught a glimpse of the frightened boy inside.

"Don't push her away. She needs to hear from you that you're getting married," she repeated. "Not from me or your sister or Marty."

"I'll talk to her later this week. I promise." He scanned the lunch specials. "What is she doing with that business of hers, anyway?"

"Oh," Gina brightened. "She's a fashion consultant. She's very good at it."

Andrew looked at her like she was insane. "She and Martha went out shopping yesterday, and Martha came back with god-awful stuff. Like these knit turtleneck shirts in pink, aqua, and some sort of coral color. Marty said it was called *shrimp*. One had little anchors on it. I don't know fashion, but I thought they were absolutely ghastly."

Gina's forehead crinkled. "What did she have Marty buy?"

"Knit turtlenecks. Two each of the world's worst colors. And these things called jeggings? Now Martha is beautiful, but pants that are spray-painted on work well for sixteen-year-olds, and that's about it." Andrew raised his eyebrows and lowered his chin. "I don't know what Kimmy was thinking, but she shouldn't start a business she's dreadful at. What name is she using on those business cards? Ellison or Ferrari?"

"Ellison."

"Well, maybe she should use Ferrari."

Gina stared at him blankly.

He shrugged. "It sounds more fashion-oriented."

"Oh, yes, of course."

When the server came, she ordered a hamburger with extra bacon and a side salad.

"No onion rings?" Andrew asked, the minute the server walked away.

"No, I don't think so. Not today."

***

She shouldn't have had that enormous hamburger, Gina thought as she walked toward the administration building an hour later. The lunch with Andrew had left her rattled and sleepy, if you could be both things at once, and she had wanted to be alert and energized when she met with Marc. She also didn't want her stomach bulging out. She wanted to smile and make jokes and ask him how he was and how his sister was, and tell him she missed seeing him. Scratch the last item. Before she opened her mouth about that, she wanted to test the waters. Maybe he was already dating someone else, or maybe, as Sydney Sheppard had hinted, he was getting back with the woman in New Mexico. Elaine, that was her name. Gina considered it a distinct possibility. He wasn't bad looking nor bad at conversation nor bad at anything else men tended to be bad at. He was good at all those things. God, she'd been an idiot.

As she walked along the brick pathway that led to the main door of the administration building, she straightened the jacket that complemented, not matched, her floral print dress. Entering the building, she walked down the hallway to the chancellor's office, and up to the receptionist. "Excuse me. I'm Dr. Ferrari. I have a meeting with Dr. Edwards in about five minutes."

The receptionist scanned her appointment, book then her computer and, finally, Gina. "He isn't here."

"I'll wait."

"He called to cancel his appointment with you. You'll have to reschedule."

She was certain that the floral pattern on her dress had wilted. "Is he ill?"

"I'm not allowed to divulge personal information," the receptionist said, curtly. "You can turn any documents in to me, if you'd like."

"Did he leave a message?"

The receptionist gave her a sideways look.

Gina reached into her satchel and pulled out the manila folder. She handed it to the receptionist and walked away.

Lost in her thoughts, she started to walk toward her house then realized the house she was walking to was gone. She pulled off her heels, turned around, and headed toward the faculty parking lot, walking barefoot to the car.

What had she been thinking? Of course, he'd find a way not to meet with her. Maybe he liked her brother and

Shauntel and Rachael, but that didn't mean he liked her anymore. I mean really, she hadn't heard from him since the fire. Not a single email. And why should he like her? She was the one who faked who she was from the start, and she was the one who ended it. Who could trust someone like her?

She threw her shoes in the back seat of her Focus and drove to the condo. When she got home, she saw Kimmy's head bobbing in the front window, waiting for the report on her meeting with Marc and lunch with her father. One thing was certain. Before she talked about anything, including their trip to Italy this summer, the two of them were going to have a little conversation about turtleneck shirts and jeggings.

***

Marc sat next to Betty on the couch in the sunroom of her group home and held her hand, the one that wasn't bandaged. If he lived in New Mexico, who would be here for her now? For the first time since he'd made the decision to leave, he was one hundred percent certain that moving back to St. Louis was the best thing to do, not just for Betty, but for him, too. "Betty, I am so sorry about your burned hand. Is it feeling any better?"

Betty nodded. "You have to wear a big mitten when you bake cookies. That's what Susan says." Susan was the new caregiver who had been hired two months ago for the daytime rotation. Marc liked her a lot. She was soft-spoken, friendly, and possessed a boatload of common sense.

"Susan is right. You need to listen to her."

Betty stuck her chin out. "Not all the time."

"Yes." Marc nodded emphatically. "All the time."

"Not at night." She smiled after she said the word *night.*

"Did you make a joke?" Marc asked, amazed at the possibility.

"Yes." She laughed with delight. "Susan is here in the day."

Marc joined in Betty's laughter.

"At night she goes to her home. I wish she would stay at my house."

He was so proud of her. Maybe when he moved back, she would consent to come to his house for dinner. He'd love it if that happened, but he wouldn't push. Baby steps, he kept reminding himself.

"Hey." He remembered what he'd wanted to show her.

"That's for horses."

"Is that another joke?"

"No. Whenever we say hey, that's what Susan says."

He reached into the manila envelope by his side and took out the three snapshots he'd found in a box when he was moving his things out of storage. "Do you know who that is?"

"No."

"That's you and me when we were kids."

Betty squealed. "Where's Mama?"

He thought she might ask that, so he showed her the next photo.

Betty eyes welled up with tears. "That's Mama." She stroked the picture. "I miss her."

"I know you do." He showed her the third and last photo. "Do you remember him?"

"Daddy."

"Yes."

She was silent for a second, then turned to him, and said, "I like the picture of you and me."

Marc put his arm around her shoulder and squeezed. "I do, too."

"Rachael reads to us," Betty said, still staring at the picture of their mother.

"Yes, I know," he said.

Betty mentioned Rachael's reading every time they talked, as though it was the first time she'd ever told him. This time, though, his sister changed the subject. "How is your friend?"

"What friend?"

"The one that came with my Rachael."

"Oh, Gina. I'm afraid she quit being friends with me."

She studied him for a moment, then put her bandaged hand over his. "You're my brother, Marc Edwards. Wear a glove when you bake cookies. It hurts when you don't. Then you to go to the emergency. That is not fun."

***

It was a lazy Sunday, and Gina stretched her legs out on the couch that Andrew would soon be moving to Boston, and made a mental note to wipe off the dried dog slobber and give it a good vacuuming before he came to get it next week. Hopefully, he wouldn't see the hairline scratch Kimmy had made on the surface of the glass table. If he did, she was ready to take total and complete responsibility for the crime.

She picked up the last of her mother's diaries that Gino brought her over two months ago, when Kimmy was in the accident and her house burned down, and considered for a moment how quickly life can change in the blink of an eye. When her kids were little, she dedicated every Sunday to spending the entire day with them, even if it meant getting up at four a.m. on Monday to get her work done. Now, with one child gone and the other almost on her way out the door, she could spend all Sunday reading on the couch if she wanted. But did she want to?

"What are you reading?" Kimmy asked as she wandered into the living room.

"My mother's diaries."

"Can I read them?"

"Yes, if you can read Italian." Gina smiled.

"She wrote them in Italian?"

"It was her first language. I'm sure when she was in her private world that's what she reverted to. When you're writing about your emotions and feelings, your first language is often more comfortable."

"Maybe I'll learn Italian." Kimmy stood next to the couch. "Can we talk about our trip to Italy?"

"Have you called Marty to set up a new shopping trip?"

"No."

"Well, then, I'm not ready to talk about going to Italy. In fact, I'm not buying the tickets until you call her and make this right."

Kimmy walked into the kitchen and came back with the cordless phone, holding it by the antenna between her index and middle fingers.

"Here," she said, as she plopped down next to Gina. "You punch in the number for me, then go in the bedroom. This is going to be embarrassing."

"I understand, honey." Gina punched in Marty's home number. "Remember when we talked about the girls in high school who grow up as opposed to those who don't?"

"Yes."

Gina placed the phone in the crook of Kimmy's neck. "Experiences like this turn you into one of the girls who grow up." She rose from the couch, picked up her mother's final diary, and went into the bedroom, closing the door after her.

To read her mother's thoughts was more than interesting. It was, informative and uncomfortable. She'd known her mother as her mother. Intellectually, she knew Francesca Ferrari was more than that, but she had difficulty seeing beyond the caregiver role that had loomed so large when she was a child.

This diary was the one her mother hadn't finished due to her death. It was the one Gina dreaded reading, because she knew it would recount Gino's final arrest and subsequent incarceration. She took a deep breath and started reading. An hour later, Kimmy knocked on the door.

"Mom, are you okay in there?"

Gina wiped away the tears. "Yes. And no."

"Can you let me in? I can't turn the doorknob. Remember?"

Gina put the journal aside and jumped off the bed.

"Have you been crying?" Kimmy asked after Gina opened the door.

"A little."

"I'm sorry about what I did to Martha."

"It's not that." She shook her head and smiled. "It's my mother." She went back to her spot on the bed, and patted the space next to her. "Come and sit."

Gingerly, Kimmy eased herself on. "You okay?" she asked Gina again.

"I'm fine. Better than I have been in a long time." She nodded toward the diary. "It's unsettling to read the thoughts of a woman and know it's your mother and that she's writing about your father and your brother and me as a young girl."

"What was she like?"

Gina took a deep breath and thought. "A lot like your Aunt Rachael, minus the sarcasm."

Kimmy crinkled up her nose.

"You know, fiercely loyal, and filled with insight. She was all those things, and soft, like Shauntel is. She never yelled. Well, hardly ever."

"Did she write about Uncle Gino?"

"Yes. She loved him very much. He reminded her of her brother, the one who helped Danny get set up with Pizza University."

"And you? What did she say about you?"

"She loved me, too. But she thought I was too dependent, too quiet, and too good." Her mother had also worried that she would let others dictate her life. It wasn't something she wanted to share with Kimmy.

"Maybe you should have fought with her more. Like we do."

Gina chuckled. "Maybe. She loved Papa with all her heart, and leaving for America with him was, she said, a spit in the eye of her father."

"Whoa."

Gina nodded, straight-faced. "It seems they didn't get along. I never knew that. My mother never spoke of my grandfather."

"Anything else?"

She nodded silently, and swallowed hard. "One big thing, but I want to tell your uncle first, and to do that I need to translate the last six months of this diary for him."

Kimmy looked at her silently, then said, "I'm sorry things didn't work out with Dr. Edwards."

"Kimmy, it was a long shot. He's moved on. He hasn't contacted me since your accident. I mean, really, what did I expect? People move on with their lives. Look at your dad. I think he and Martha will be happy together. That doesn't upset you anymore, does it?"

Kimmy shook her head and continued to stare at her. It was the same look she had on her face at thirteen when she'd taken five dollars out of her purse and got caught in the act. "I'm going shopping with Dad and Martha tomorrow," Kimmy volunteered. "I think Dad wants to come along to make sure I don't do Martha in again. Then they want me to stay for dinner. He said they want to tell me something important."

"Hmm."

"Yeah, it's probably some revelation about a protein diet derived from seaweed, soy, and tofu. Can we talk about Italy now?"

"Sure."

"I called Aunt Rachael to see if she'd take Hairy while we're gone."

"And what did she say?"

"She said she couldn't because she works all day at the book store, and Hairy pees on things. So, I called Uncle Gino."

"And he said no dogs in a bakery?"

"He said he'd be happy to."

Chapter Sixteen

The trunk of Gina's Ford was full of luggage, and Hairy sat in the backseat with his nose sticking out the three-inch crack of the right rear window. He looked as though he'd died and gone to heaven, she thought, smiling. God, how she would miss that dog this summer. She adjusted her sunglasses as she and Kimmy barreled down the I-70 toward St. Louis, driving straight into the early-morning sun.

Her daughter's last set of casts came off the week after she graduated from high school, replaced by removable arm braces made of Velcro and plastic. By the end of summer, Kimmy would be done with them as well, although the orthopedist made it clear that cartwheels and hand springs were not in her daughter's immediate future. The two of them had their final and last argument about cheerleading, regarding the orthopedist's words. This time, though, the sides were reversed. Gina kept repeating to Kimmy that if she wanted to do cheerleading again, she would get her whatever help she needed.

Finally, Kimmy hauled off and yelled at her mother, "Yeah, I know, free to be you and me. Just like the Marlo Thomas song. Only this time, respect the fact that I'm also free to say no, I've moved on. Okay?" And that was that.

She glanced at Kimmy and marveled at the resilience of youth. With all that had happened in the last few months, her daughter was still ready to dive into their adventure in Italy. Every now and again, she would catch a sad and wistful expression on Kimmy's face, although it was quick to fade when she saw Gina staring at her, as she was right now.

"You okay?" Gina turned her eyes back to the highway.

"Yeah. Who wouldn't be?" She shrugged. "I'm going to Italy for the summer. How many people get to do that? And it's on your dime, too. Of course, I'm okay."

"I mean, are you okay with everything else?"

"You mean like Jenn, and Dad and Martha, and the house, and the fact that I don't know what to do with my life?"

"Yes."

"Well, I don't think I'll ever get over the fact that Jenn died and I didn't, but that's more of a reason for me to do something with myself. Something good. And it was nice of Dad and Martha to come to my graduation, and even nicer of Dad not to talk about himself during the entire dinner like he usually does. He actually asked me a question about my future, when Martha poked him in the arm to say something. Honestly, Mom, I think she may be too good for him."

If Gina could have pinched her inner arm while driving she would have. "Kimmy, your dad's a bit insecure. I think that's why he talks about himself so much."

"Yep. It's an aspect of narcissism." Kimmy shrugged. "That's the term Danny uses."

"Does he? I'm sorry your father's like that."

"It's not your fault. That's like me blaming you for being born. Why waste your time? If he wasn't my dad, then I wouldn't be me or have Danny or Aunt Rachael. Or you." She turned to stare out the side window as she spoke. "When you're a kid, you know things, but you can't talk about them because you don't know how. You don't even know you know them—you just feel them. I knew Dad was like that. I just didn't have the words." Kimmy sighed. "Also, I didn't want him to be that way, so I told myself I was wrong to feel like that. But look at how he treated Danny."

"Kimmy—" Gina started then stopped. Why should she keep smoothing things over for Andrew?

"It's okay. He's my father. I already decided that I don't want to excommunicate him like Danny did. I need to figure out how to deal with Dad as he is. I'll never have the kind of relationship with him that I have with you. If I have one at all, it'll be different."

Gina kept her eyes on the road. "That's pretty insightful. You sure you don't want to get a degree in psychology?" *Oops.* "What I mean is, you're multitalented, and whatever you do you'll be good at."

"Thanks. I've had lots of time to think lately. And Danny and I have been Skyping." She turned away from the window to face Gina. "You know, you don't quit on us, Mom. You don't quit loving Danny or me, even when you don't agree with what we do or when we do something stupid like burn the house down."

Gina nodded but stayed silent. She'd been brought to tears too much lately.

"Sydney came by yesterday when you were at your office."

She cleared her throat. "Really?"

"Yeah. We talked. We talked about Jennifer and the fact that we weren't friends anymore after that and how much it hurt her when that happened." Kimmy sighed and ran her fingers through her hair. "I guess I always knew, and I feel bad about it. But I had to be someone different. Different from you and Danny and Dad."

"I understand."

"Anyway, she's doing great. She's going to George University in the fall on a scholarship."

"Good for her."

"And you're not going to believe this one."

"What?"

"Well, I'm going to help her pick out some clothes. For college. Things that will make her look smart and sophisticated. Like she's in command."

"Wow."

"Yeah, well, that's the look we're shooting for. I'm doing it for the practice. And she asked me. Weird, huh?" Kimmy looked out the window then back at Gina. "We also talked about you and Dr. Edwards. You really liked him a lot, didn't you?"

Gina stiffened. She hadn't expected the conversation to go this way. "At the time, but it didn't work." She added quickly, "And not because of you and the accident and the fire."

"Sydney wanted me to tell you that when you came down to Dr. Edward's house, a while ago, she made up a lie. She said there wasn't a list of women who stopped by. Only you. Oh, and the woman in New Mexico, he isn't getting back with her. Syd says she doesn't like dogs or cats."

"Oh." Rather than let any emotion leak from the bomb Kimmy had plopped in her lap, Gina gripped the steering wheel harder and kept her eyes glued to the highway.

"She feels really bad about it, Mom. She said that Dr. Edwards was really sad when you didn't see him anymore. It's my fault."

"Kimmy, we've talked about this. Sometimes things don't work out, okay?"

They rode in silence for about ten minutes. Kimmy looked out the window, while Gina drove and digested everything they'd talked about.

"I think I'd like to know Uncle Gino and Shauntel better," Kimmy said, breaking the silence. "Danny thinks they're great."

"That's a good idea."

"He said they're authentic. Danny uses that word a lot. And it's awfully nice of them to watch Hairy."

And it was. In all honesty, Gina was still surprised that her brother had consented.

"You know Aunt Rachael told me that Dr. Edwards is moving to St. Louis in August."

"I thought he was moving there in December when the job in Columbia ends."

"No, Aunt Rachael told me he resigned early. She said he was disgusted about something. Something to do with the chancellor."

This was news. She glanced at Kimmy out of the corner of her sunglasses and found that her daughter was scanning her face for any and all reactions. She wasn't going to give her any encouragement. Not an inch of her body language would reveal the fact that she was stunned Marc had ended his sabbatical early.

Kimberly continued. "Maybe you could go talk to him sometime when you're in St. Louis after we get back. Tell him you know that he didn't keep a list of other women."

Gina eyed her daughter, then looked back at the road. "It's a little late for that. Like you said about cheerleading, that ship has sailed." She was quiet for a moment then the words tumbled out. "He didn't call or even email when he missed our appointment."

Kimmy looked away quickly. "Sydney told me his sister burned her hand, and he had to go to the emergency room to get her."

Why hadn't Rachael told her any of this? Surely, she knew. Come to think of it, she didn't talk about Marc at all anymore. "Is she okay?"

"Yeah."

"He would have called if he was interested." She took her eyes off the road for a second and glanced at her daughter. "Sometimes you need to let it go."

"Maybe he thinks you're not interested. Maybe he's waiting for you to call."

"Kimberly, that ship has—"

"Ships can redock."

"Can we talk about something else?"

Kimmy raised her eyebrows and cocked her head. "Sure. Didn't you say that we're not going to be around forever? Pretty soon I'll be starting my own life, and Danny already has."

"That's sounds like something your aunt would say, not me." Actually, it was more like something she would think but never say, unlike Rachael.

"Come on, Mom. If there's someone for Dad, then there's gotta be someone for you."

Gina shifted in her seat. "I know when you're eighteen you think that everyone in the world can be happy, and that it's your job to be the matchmaker. Jane Austen wrote an entire novel about this very topic. It's called *Emma*."

Kimmy sniffed. "I've read it, and I've seen the movie. Emma was a blond busybody, and I'm not even a blonde. And just as a side note, *Emma* ends happily."

"Sweetheart, it's called fiction for a reason. And just as a side note, Jane Austen herself had dark-brown hair."

"I want to know, in case I meet someone else to fix you up with, what is it that you liked about him the most?"

"Kimmy—"

"Aw, come on, Mom. We've got a whole hour left until we make it to Uncle Gino's. We have to talk about something."

"Okay, okay. Five things."

"Five things right off the top of your head, huh? Yeah, like that ship has sailed. Just tell me one."

"No. That's what I liked about him." She turned to make sure her daughter was listening. "He almost died a few years back, and when he didn't, he decided to find five things every day that made life worth living. You know, like the way your kitchen smells when you're cooking or Hairy's tail wagging when you walk through the door."

"Well, it wouldn't be his breath." Kimmy turned around and gave Hairy a reassuring pat on the head.

"No." Gina laughed. "It certainly wouldn't be. Anyway, that's the thing I liked about Marc the most. He could make me see how stupid it was to get all steamed up about something that doesn't really matter and miss the good things in life. The little things, like…" She suddenly remembered their talk months ago. "Water."

Kimmy raised her eyebrows. "Water? Okay, whatever. Where did you meet him? I asked you once, and you never told me."

"I met him when I was in Italy last winter. He thought I was Italian."

"Whoa, you mean you met him in Italy, and he actually ended up in Columbia, down the hill from you?"

"Weird, huh?"

"Really weird. Talk about fate. Maybe you knew him in a past life or something, and he was your true love, and it ended badly, and now you have another chance."

"Highly unlikely." She hated fate. Things happened for a reason, and when humans didn't understand the reason, they called it fate. It was as stupid as thinking you heard voices in the Pantheon.

"Where in Italy?"

"Rome."

"Where in Rome?"

"What is this, twenty questions?"

"Whatever it takes. Where in Rome?"

"At the Pantheon."

"How come you never told me?"

"Because it was private, and now it really doesn't matter because like you said, I'll probably never see him again."

"Can he speak Italian?"

Gina laughed, remembering. "Yes, but not that well. He gets his prepositions wrong, and some of his verbs and adverbs."

"Oh my," Kimmy said, mockingly.

"Hey, those words can get you into big trouble if you don't get them right. They can lead to some enormous misunderstandings." She turned to Kimmy. "Let's talk about something else. Okay?"

"Fine. Let's talk about the Prada outlet instead. I have our trip there all worked out."

***

Gina had been waiting for the dinner at Gino's to be over for the last two hours so she could get away with Rachael and they could talk in private, but everyone kept talking, and eating, and laughing. Finally, she nudged Rachael out the bakery door, to walk Hairy around the block, telling everyone that he absolutely needed to get outside—and quickly.

"Why didn't you tell me Marc's sister burned her hand?" Gina asked her, the second the door to the bakery shut.

"Why didn't I tell you? Because the last time we talked about Marc we almost had—in fact we did have—an argument, and you told me that you didn't want to talk about him with me ever again. That's why."

"But this was about his sister."

Rachael raised her eyebrows and glared at Gina. "Next time give me a list of acceptable topics connected to Marc Edwards, but aren't directly Marc Edwards, and I'll make sure I adhere to it."

"Okay, okay." Gina stopped while Hairy relieved himself on yet another mailbox post. "I wish you were coming with us."

"I have the store to run, and I'm going to see Betty and her friends at the group home. All in all, it'll be a great summer. They call me Book Lady. And I'm thinking about getting a dog. Maybe two, like Marc has."

"I thought you said you were like a tuna sandwich. You know, you eat by yourself."

"I am, but every once in a while, it's good to have a few chips with the meal."

Gina smiled.

"Besides, you don't need me to run interference between you and Kimmy anymore. You two are fine." Rachael smiled approvingly. "Hey, guess who asked me to be a witness at his wedding?"

"I can't imagine."

"Yeah. Even though he's a self-absorbed brat, he's my brother."

They made it around the block and were turning into the bakery, when Rachael stopped at her car and popped opened the trunk. She reached in and pulled out two large photo albums.

"What's this?" Gina asked, as Rachael held them, beaming at her.

"It's every picture of you and your parents and the kids we could find. Gino, Shauntel, and I put them together. I know it doesn't make up for what you lost in the fire, but we thought it would help."

"God, Rach, how thoughtful." Gina felt her eyes start to water. "I can't thank you enough."

"You've been through a lot, Gina, and the kids are okay. Both of them." Rachael turned her eyes to the albums. "I thought about waiting until you got back to give it to you, but I wanted you to see what we'd all done together, and I wanted you to know that your brother was a big part of it."

Gina nodded silently and tried to wipe her tears away before they took Hairy back inside Gino's upstairs apartment. She wasn't ready to look at the pictures. It was all so emotional, looking at times that had passed and would never be again. She'd had a family, a house, a marriage, and now it was all gone. Kimmy and Daniel would go their own way and make their own memories. She was no longer their conductor, she was the audience, and that was as it should be.

Rachael must have read her mind. "Hey, I'll keep this album for you until you get back. I don't think you want to be lugging them around in your suitcase." She placed it back in the trunk of her car. Rachael hesitated, then spoke, "Look, I know you don't want to talk about Marc. We all know you don't want to talk about Marc, but there's something I need to tell you."

Gina sighed. "Okay, shoot."

"He's headed for Italy, too. He left yesterday."

Gina blinked. "That's nice. Italy is a big place. I'm sure he'll have a wonderful time, and I'm sure I won't run into him."

Rachael's eyes narrowed. "Okay, Venus, you've been informed. Still need a ride to the airport?"

"Yes, if you don't mind."

"No, I don't. One more question, though, and no, it's not about Marc."

"Great."

"Did you tell Danny about Andrew getting married?"

Gina nodded nervously. "I sent Daniel an email about it, but I haven't gotten a reply, and I'm not pushing it. We'll be together in two days, and we can talk then if he wants. It's his choice."

Rachael closed the trunk and frowned. "Do you think the two of them will ever talk again?"

"I don't know. Ever again is a long time."

***

It was early, and Gina, all packed and ready to go, was up almost as early as her brother, who had been busy baking bread and biscotti since four in the morning for the opening rush. This was it, the day she and Kimmy were taking off to see Daniel in Naples then do a tour of Rome and Milan.

"Here." Gina pushed a manila folder toward her brother across the wooden worktable in the back of the bakery.

The two of them sat on opposite sides of the table, on the stools they'd carved their initials into years ago when they were children.

"What's this?" Gino asked, staring at the folder. "Directions for Hairy?"

"No." She smiled and shook her head back and forth. "I translated Mom's last journal for you."

He put his mug of coffee down. "The one right before she died?"

"Yes." She'd rehearsed what she was going to say to her brother at least ten times so she wouldn't start crying when she told him. It didn't work. She reached up and wiped the first trickle off her right cheek. "Gino," she began but was quickly interrupted.

"I know. I killed her. We've already talked about this." He moved his head back and forth as though it hurt to do it. "Please, don't—"

"No," Gina broke in. "You didn't. She had a heart condition. She knew she was going to die, but she didn't think it would happen so fast. She didn't tell Papa, either. Unless he read her diary, I doubt he ever knew. She was waiting until you got out of prison to see you, and to tell everyone then. Gino, she just ran out of time."

"But she wouldn't have if I hadn't done the things I did."

"Not true. Her heart was weak, she had cardiovascular disease. Nobody ever caught it when she was younger."

Gino put his hand on the folder, then took it off as though it was hot and would burn his fingers. "Whatever Mama went through, whatever was wrong with her, I still…" He stopped, and then began again. "There was no excuse for what I did. I hurt her."

"Hurt, yes. Killed, no. You didn't break her heart."

"Metaphorically speaking, I did."

"Well, there's a big difference between metaphorically doing something and really doing it." She watched her brother consider her words. "Look, she worried about me too. All the time."

"You're lying."

"No, I'm not. She thought I was too good, too nice, and that people would take advantage of me because I worried so much about what other people thought."

A hint of smile played on Gino's lips, but it disappeared quickly. "You wouldn't have worried about that if I wasn't your brother."

"Maybe. Maybe I wouldn't have studied so hard or read so many books if you weren't my brother either. And was that a bad thing?"

"No. Look at you. Cornell PhD, professor, writing papers about washing your hands." He smiled playfully

"Okay. Stop right there, Gino."

He turned serious, once again. "You know, I'd never do anything to hurt you, or Kimmy, or Danny. You know I was trying to help him, right?"

Gina nodded and reached across the table, pushing the folder an inch closer to her brother. "Just read it. Okay?"

"Okay." He pulled the folder over next to him and stared at it as though it would explode any minute.

"And one more thing." Gina slid off her chair and walked over to Gino's side of the table. She put her arms around her brother's tattooed ones and hugged him hard. "I'm really glad you're my brother."

***

Rome wasn't the same in summer. It was humid like St. Louis, with almost as many Americans. Americans, who thought Gina was a native and asked her in horrid and broken Italian that always seemed to sound like Spanish how to get to the Colosseum. After she overheard Danny deliberately giving incorrect directions to a couple of tourists, who he later claimed were disgustingly obnoxious and deserved it, she took over being the direction giver of their group.

They spent the first two weeks in Naples, visiting family and touring the Amalfi coast. Kimmy went to the Naples Museum of Archeology four times, with follow-up trips to Pompeii, Herculaneum, Stabio, and Ostia. She wanted to see the sites where the mosaic collection came from. Except for cheerleading and clothes, her daughter had never seemed so interested in anything before.

Kimmy's outings gave Gina the opportunity to talk with Daniel by himself. She wanted to understand why he'd left his dissertation when he was almost done. Daniel was going back to school next week. Pizza University, not graduate school. He and Gino had plans to open a certified Neapolitan pizzeria in St. Louis. And he would write. That's what he wanted to do, he told her, not write about other people's writing, but write himself. Inside, she was still afraid for him, but it was probably something all mothers went through on the cusp of finally letting go.

The three of them were happy together, chumming around. She loved watching Daniel and Kimmy interact. Her children liked each other. When had that happened? She turned around to see them a block behind her, messing around with their phones again. Why play with your phone when there was so much to see? She stopped and waited for them to catch up.

"You know, you're in the epicenter of Western civilization."

"I thought that was Greece," Daniel said.

"No. It's Rome," she said emphatically. "Just ask any Italian. They'll tell you. Why don't you two put those phones away?"

"Because then we wouldn't look Italian," Kimmy said.

Danny laughed.

"Whatever you're texting can wait. It can't be worth what you're missing. Do you know that we just passed Santa Maria? It's built on top of the original Roman house the early Christians used to secretly worship in, and you missed it."

"Let's go to the Pantheon," Daniel said.

She knew one of them would bring it up eventually. "We haven't seen Hadrian's market yet."

"Let's see the Pantheon first," Kimmy said. "We can double back to the market later. Didn't you say the gelato was really good there?"

"It's good everywhere." Daniel cut in. If looks could kill, her son would be buried and in the ground from the one his sister flashed his way. What was up with those two? They'd been getting along so well.

"There's a gelato shop at the Trevi Fountain," Gina said. "We haven't been there, either."

Her children replied in unison. "Let's go to the Pantheon."

"Why don't we have lunch first?" Anything but the Pantheon.

"If we walk to the Pantheon, we'll work up an appetite for lunch," Daniel said.

Gina took a deep breath. "Fine." She was going to have to face it sooner or later, so it might as well be sooner. "You two try to keep up with me, okay?" She marched ahead like a Roman foot soldier on a drill.

Without a word between them, they turned the last sharp corner of the last narrow street together, and there it was. Just like the first time she saw it, it took her breath away. All that the Pantheon had witnessed and still, it stood. Romans had walked into that structure for over two thousand years, celebrating life, mourning death, and hoping against all odds to be given a solution to their problems, like she had. But she hadn't listened. She hadn't been ready for the answer.

"You okay, Mom?" Daniel asked.

"Yes. It's just, this building amazes me every time I see it."

"Let's go in."

She didn't feel worthy. She was the woman who'd been given a gift and walked away from it. "You two go. I want to sit by the fountain for a few minutes." She couldn't tell them she was about to cry. She motioned with her hands like a good Italian, shooing them both away.

Her children walked through the colossal doors into the building. She watched them go, wishing for them all that was good in life, and hoping they would savor the bits and pieces of joy that flitted past each day. That's what Marc had taught her. That's what the experience of meeting him had been about. That's what the voice in the Pantheon, her voice, had been trying to say.

Someone sat next to her, invading her personal space. As she turned to get a glimpse of the interloper, she convinced herself for a split second that it was Marc. But of course, it wasn't. It was a young man, making room for a young woman who was approaching him with two containers of gelato. Gina could tell by the look of familiar endearment they gave to one another that they were in love.

She thought Marc would come. Surely, he had heard from Sydney Sheppard or Gino or Rachael that she would be in Italy this summer. She envisioned him sitting next to her with espresso and a cup of gelato, gazing at her like the couple to her left were doing right now. But he wasn't going to come. It was a silly thought. He'd moved on, and she didn't blame him.

Today, she would avoid god's eyeball, the oculus in the Pantheon's ceiling. She didn't want it glaring at her accusingly, asking why she'd come back when she hadn't listened in the first place. She stood slowly and made her way into the Pantheon, ready to take her medicine.

But there was no medicine to take. Today the Pantheon was just the Pantheon, an amazing, intact, and ancient structure with a hole in the middle of the ceiling that was just a hole. It said nothing to her, and she said nothing to it. She spied Kimmy in the back, texting away and walked over to stand beside her.

"Kimmy, you're going to get to be my age someday and realize you've spent your whole life glued to a portable piece of technology instead of living."

"Sorry." Kimmy didn't bother to look up. "I'm trying to help two people."

"You're not playing Emma again, are you?"

"I'm resigning as of this very second." Kimmy smiled and dropped her phone into her purse, then her face clouded over. "There's something I need to tell you, okay? And I feel really horrid about it. It's worse…it's way worse than Martha's turtleneck shirts. It's even worse than her jeggings."

"Okay."

Kimmy took a deep breath. "After the accident, when I was bummed about Jennifer, and you and Dad and I not living together, like I thought we were going to, I thought maybe if I could keep you away from Dr. Edwards, you and Dad still had a chance. So I broke into your email account...well, I didn't really break into it. You left it open on Dad's desktop, so it really wasn't a break-in, technically speaking. Anyway, I deleted Dr. Edwards's emails before you saw them, and then I marked his address as junk mail, so it wouldn't go into your inbox. It wasn't easy with those casts on." She added quickly, "Not that I'm proud of doing it in the first place."

Too stunned to speak, Gina gaped at her.

"Mom, it was a horrible and unethical thing to do, and childish. I feel so bad about it, but I couldn't tell you. I tried a couple of times, but I just couldn't. Here you were helping me, and look what I did to you. I am so sorry. I hope you can forgive me. Someday."

Gina managed to close her mouth but stood there blinking like someone had taken a picture using a flashbulb close to her face.

Kimmy continued. "Danny and I are going to make some sibling memories all on our own. Just the two of us. We're going to a spa, and I'm introducing him to manicures. Really, would you want to buy a pizza from someone with nails like his? Have you seen them? And then I'm taking him shopping and teaching him what I taught you about dressing, only man-style. Free of charge, of course. I love you, Mom. And so does Danny. Trust that, okay? And I'm really, really sorry."

She stared at her daughter, more stunned than upset. If simultaneous thoughts could go through her head, they would be, *I can't believe you did that, how did you pull that off with casts on both arms, and Marc really did try to get in touch with me.*

Kimmy reached up and gave Gina a hug. "I'm way too young to be giving my own mother advice, but there's something Uncle Gino told me that I've been thinking about lately."

"What?" Gina managed to squeak out the question.

"Sometimes life gives you a gift if you're smart enough to take it. We'll see you back at the hotel." Kimmy turned and walked away.

If she ever worried about her children again, she was going to see a shrink. Obviously, they were well on their way to maturity—with a few regrets and struggles here and there to come. But wherever it was they were going, they would get there.

She stared at the oculus in the ceiling one more time, then gave it a wink, and walked outside to sit and take it all in. The Pantheon was beyond description in so many ways.

Someone gently nudged her then shoved a cup of gelato her way. "I got you fig. They say it's a gift from the gods if you believe in that sort of thing. I'm not real sure about that stuff."

She stared at Marc, open mouthed. "How did you know I was here?"

"I could lie and tell you the fates brought us together, but they didn't. Or maybe they did, and your daughter was their agent on earth."

"Marc, she's no angel. Let's be clear about that one."

"She's been texting me since before you left for Italy." He answered her next question before she asked it. "She got my number off your brother's cell phone. Pretty slick. And she told me about her email caper and apologized profusely. Hey, it takes guts to fess up to something like that and take the heat."

Beethoven's "Ode to Joy" burst from Marc's pocket.

"You kept that ringtone?"

"I meant to get rid of it the day after Valentine's Day, but for some reason, I couldn't. I like joy."

"Me, too." And she did, finally. She'd never told anyone about the voice in the Pantheon that day. She'd been too embarrassed. The world was logical, and things happened for a reason. Didn't they? Eventually, she'd tell Marc about the voice. In a month or two, maybe, but certainly not today. Then again, maybe it would be her secret for the rest of her life.

He reached into his pocket and grabbed his phone. "It's your daughter. She probably wants to know if I made it here."

"Don't answer." She stared at him, silently scanning the freckles on his face.

He looked at her sheepishly. "I was supposed to beat you to the Pantheon and be sitting on the fountain waiting for you, like when we met. Your daughter had every detail planned out, but I drew the line when she wanted to pick out clothes for me to wear. Anyway, I was late because I told the cab driver to take me *around* the Pantheon when I meant to tell him to take me *to* the Pantheon. So we got stuck in traffic."

"Is that sort of like, I work *at* Columbia, not *in* Columbia?" God, was she glad to see him.

"Sort of." He smiled. "You want to go sit down? Maybe talk a little. Or not. We can just sit there and people watch."

"Sure."

They sat together in silence, holding hands, watching the people go by, and taking back up where they left off, as though nothing had ever happened. He'd never been the budget cuts man, he'd never bought her an espresso maker, her house had never burned to the ground, and Kimmy had never deleted his emails.

"I'm going to get us some espresso." Gina stood and was off in a flash. When she was making her way back through the crowd, and they located each other, the expression on Marc's face, when he saw her, was one of familiar endearment, like the couple earlier today.

His phone made a mechanical sound as she sat down, and he pulled it out of his pocket again.

"Is it who I think it is?" Gina asked.

"Yes. She texted me to tell you that they were going to the Prada outlet on their own and that they'd meet back up with you in a few days. She also said to tell you she is way better than Emma. Who's Emma?"

Gina laughed out loud.

"I love your laugh." Marc stood and drew her up to him. "I should have called you after I missed our appointment, but you hadn't answered any of my emails, and I was scared to get turned down again. My sister hurt her hand. That's why I wasn't there."

"I know.

"I told the office assistant to ask you to call me, but you didn't."

"She didn't tell me that, but I should have anyway."

"I should have, too, but I was scared." Marc looked at her pleadingly. "I've messed up so much in my life, and I don't want to mess up with you. You mean too much."

"If we mess up, we'll fix it. Together," she said, fiercely.

"I think I love you, Gina. I'm sure of it, in fact."

"If I'm going to make you the first of my five things every day, I certainly hope so."

He kissed her hard in front of the tourists, the Italians, the Pantheon, and whoever or whatever was, maybe, up there wishing them—joy.

"I love you, too." And she did. She was certain of it this time. "And I miss your email jokes and hearing your five things."

He bent down and whispered them in her ear. "You, you, you, you, and you."

About Lynne Marino

Lynne E. Marino was born and grew up in St. Louis, Missouri, where she was always the first in line for the Bookmobile. She has spent most of her adult life in the Southwest, still reading away. Now she writes her own stories. She currently resides in Tucson, Arizona.

Social Media

Blog:
https://lynnemarinoauthor.wordpress.com/2018/01/02/lynne-marino-author/

Facebook: https://www.facebook.com/lynnemarinoauthor/

Acknowledgements

I would like to thank the group at Solstice Publishing for this incedible opportunity. I would also like to thank Joan Dempsey and Ginny Glass for their editing expertise and willingness to work with me. Finally, I would like to thank my critique partners Jill Hannah Anderson, Kerry Morgan, Ann Markow, Sylvia Wright, and Judy Grout for their infinite patience. Someday I will know where all the commas go, and I will put them there. Promise.

If you enjoyed this story, check out these other Solstice Publishing books by Lynne Marino:

The Cha-Cha Affair

Stephanie Ledger isn't a Scottsdale princess anymore. Her messy, never-ending divorce has left her with an empty upscale house, and an even emptier bank account. She swears that she doesn't want another man in her life-ever, until she meets Joe Schmidt at a ballroom dance class, and the sparks begin to fly.

The more time Joe spends with Stephanie, the more he wants their fledgling partnership—on and off the dance floor—to be something more. Unfortunately, he works for the IRS and they are investigating her soon-to-be-ex-husband's finances, and Stephanie herself. Joe knows that if she ever finds out, he's toast.

Still determined that she'll never fall in love again, Stephanie ropes Joe into a riotous caper to get some leverage on her lying, lecherous husband in the hopes of finally bringing her divorce to a close. The duo dance their way in and out of trouble, and into each other's heart, until Stephanie discovers what Joe has been hiding. But will she also discover what everyone around them already knows? While the two of them together may be annoying and imperfect, they are also annoyingly perfect for one another.

https://bookgoodies.com/a/B07FCTNTRQ

www.ingramcontent.com/pod-product-compliance
Lightning Source LLC
Chambersburg PA
CBHW070445030726
47503CB00004B/910